ANY WAY
YOU
WANT IT

ANY WAY YOU WANT IT

KATHY LOVE

KENSINGTON PUBLISHING CORP.

http://www.kensingtonbooks.com

For all my new friends in New Orleans

Acknowledgments

As always, special thanks to The Tarts.
I love our talks, our plotting and the wine.

Thank you to my dear friend Erin McCarthy.
It's been quite a year
and all sorts of ridiculous!

Thanks to the friends who are always there to keep me sane.
Julie Cohen, Erin McCarthy (again), Lisa Cochrane,
Arianna Hart, Kristi Ahlers, Jordan Summers, Christy Kelley
and my mom.

A special thanks to Sonny Kane, who helped
bring The Impalers to their wonderful undeaths and
answered all my endless, and often clueless, questions
about music.

And all my love to my family.

Chapter 1

" *That* is what you are offering the most famous and powerful voodoo priestess in New Orleans?" Maggie glanced at her friend Erika, then back to the cracked, weathered tomb, then to the items cradled in her palm.

"I just scratched Xs into her final resting place, I can't imagine she'll mind these."

"She doesn't mind the Xs," Maggie's other friend, Jo, said, skimming the voodoo book she'd bought at one of the strange little shops along Dumaine Street. "They symbolize your three requests."

"I get three?" Maggie managed to ask seriously. "Just like with a genie?"

"Genies don't exist," Erika stated, as if the very idea was so ludicrous she couldn't believe Maggie had even mentioned it. So Maggie didn't bother to point out they apparently believed in the wish-granting powers of a voodoo queen, who'd died sometime over a hundred years ago.

Maggie looked back to the tomb, which was covered in Xs and other symbols designed to communicate with the long-dead woman laid to rest inside. Obviously others believed too, but Maggie couldn't help feeling it was all a little silly. Still, she had made the Xs. So she wasn't completely dismissing the idea, was she?

"Erika's right," Jo said, glancing up from the book long

enough to raise a disdainful brow at the objects in Maggie's cupped hand. "Marie Laveau expects something better than that. It says she expects items that are personal to the one making the request; an offering that has the giver's energy attached to it."

Maggie stared at her usually sensible friend. They were talking about a dead woman, weren't they? As far as Maggie knew, the dead really didn't expect much at all, but she decided not to mention that to her suddenly very superstitious friends.

"Well, there's nothing personal about those," Erika stated, eyeing Maggie's choice of offerings with a grimace.

"Well, they're all I've got. Marie can take them or leave them."

Both of her friends frowned at Maggie's cavalier attitude. If Maggie wasn't mistaken, they also appeared a bit nervous, as if they expected Marie to unseal her tomb, march up to them, and start complaining in person. Or maybe worse. What *did* dead voodoo queens do when they got an gift they didn't like?

Maggie looked down at the items in her palm. Maybe she should rethink all this. She laughed slightly that she was actually worrying, too—although she had to admit her chuckle sounding a little strained, even to her.

Maggie could understand Erika's reaction to all this. She was more open to the idea of magic and ghosts and other paranormal phenomena. But Jo? Maggie never would have guessed her sensible friend would buy into this.

"You two are taking this all way too seriously," Maggie said as she stepped forward to place the offering beside a vase of now wilted, but obviously once beautiful, and probably expensive, flowers.

"I would at least leave the ChapStick," Erika said, just as Maggie would have placed the offering beside the others.

Maggie glanced back to them. Erika nibbled her bottom lip, eyeing the tomb worriedly. Jo didn't look up from the book, but did nod in agreement.

Maggie shook her head. "What does Marie Laveau need my ChapStick for? I'm not suffering dry and cracked lips for a dead woman. I'm leaving these," Maggie said, deciding then and there she wasn't going along with this any more than she already had. She dropped her gift onto the cracked step of the tomb. "I'm pretty sure Marie will be fine with this."

Again her friends cocked doubtful eyebrows. Then all three friends stared down at the offering—two sugar-coated pecans—covered with a fine smattering of lint.

"Weren't you the one who said they were delicious and addictive—the veritable crack of the nut world?" Maggie asked Erika, suddenly feeling the need to defend her decision.

"They are—but not after they've been floating around the bottom of your pocketbook."

"They're only a little worse for wear." Maggie realized her own voice sounded noticeably doubtful now. Great, the superstitious duo were getting to her.

"Well, you've already left them," Jo said with a resigned sigh. She snapped the book shut. "Make your wishes."

"And make them something exciting," Erika said, then added, "and naughty."

Maggie frowned at her friends. "Who are you two? And what have you done with my normal friends?"

"Oh, please, you always knew we were freaks. Just make your wish—before she realizes what a crappy offering you left her," Erika said.

"Make the wish you want," Jo said, shades of the sensible friend returning—sort of. She was still talking about the wish as if it was going to actually happen.

Maggie shook her head, amused and exasperated all at once. But then she closed her eyes and concentrated. She didn't even know what she wanted for a wish. On the off chance it did work, what would she want?

Her thoughts drifted back to why she was here in New Orleans. She was trying desperately to forget the past six months. So what would help her do that?

"Wish for a gorgeous man and a hot, sexy fling," Erika said, from close to Maggie's right shoulder. Maggie's eyes popped open and she shot her friend a shocked look.

"Erika!"

"It's a good wish," Erika said.

And Jo gave her a halfhearted shrug, as if she would like to deny it, but just couldn't.

Did she really seem that much in need of a good roll in the hay? She decided she probably did. She made a face at her friends, then closed her eyes again, attempting to think of something more realistic, more obtainable. And not so . . . well, frankly, ridiculous.

But Erika's suggestion kept popping back into her head like the repeating chorus of a pop song, irritating yet oddly compelling.

A hot fling. Yeah, like that was ever going to happen. To her.

She squeezed her eyes shut even tighter. What did she really want?

A strange, nebulous image of some man appeared in her head. Great, now that the idea had been planted, she was even getting images of the man she'd want to have a fling with. Yikes.

Ah, what the hell. It wasn't like Marie Laveau's spirit or whatever was going to rise from the grave and grant her wish anyway. And if by some miraculous twist of spiritual fate she should meet a gorgeous guy who wanted to have a hot, sexy fling—with her, which would never happen—it would certainly prove Marie Laveau was fine with lint-covered pecans. Or that she had quite a sense of humor.

Chapter 2

"I ate way too much," Maggie groaned as she stepped out onto the sidewalk.

"I drank way too much," Erika said and giggled. Maggie laughed too. They'd all had a bit too much to drink.

But this was vacation, Maggie thought, and if anyone deserved to get a little tipsy, she did.

The sun had set beyond the ornate, yet run-down buildings while they were in the restaurant. Now the side street was dim, all the bright colors of the day muted to varying shades of gray. But the air was still warm and heavy with humidity, and the shadows and hair-frizzing dampness didn't dull the energy crackling in the air.

Maggie had sensed that energy as soon as she'd arrived there, that afternoon. She could admit it to herself now that she was feeling a little more . . . open, with the expensive chardonnay heating her blood. It was an energy that had nothing to do with the excitement of going on vacation for the first time in years, or being in a new city.

Oh, she'd definitely been excited about going on this trip. Getting away from her dull box of an apartment outside of Washington, D.C., was much needed, as was getting away from her job. She loved her job, but as her friends said, it was a job where she could hide away with her moldering sheet music and avoid life.

Yes, she was excited, but this was a different feeling from that one. This wasn't an exhilaration inside her, it was more of an energy around her. As if the city had its own aura. Its own life. And she was now caught up in it, pulled right into its essence.

She chuckled to herself. Here she'd been finding it amusing that her friends were getting all mystical—she was doing the same thing. Of course, the wine might be helping her with that too. But whatever it was about New Orleans, she was glad to think about something other than her often very, very dull life. And Peter. That situation certainly hadn't been dull, but it had been the kind of escapade she could have easily done without.

Ack! She wasn't going to let him sneak into her thoughts—not even for a minute.

She was going to think about the wonderful vibe of the city. She stopped walking and took a deep breath.

As soon as she'd stepped out of the cab and set her feet on the gritty, cracked streets of the French Quarter, she'd felt something. A latent dynamism, a crackling hum in the air.

She giggled slightly under her breath. Okay, maybe the three glasses of wine had been a bad idea. It was making her thoughts rather out-there. She was getting as suddenly and strangely cosmic as her friends. But she did feel more alive here.

As if to accent her thoughts, Jo paused outside a small cafe, little more than a hole-in-the-wall.

"Listen to that," she said, swaying to the lively zydeco drifting out onto the street. She began to dance as if it was the most normal thing in the world to break into a jig on the sidewalk; as if being here energized a person so much that they just had to dance.

Erika joined in, possessed by that same need, but Maggie could only sway along with them—she was too busy listening to the music. Music—with its own power, its own life force.

Maggie could hear the horns and the snare drums and the accordion. In her mind, she could see the notes dancing, skipping over the staffs like her friends danced across the cracks in the pavement.

Maggie smiled, closing her eyes, wanting to see the music more clearly.

"Come on," Jo called, her voice shattering Maggie's thoughts, sending the notes scattering. Maggie opened her eyes, having no idea how long she'd stood there absorbed in the song.

Her friends had moved on and were waiting at the intersection for her.

"I like that music," Maggie said as she joined them.

"Is there any music you don't like?" Erika asked.

"Not much," Maggie said. "After all, music is my life."

"But," Jo said pointedly, "you are not here to think about your work. You can think about dancing. You can think about singing."

"I did see a karaoke bar when we were riding into the Quarter," Erika added.

"No karaoke," Maggie insisted.

"You can even *play* music," Jo said, continuing her train of thought.

"Where would I do that?" Maggie asked, but Jo was not going to be distracted.

"But you cannot think about music in the context of your work," she said.

"That's right. You are here to live a little. Not work."

Maggie sighed. "I like my work." Not to mention she hadn't been thinking at all about the items she'd received in the mail just a day before she was to leave for this trip. Well, not until her friends mentioned work.

"I like my work too," Jo said. "But I don't intend to think about kids or grammar or reading comprehension. I want to dance."

"Yeah, me too," Erika agreed.

Maggie laughed, but she lingered behind, still hearing bits of the music. Still seeing the notes in her head. The way they would look written down. Some bits she couldn't quite see.

Having heard the song just this one time, and now from a distance, she couldn't see it exactly. But she could make out most of it. Black and white notes dancing the different beats of zydeco across sheets of paper.

"Are you coming?" Erika said, as they started down the street away from her again.

"Where are we going?" Maggie asked, doubling her steps to catch them.

"Bourbon," her friends said in unison, then they dissolved into tipsy laughter.

Maggie smiled too, but then she shook her head. "Why don't you two go on? I'm kind of tired." Which wasn't untrue. Their flight had left Dulles Airport at six that morning, and they had only dropped off their luggage at the hotel before they went right into tourist mode. They were staying right on Bourbon Street, but she knew her friends were not headed there to go back to the hotel. And Maggie really did feel the need to rest.

Even now, this newly sensed energy was swirling around her, making the air thick and her head a little woozy. The wine wasn't helping, but she didn't really believe it was the alcohol—not solely.

"No way," Jo said, catching Maggie's elbow, pulling her along. "You are not sneaking off to read or listen to classical music or whatever boring thing you normally do."

"Right," Erika agreed.

Maggie laughed, but she did try to get her arm out of Jo's grasp. Jo wasn't letting go—not without a fight, it appeared.

"Those things aren't boring," Maggie argued. Besides, Jo read twice as much as Maggie did, and she had a healthy knowledge of classical music. They'd attended many symphonies together.

"Okay, they aren't," Jo agreed. "But they aren't what you do on vacation. Especially a vacation in New Orleans. Hotel rooms are for sleeping only."

"Well," Erika said slowly, "and other things."

Jo thought about that, then nodded. "Right, but that usually ends in sleeping."

Maggie frowned for a moment, losing track of what they were talking about briefly, then she understood.

She shook her head. "I don't remember you two being quite so sex obsessed."

"And you aren't sex obsessed enough," Jo informed her. "Now come on, you can't come to New Orleans and miss Bourbon Street."

"I'm here for ten days," Maggie pointed out. "We could wait a night. I am honestly tired."

"No," Erika and Jo said, speaking again at the same time—a habit that was actually getting a little irritating, Maggie decided—as Erika caught her other elbow, and her friends pulled her down the sidewalk. She gave in, allowing them to lead the way.

"Erika and I are only here for five nights. And we need them all," Jo said.

Maggie sighed. That was true. Her friends were leaving her early, something she was not happy about. What would she do in a city like this alone? She'd already noted this was a place filled with couples and groups.

She supposed she'd better take advantage of having both her pals here. Her pace picked up.

Even unfamiliar with the layout of the city and muzzy from the wine, Maggie didn't need to be told when they reached Bourbon Street. She blinked at everything around her. The flashing lights, the loud, slightly distorted bass of bands singing party favorites, the distinct smell of trash, beer and . . .

Was that vomit?

Add to that neon signs that said things like LIVE SEX ACTS and FULL NUDITY. Holy cow.

"This is . . . something," she managed, peering around, not sure where to look next.

Even Jo and Erika, who were definitely worldlier when it came to bars and partying, gawked in awe.

"This is pretty amazing," Erika finally said, after they'd all stood mesmerized by a pair of female mannequin legs in black stilettos, kicking in and out of a club's windows.

"You definitely don't see that every day, do you?" Jo said.

Maggie almost said that she'd never seen that, period, when her attention was seized by a distinct strain of music, somehow reaching out to her over the warring chords of "Jessie's Girl," "Living On A Prayer," and "Summer of '69."

Without thinking, she took a step toward the sound, and then another, until she'd zigzagged through the crowds of revelers to a bar on the corner of Bourbon and some cross street.

She stopped on the sidewalk, staring at the building. The place was shabby, paint peeling from the wood, the sidewalk around it crumbling and layered in filth. But from her spot on the street, she could see the stage through huge open windows; a band was setting up. And she could clearly hear that distinct melody. Piano notes swirling through the air, a sound as out of place in this world as she felt.

Again, her feet moved until she found herself in the bar, standing in front of the stage, peering up at the person playing the music. Music that no one else should know.

Well, no one but her and possibly a few other authenticators. And the person who wrote it, of course, but that person was long since dead.

"Wow," Jo said from beside her, dragging Maggie's attention away from the music. "Good eye. That guy's pretty darn hot."

Maggie blinked back at the stage, for the first time noticing the man actually playing the music. He was tall with long hair in a shade somewhere between chestnut brown and dark mahogany, cascading over his broad shoulders.

He was looking down at the keyboard, his hair falling forward, shrouding most of his features, so that Maggie wondered how Jo could tell whether he was hot or not.

The thought quickly vanished as she watched his long fin-

gers travel over the keys, playing a particularly difficult combination of chords. Exactly the combination she'd read before she'd left. A fusion of notes that seemed to be a signature
of sorts, the signature of a composer she was willing to bet
this guy from a cover band on Bourbon Street had never even
heard of.

Yet here he was, playing it. Playing a piece that no one
knew. An undiscovered composition probably by a little
known composer.

Then two things happened at once: the beautiful, haunting
tune abruptly switched into the intro to the classic eighties
rock ballad "Sister Christian," and Maggie realized that the
musician was staring directly at her. And she was staring back.

"Ah, man, he has a lazy eye," Erika said with a disappointed sigh.

Maggie heard her friend's words and regret, but they didn't
seem to quite reach her, as if they echoed from a distance or
through a somnolent haze. She just kept staring at the man,
unable to look away, even though everything in her told her
to.

"There is something up with his eye, but I don't think it's
lazy," Maggie heard Jo say.

Maggie wanted to speak, to say there wasn't anything
wrong with his eyes, but the words in her head couldn't fum-
ble their way past her lips.

All she could manage was to focus on him—on the eyes in
question. Eyes that seemed to match the music he'd been
playing: complicated, intense, haunted. And just as the music
held her entranced, so did his gaze.

Until finally, a small smile curved his lips and his gaze left
her to concentrate on his keyboards.

Maggie actually jerked, as if some invisible line had been
cut between them, and she was freed. The room tilted for a
moment as the whole world seemed to shift on its axis. Then
it slammed back into place.

On rubbery knees, she walked toward the bar.

"Where are you going?" Erika asked.

"I need to sit," Maggie murmured, relieved to find a vacant stool, which she collapsed onto. What had just happened?

"I think that guy was checking you out," Jo said, wiggling her eyebrows.

Maggie ignored her as she tried to visualize the sheet music she'd just begun to study before she left her office for this trip. She could see the notes, scratched across the page, ink faded on yellowed, brittle paper. Faint notes, but still there. Like the already fading notes of what she'd thought she'd just heard. Those notes gone now amongst the chords and rhythms of the rock ballad.

"What's going on?" Jo asked, when Maggie continued to stare off, lost in the images in her head.

Maggie shook her head, not quite ready to say aloud what she was thinking. It seemed so ridiculous.

"Maggie, I can't believe just having a guy notice you has you that shaken," Jo said, wedging herself between Maggie's stool and the one next to her. The businessman seated on the neighboring barstool, who Jo had bumped into, turned to glare at her. His annoyance faded as soon as he saw Jo's profile, her lovely features accented by cropped, glossy brown hair and big dark brown eyes.

Jo didn't notice the man twisting on his seat to peer at her. Nor did Erika notice his friend, checking her out as well. Erika, with her thick midnight black hair and killer smile. Then again, attention from men was a common occurrence for both her friends. Not for Maggie, however, with her less than lithe form and limited fashion sense.

Then she recalled the link she'd felt when she'd met the eyes of the man on the stage. A connection had coursed between them, strong and . . . almost alive. A feeling she'd never in her life encountered. Of course, it wasn't his attention that had shaken her. Okay, maybe it had a little, but she wasn't sure that what had occurred between them was even attraction.

It was almost as if they were both in on a secret. A secret

he acted like only they knew. Of course, she wasn't actually in on that secret, was she?

Was it the music? Was that what they'd shared? Did he know she knew the piece he'd been playing?

And she did know it. Maggie was certain. Okay, she had only given a few of the pieces a cursory glance as she readied to leave for vacation. Certainly, packing and getting ready to leave could have made her less observant than usual. And there had been dozens of compositions that needed authenticating. Literally dozens. Symphonies, concerti, and sonatas. Even what appeared to be a complete opera.

Quite a discovery, and she couldn't resist sneaking a little peek, even though she couldn't really do any intense analysis until she got back.

Still, even with her brief perusal, she knew the keyboard player up on that stage had been playing one of the pieces she'd seen. A sonata.

She wasn't wrong—although now, with yet another classic rock standard playing behind her, she was starting to question her own memory.

"That guy—on the keyboards," she said, still hesitant to say the words aloud, because they were so implausible, "he was just playing one of the pieces I'm researching. A piece that may very well have never been seen by any musician other than the composer."

Her friends stared at her. They thought she was nuts too.

"Oh, no," Jo said, shaking her head. "No, no. You are not going to think about work."

"That's right," Erika agreed. "You are too obsessed with it as it is. You are not going to think about it now."

"But I wasn't. Not until I heard what he was playing." Maggie knew what she heard. Even though she knew it wasn't possible.

"How would some musician on Bourbon Street know the stuff you research? Aren't they lost pieces of classical music?" Jo frowned, then waved for the bartender.

"Exactly," Maggie said. "But I know it was one of them. In fact, it was the last piece I looked at before leaving the office."

Maggie cast a look between her two friends. Erika's eyes shone with concern. Jo frowned, the downward curve of her lips somewhere between worry and exasperation. And neither one looked as if they believed her.

"You know what I think," Jo said, after ordering something from the bartender that Maggie couldn't quite hear over the newest rock anthem pounding behind her. "I think it just reminded you of that piece. And wasn't that the large collection you and Peter were supposed to be working on together?"

Maggie nodded. This job was one of the few things she'd gotten to keep when Peter left.

"Maybe subconsciously you were thinking about work and Peter. I know it's hard to let go of what happened, but you've got to, for you." Jo's eyes now looked more worried than irritated.

Was she that hung up on Peter? Still? Maybe.

The bartender, a bouncy gal with a multitude of dyed braids sticking up from her otherwise shaved head like so many colorful antennae, appeared with three beers. Before Jo could reach into her purse for her wallet, the businessman still pressed beside her took that moment to turn and offer to buy their drinks.

Jo smiled, easily flirting with the man. Maggie watched, momentarily distracted from her own strange train of thought. Flirting was an art form, just like music. And a talent that she'd been born without, just like music.

She glanced over her shoulder, back toward the stage. The man who'd been playing the keyboard now stood at the mic.

For the first time she realized it was his voice that filled the shadowy bar. A good voice, a bit higher than she would have guessed—something about his features suggested he'd have a husky voice. But the tone was strong and melodic, and a little . . .

She realized her skin tingled and she was holding her breath deep in her chest as she listened. His voice was . . . sexy. Very sexy.

She forced herself to turn back to the counter and take a sip of her beer.

"I'm thinking that the fact you thought you heard that music is a sign," Erika said, startling Maggie from her intent concentration on that voice.

"What?" Maggie blinked. Again it was as if the man had mesmerized her, now with his singing rather than his eyes or his playing. What was it about him that was so entrancing to her? Aside from his knowledge of undiscovered sonatas.

"I think the fact that you *thought* you heard that man playing the very song you were just researching is a sign. Because he couldn't know it. As you said, it's not possible. So maybe you just thought you heard it. Maybe it was some weird cosmic occurrence to lead you to this bar, to see him. Maybe Marie Laveau wanted you to meet him."

Maggie stared at her friend. She was serious.

Maggie turned slightly on her seat and glanced back up to the stage. She considered the idea for a fraction of a second, then nearly laughed. Erika was definitely more esoteric than either herself or Jo. And apparently more romantic too. But this was definitely one of her more fantastic theories.

But the laugh died on her lips.

He was watching her again. His eyes—she couldn't quite make out the color from this distance—locked with hers. For the first time, she noticed what her friends had mentioned; there was something different about his left eye. Although it definitely wasn't lazy. It was . . .

"Just look at the way he's watching you," Erika said. "He's into you."

Maggie immediately broke her gaze from his, feeling heat

burn her cheeks. She shook her head. "You're making too much of all this."

She knew she was saying that for herself as much as for Erika. When she met that man's eyes, she did feel like something brought her here. Which was crazy. Absolutely crazy.

Her friends were right, though. She had to have imagined what she heard. Without looking back to the stage, she turned on her barstool and focused on her beer, paying unusually close attention to peeling off the label. She needed to let this go. Picking up the beer, she took a sip, then grimaced.

She'd liked the wine with dinner better. There, she decided. Everything could be blamed on the wine. She'd been tipsy and just thought she heard that rare, haunting, beautiful music. That was the only reasonable explanation.

It had to be.

Chapter 3

Ren watched the bar from his vantage point on the small stage. People danced and drank and generally acted rowdy and often ridiculous. The usual.

Okay, scrap that, most people acted that way. Except one of them. His attention was focused on the curvy woman with tousled hair. Hair the shade of . . . what was that color called? Strawberry blond? Hell, he didn't know, but it was a good color.

He watched and sang the lyrics of a Journey song, reciting the words with little thought. It wasn't like he hadn't sung the same song thousands of times. Hell, maybe millions. He'd been in New Orleans, working on Bourbon, longer than was probably safe. But then, this was a city of transients. People didn't stay here long enough to notice that he hadn't changed one bit in the last ten years. And the return visitors were usually too drunk and into their partying to really give his looks much thought.

This was a strange place, where he could be the center of attention and be invisible all at the same time.

He glanced over to a group of revelers on the dance floor. Five woman, scantily clad, flashing legs and cleavage, and working very hard to get him to notice them.

He smiled. Predictably, they giggled and whispered to each

other and began dancing more determinedly. More leg. More cleavage. The usual.

And while that was good—Ren did enjoy women—the best part was that he could spend the night with one of them, maybe more than one of them, and then they went back to their lives. Ren would be nothing more than a vague memory—just as they were to him.

Bourbon Street was famous for the best time you didn't remember. And that worked out well for him. The people were predictable, and he could easily get lost amongst them.

Plus the atmosphere here effervesced with energy, with life, which made it very easy from him to survive. He breathed in deeply, pulling the vitality in the air deep into his body, feeling it fill him. Human life force, which fed him.

Women, sex, and human energy. This darkened, run-down bar provided all the necessities he required.

His gaze moved back to the woman at the bar. But what about that one? There was something very different about her. And not just her rather conservative clothes and lack of exposed skin.

He smiled. Although that *was* different.

No, what intrigued him was that when he'd been playing the keyboards, something he rarely did, he could have sworn she'd actually recognized the piece. He'd been fooling around while the rest of the band set up, and on impulse, began to play a sonata he'd written when he was only fourteen.

He'd played the piece publicly only once—for his father's birthday gala. Not that anyone in attendance had known the smug, pompous bastard was his father. And that Ren was not just his father's favorite discovery, a child prodigy, a performing monkey.

Ren had played the piece—honestly believing his father would be so impressed that he would announce to the *ton* that the gifted child seated before them performing his heart out was, in fact, his son. But dear Daddy hadn't, and Ren had thrown the piece away—because while his father loved his music and his talent, he'd never had a moment's love for his illegitimate son.

Ren frowned slightly, even though his voice remained positive as he sang, telling the audience that any way they wanted it, that's the way they needed it.

He couldn't even say what made him think of that song tonight—not the Journey song, which he sang every night he worked. That sonata. He hadn't thought of the piece in decades. Longer than that.

Yet he'd impulsively played it, and when he'd looked up, the curvy strawberry blond had been standing right in front of the stage, staring up at him like she was seeing a ghost. Wide-eyed, shocked. And he could have sworn he saw recognition in her eyes, too.

Ren finished singing, offering a routine thank you to the crowd swarming the bar.

"Dude, what's going on tonight?" his lead guitarist, Drake, leaned in to ask. Drake was a vampire, too, but Drake was a run-of-the-mill bloodsucker, while Ren had the dubious distinction of being a lampir, an energy sucker.

Ren frowned at his bandmate. Okay, with his goatee grown long, head shaved except for a long queue ponytailed on the back of his head, and a skull shirt, Drake was far from run-of-the-mill. And he'd been a pirate in life.

"What do you mean?" Ren asked, not following Drake's comment.

Drake frowned, which made him look almost sinister, except Ren knew he was harmless. Well, unless crossed. Okay, he was still a pirate, really.

"You sang the same lyric three times."

Ren frowned. "No I didn't."

"You totally did," Johnny said, appearing from behind his drums, heading down off the stage. Johnny had been a gangster in his former life. Unlike Drake, he didn't look the part at all now, in his tie-dyed T-shirt and ripped jeans.

Ren frowned at the drummer's sudden desertion, but then

decided that maybe he could use a little break as well. He announced the band would be back in ten. The sound guy, a really annoying human with far more attitude than he deserved to have, started the pounding beat of dj'ed dance-pop before Ren could even finish his announcement.

Normally that really pissed him off, but tonight Ren was too preoccupied with other thoughts to be bothered. Instead, he pretended to busy himself with some of the equipment—the best method to avoid the five busty, leggy women, who were already rushing the stage to talk.

But there was no need to worry. The other band members were more than happy to greet the women. And that gave Ren opportunity to cast more looks over at the one at the bar.

Most of the set, she'd sat with her back to the stage, sipping a beer. He'd deduced she was with two other women. Her friends had befriended a couple of men at the bar and were now chatting and dancing with them, while Miss Curvy sat alone.

He checked the bass levels on the amps, which were fine. Which he knew already. Were the men here tonight bloody blind? She was the most intriguing woman in the room.

Then he decided he was glad she wasn't getting the usual regiment of drunks hitting on her. That idea bothered him more than he cared to consider. He checked the treble. Also fine—as he knew.

He straightened up from the equipment and looked her way again. She was wearing a black blouse with a pair of black, cuffed pants and black shoes. Nothing exciting about that. He cast a quick—a very quick, because it was never wise to make direct eye contact with horny women if you were trying to avoid them—look at the barely clad ladies. What they'd chosen to wear was tight, bright, and accompanied by high heels. All selected to attract attention.

He looked back to the other woman. She looked as if she

wanted to fade into the shadows. She didn't want any attention whatsoever.

And before he realized his intent, he was strolling down the steps of the stage, heading right in her direction.

Maggie took another sip of her beer, hoping the bitter liquid would make her a little more relaxed. She wanted to get back to that warm, cheery feeling she'd had when she'd left the restaurant. But she was rapidly realizing she wasn't a beer drinker, especially lukewarm beer.

She drew in a deep breath. At least the band had stopped playing, and she was no longer surrounded by that voice. She wasn't a big Beyoncé fan, but at least the woman's voice, which now surrounded her from the sound system, didn't make her insides feel all funny.

She looked over at her friends, who conversed animatedly with two new men—sailors all decked out in their dress whites. She had no idea where the businessmen had disappeared to.

She shook her head, amused at the attention her friends were attracting. They were amazing. But instead of the usual twinge of envy, she only felt tired. She wanted to head back to the hotel. The events of the day had caught up with her, and she just felt drained.

But she knew if she told her friends she was going to go, they'd insist on walking back with her, even though—and sadly, it had taken her most of the night to realize this fact—they were actually in a bar right across the street from their hotel. Still she knew her friends would leave with her, and she didn't want to ruin their fun.

Erika started dancing with one of the sailors, laughing at something he leaned in to say. Her laughter lit up her face, making her features stunningly lovely. There was a part of Maggie that wished she could be like that. A flirt. Comfortable with the opposite sex. She never had been though. Not until Peter—and well, that hadn't worked out well, had it?

Maggie glanced toward the stage, telling herself she wasn't looking for anyone in particular, even as she searched for long hair and intense eyes. She promptly assured herself that it wasn't disappointment she felt when she couldn't locate them.

Her gaze moved back to her friends. Jo and her new friend had joined Erika and her guy. They all danced and laughed.

Again Maggie smiled. Okay, maybe this time a touch of envy tightened her chest.

"Are you having fun?"

Maggie started, literally jerking in her seat at the voice so near her. Strange, that she could be so startled when the bar was already loud.

Then she saw who spoke to her. The musician. The one with the strange eyes. Now, close up, she could also add a great smile to his description. White teeth with the corners of his lips curled slightly, giving his grin a Cheshire-cat quality. And she'd been right, his speaking voice was indeed husky, like the rich, warm brush of heated velvet.

"Umm, yeah," she managed to say, trying not to stare at his mouth. But when she moved her gaze, she was staring into his eyes, and that made her uncomfortable too. She opted to look at the button of his shirt. Except just above that button was a V of bare chest covered in faint whorls of dark chest hair.

She looked down at her hands.

"Can I get you a drink?"

She glanced up at him, half expecting that he was talking to someone else now, but his eyes were still locked on her. In the blue and red light cast by the neon beer signs behind the bar, the eyelashes of his left eye looked faintly purple. She blinked, sure she was seeing things. Either that or the wine from dinner hadn't worn off as much as she'd thought.

"No, thank you," she finally said, her gaze returning to the buttons of his shirt, the one below the top one, so she couldn't see the chest.

"Stacy," he called, gesturing to the bartender with the braids springing out of her head. Once he caught her attention, he nodded. She nodded back and bounced away. Apparently her braids really were antennae; he didn't even have to speak to communicate with her.

"Are you visiting here?"

Maggie blinked up at him. Was he still talking to her? Surely her inability to speak had bored him by now.

"Yes. From Washington, D.C."

He looked impressed. Then he tilted his head slightly as if he was studying her. The pose made his hair fall forward, framing his face.

Maggie had never been crazy about long-haired men. She never thought about it either way, really, but there was something breathtakingly beautiful about the contrast of his long, silky hair and the masculine line of his jaw. Her fingers twitched as the sudden urge to touch the shiny length jolted through her.

Oh yeah, the wine was still in her system. No doubt about it.

The bartender appeared with a bottle of something. "Here you go," she said with a wide smile, then bounded away to take another patron's order.

Ah, Maggie realized, he'd just been making small talk while he waited for his drink.

"It's loud in here," he said as he leaned forward, reaching past her to grab the bottle. She could feel him as if he'd brushed against her. His body seemed to fill the space between them—even though he didn't come close to touching her.

She nodded, taking in a steadying breath. Why did this guy have her so shaken? He wasn't flirting. He was just chatting. Why did she feel so flustered? Why couldn't she play it cool like her friends did? After all, this guy was *not* feeling the same vibe she was. No way.

"Maybe you'd want to—"

The musician's question was cut off as one of the other

band members, a heavyset guy with very short hair and a black AC/DC T-shirt, came over and slapped him on the back. "Come on. Time to play, my friend."

He nodded, then turned back to Maggie. "Are you going to hang around for the next set?"

She nodded, even as her lucid mind reminded her that she'd wanted to go back to the hotel minutes earlier. Somehow, her brain and body didn't seem connected.

He smiled again. He did have a great smile.

"Good. I'll talk to you after."

Again she nodded automatically.

As soon as he headed back to the stage, Jo and Erika were at her side.

"What did he say to you?" Jo asked.

Maggie blinked, surprised they had even noticed the brief exchange. "He asked if we were staying for the next set."

"Hell, yeah, we are," Erika stated, glancing over her shoulder at him. Maggie did too. He was positioning himself in front of the microphone, long finger curling around the stand. He was looking at her.

Them. He must be looking at them. Probably realizing the cuties were her friends.

Then he smiled, and his eyes were definitely on her. Heat burned over her cheeks.

"Why does he want me to stay?" she pondered aloud.

Jo made a noise very close to disgust. "Because you are lovely and he wants to talk to you."

Maggie cocked a dubious eyebrow. She knew she was smart and she knew she was passably pretty. She also knew she could be fun—even if it was hard to tell now, when she was overwhelmed by the general weirdness of this night. But she also knew she was not the type to attract a musician in a rock band.

They went for . . . she watched as the drummer was dragged away from a gaggle of busty, beautiful women by one of the other band members.

They were attracted to women like that.

Especially a musician who looked like the one who'd talked to her. He really was gorgeous. That could be the wine and warm beer talking, but she didn't think so.

"He must say that to everyone," she decided. He was probably just a friendly guy.

"He didn't say it to me," Erika said.

"Or me," Jo added.

Maggie frowned. "What do I do?"

"You stay." Jo nodded at her as if the suggestion was a done deal.

And Maggie supposed it was. After all, she was too curious a person not to see why he wanted her to stay. Yeah, right, and that was the only reason.

Chapter 4

"What is he doing?" Erika asked, frowning at the stage.

Maggie didn't respond. She just watched as the musician, who she'd waited for like a groupie, fiddled with some of the sound equipment, oblivious to her, still seated at the bar. They'd finished playing nearly fifteen minutes ago, and he hadn't approached her.

"I think maybe we should go. I feel stupid just waiting here," Maggie said, keeping her voice even, trying to hide her humiliation.

What had she been thinking? That he'd really intended to talk to her again? After all, this was New Orleans. He'd probably had twenty conversations tonight just like the one they'd shared.

She glanced around the dim, run-down barroom, looked at the thinning crowd. She was the only one who'd waited. Even the tipsy group of wild women who'd worked all night to get the band's attention, especially his attention, had left after the band stopped playing.

Maggie glanced at her friends. Both Jo and Erika looked pained and annoyed for her. Although she knew they meant well, their sympathetic expressions didn't help. They just made her feel more pathetic.

Maggie rose from her barstool, turning to check if she'd

left anything behind, only to realize that all she had was her purse—and that was in her hand.

She pulled in a deep breath, attempting to calm herself. She'd managed to stay composed through the band's long set. There was no point to falling apart now.

In fact, she decided, this was for the best. What did she really expect to happen anyway? That Erika's prediction had come true, and whatever happened with the musician and the music was Marie Laveau's doing? That a voodoo priestess had somehow led her here? It was time to go back to the hotel and crawl into bed, as she'd been longing to do all night long.

She glanced back at the bar again, looking for what, she didn't know. Darn, she was flustered.

"Okay, let's . . ." Her words faded as she turned back to her friends to find herself staring at a V of chest and dark hair. Both familiar.

"Were you leaving?"

Maggie hesitated. Something inside warned her she should just say yes and head back to the hotel. After all, she was out of her element with this man. He had probably just come over now because he realized that, silly person that she was, she had actually thought he meant what he'd said earlier. So, now he felt obligated to come speak to her.

"It's still loud in here. And hot," he said, tugging at his shirt, which again drew her attention to his chest. He gestured to one of the side doors leading to the street. "Want to step outside with me?"

Maggie hesitated. While the bar had emptied out considerably, the pop music did make it hard to talk. And humidity did make the air thick and damp. Although she noticed he didn't appear sweaty at all—not even flushed. She suspected she did.

She glanced at Jo and Erika. Erika grinned, widening her eyes with encouragement. Jo wasn't as eager as Erika, but she didn't give any signal that she thought Maggie should avoid him.

Maggie nodded. "Sure. It is kind of loud."

Again that amazing smile appeared. He started to reach out as if he intended to touch her, perhaps place his hand on the small of her back, but then he dropped it back to his side.

"This way," he said, again gesturing to the side door.

They stepped out onto the sidewalk, a cracked slab of stained concrete. The street they stood on ran perpendicular to Bourbon. Bourbon was still alive with partyers, despite the hour.

"I'm Ren Anthony, by the way," he said offering his hand.

"Maggie Gallagher," she said, accepting his hand, immediately remembering his hands as he held the mic. She'd thought he had nice hands then, but touching them, she realized they went beyond nice. They were . . . lovely. Long fingers and broad palms, an artist's hand, strong and sculpted, but with a slight roughness of calluses, as if they'd known physical work too. Her body reacted instantly; energy zinged up her arm and throughout her body. Then he released her.

"Does anyone ever sleep in this city?" she asked, grabbing onto the first thought that came into her mind.

Ren turned to watch a large group of what appeared to be middle-aged men and their wives wander down the middle of Bourbon, loud and giddy.

"During the day," he said. Then he turned back to her. "Did you come here to sleep? Because if you did, you *are* in the wrong place."

She recalled her friends sharing a similar sentiment with her earlier. Although Maggie hardly saw it as a sign, Erika would. Maggie wasn't that impractical, though. After all, New Orleans was a party-all-night kind of place.

But she did consider his question. "No. I didn't come here to sleep."

"So what did you come here for?"

Maggie met his gaze, realizing for the first time since they'd stepped outside that she'd been avoiding looking at him. But he'd managed to ask the question of the night, and that surprised her. What had she come here for? What did she expect from this vacation?

For the first time, she considered the idea seriously, that it might not just be to relax. Maybe she was looking for the fling that her friends said she needed. She considered telling him that, but she didn't have the courage. Her gaze left his and dropped back to the stained sidewalk.

"Does my eye bother you?"

Maggie's head snapped up. What? Why would his eye bother her?

Then for the first time, she realized why one eye looked so different. She'd noticed it was different back in the bar, but out here, surrounded by streetlights and the lights of the other buildings, she could see why it looked unusual.

While the lashes of his right eye were dark brown, a shade or two darker than his hair, the lashes of his left eye were perfectly white. Devoid of all pigmentation.

She couldn't help but stare for a moment. It was so dramatic. And fascinating to look at.

Finally, she remembered he'd asked her a question.

"No. Your eye doesn't bother me. It's actually rather interesting."

He smiled slightly—not the same as the smiles she'd seen before, though. This one looked hard, somehow. It didn't quite reach his eyes. "You're not worried it could be an evil eye or something? This is New Orleans. Voodoo and all that."

There was a joking quality to his tone, yet like his smile, the amusement didn't seem to reach his eyes.

"Well, I'm not sure about all the voodoo," she said, offering him a small smile, "but I'm pretty sure your eye is fine."

She smiled until she realized his gaze was locked on her lips. His eyes moved up to meet hers. A zing of awareness shot through her just as it had when their eyes met while he was onstage. The haunting strains of the song he'd been playing suddenly echoed in her mind.

"So is this just a vacation?" he asked, drawing her back to

the moment, the music and the strange energy shattering and rippling away like the still waters of a pond when a rock is thrown into it.

"Yes." She pulled in a breath, trying to gather herself. "For ten days. We're staying right there," she pointed to the large, many-windowed hotel across the street.

His gaze followed her gesture and held there long enough that Maggie began to wonder what held his attention so. Then he turned back to her.

"You probably shouldn't announce that. Unless you want strange men to follow you home." He smiled, the curling at the edges returned, though something was different about his eyes. "Do you?"

Maggie blinked, still trying to understand the strange, almost haunted look in his eyes.

"Do I what?" She totally missed what he was asking.

"Do you want strange men to follow you home?"

Her body reacted to the question instantly. He was flirting with her. Unbelievably, he really was. She had no idea how to deal with that.

"So do you live in the French Quarter?" she managed to ask, opting to ignore his question and get the conversation on some sort of normal ground.

He nodded, and again she noticed how silky his hair looked framing his face.

"I live on St. Ann," he told her. "Why? Did you want to follow *me* home?"

She swallowed. Wow, she really was out of her element here. Guys did not flirt with her. They just didn't. Except this one, and she had no idea how to respond. Her gaze dropped to the ground. Gum, beer caps, crushed cigarettes—these things she could understand.

Then a hand touched her, strong fingers gentle as they nudged her face up so her gaze met his.

"I make you uncomfortable, don't I?"

Maggie licked her lips, trying to breathe, trying to speak as more sizzling awareness zipped through her, stemming from the place where his fingers touched her chin, then radiating outward in whirling spirals throughout her body.

She managed to shake her head. He did make her uncomfortable but not in the way he thought. He made her awkwardly aware of how attracted she was to him. And how little she knew how to handle something this intense, this strong. Peter had never made her feel so . . .

She let out a pent-up breath. So strange. She pulled in a slow breath to replace the one she'd released.

His gaze returned to her lips.

The one and only thought going through Ren's mind was that he wanted to kiss this woman. She had a small mouth, bowlike, sweet, and he wanted desperately to taste it. But given the way she'd frozen when he'd touched her, he didn't think she'd be very receptive to a kiss.

Man, he'd lived this life way too long. Only in New Orleans, only in the bar scene, was it even remotely acceptable to make out with a woman that you'd said less than fifty words to. Add that he was a musician, and he could usually knock off another twenty-five words.

But this woman wasn't a part of that world . . . his world. She had an intelligence and innate innocence that was clear in her wide gray-green eyes. Even in the way she held herself—a little closed off, a little distant. As if she knew she was too close to something dangerous. The virtuous standing before the fires of hell.

What? When had he gotten so colorful in his thought processes? Night after night of the same old rock and roll and the same debauchery had drained all the creativity out of him. Even back at his most creative, that image would have been a tad dramatic.

For a moment, his gaze left her and focused on the building she'd pointed to earlier. A large, popular hotel . . . now. The original building, The Opera House, was gone. The beautiful building once filled with music and applause and talent, gone, reduced to ashes.

Perhaps the fire analogy wasn't so far off after all. It certainly was a good reminder of what could happen if he got too involved with a mortal. He destroyed them, and he could easily destroy all the appealing things he saw in her.

But instead of walking away, as he should have, he returned his attention to her. Maggie. He studied the woman in front of him.

Was it so wrong to simply talk with her? To let her freshness clear away a little of the dirt that had settled into him? But he wanted to do more than talk, didn't he? That's when things got tricky; that's when he was playing with fire.

Or rather, he was allowing her to play with fire. He slid another glance at the hotel, a looming reminder of how dangerous things could get if he went too far.

But instead of ending things here and now, he asked, "So what do you do back in D.C.?" A safe enough question. For both of them.

But again, she regarded him with a wariness that easily rivaled that of a cornered rabbit.

"I'm an authenticator. I do a lot of work for the Smithsonian and other museums."

Interesting. "What do you authenticate?"

Again she seemed reluctant to say, but she did. "I actually research and authenticate classical music."

Now it was Ren's turn to freeze. Classical music. Was that why she'd reacted the way she had when he'd noticed her there at the stage, staring up at him as if she was seeing a ghost?

Of course, she *had* been seeing a ghost. But there was no way she could know that. That piece had never been heard outside of his father's music room. Played in public once— and then forgotten. Except by him. It was still there, even after he longed to forget it, forget that night.

"You are a very good pianist," he heard her say, and he shoved that long-ago night out of his mind.

"Not really."

"That song you were playing at the beginning of the night—"

"You know, it is late."

His abrupt words shut her down instantly. He knew they would. It wasn't hard to crush a butterfly—and she was fragile and delicate as one. Just as he'd seen the pureness, he'd seen the vulnerability too, right from their first gaze.

But he could not talk about this, even though she couldn't possibly know who he was. He wasn't a pianist anymore. He wasn't a composer. Renaldo D'Antoni was dead. A ghost.

"Oh," she said, pink coloring her cheeks. "Right. I didn't mean to—"

He couldn't listen to her apology when she had no reason for making one. "I just didn't realize the time. And I have a long night tomorrow."

"Right," she said again. Then she glanced around her, and for a moment he wondered what she was searching for. Then he recalled her friends.

The two women appeared as if they'd been watching. They stepped out of the bar to join them on the street, right at her side once they were aware Maggie needed them.

Ren liked that they'd remained close. New Orleans could be a dangerous city. It made him feel better to know his butterfly wasn't alone.

They flanked their friend like tall, lovely bodyguards.

"Maggie," the one with short brown hair asked, "who's your friend?"

Ren could tell the friend's inquiry was really just a way to gauge Maggie's feelings. He watched Maggie closely too, even though he knew her emotions. He could feel them in the air—she was embarrassed. He hated that feeling on her. It was like a noxious perfume, as noxious as her wariness. More so—because embarrassment also involved pain.

But he managed to remain stoic as he offered a hand to the friend.

"Hi, I'm Ren."

"Jo," she said, not offering him a smile and only accepting his hand for a moment.

Jo wasn't a vampire, but she obviously could sense her friend was uncomfortable. Of course, Maggie's emotions were easy to read, every one of them flashing in her eyes.

"And I'm Erika," the black-haired one said, regarding him with a small smile, and a look that was more speculative than judging.

But both women were ready to protect their friend. That should have made him feel a lot better, but instead he was filled with an odd desire to join her friends' ranks. Maggie seemed to need protection.

Yeah, from you more than anyone, he thought.

He immediately decided he'd been wrong to even approach this woman. She wasn't his type. Totally wrong. He should have chatted up the buxom babes who'd shimmied on the dance floor all night.

Maybe it wasn't too late to find them. Then he looked back into Maggie's big eyes, and a sinking feeling told him it was already way too late.

"Nice to meet you all," he said, stepping back from the women. "I hope you have a great time in New Orleans." He didn't even bother to temper the abrupt goodbye. The whole point was to make sure she didn't return.

Maggie Gallagher was a risk he couldn't take. Who knew a butterfly could be so dangerous?

Chapter 5

Maggie picked up the beignet, taking a huge bite. Powdered sugar dotted the front of her shirt, and she didn't rush to brush the powder away. Instead, she closed her eyes and savored the mixture of chewy dough, sweet sugar, and just enough grease to make the pastry heavenly. Yes, she was comfort-eating, and she really did not care.

"That guy was a twit," Jo said, pulling off a corner of her beignet and popping it in her mouth. Erika nodded, doing the same thing with her pastry. Neither of them had a speck of sugar on their clothes. Damn them.

"What was his name again? Ren? What kind of name is that?" Erika rolled her eyes as if the man's name was an offense to the human race, rather than just a little different.

"And his eye was weird," Jo added.

Maggie swallowed and reached for a napkin. "It was unusual, but I didn't think it was weird." She brushed away the dusting, glad the peasant blouse she wore was mostly white.

Jo shrugged. "Whatever. You can do better."

Maggie didn't argue—but she didn't agree either. Truthfully, she hadn't talked to the man long enough to know what he was like, really. She did know that he seemed to run in varying degrees of hot and cold, but she wasn't sure that was justification to hate him. After all, he hadn't done anything particularly wrong.

Oh, she'd definitely felt mortified at his abrupt aloofness and departure. But really it wasn't that strange.

She wasn't a man-magnet, and he'd likely realized that very quickly once they'd gotten outside. She'd made conversation as if English was her second language. Her body had gone into overdrive every time he'd looked at her, as if she was some inexperienced schoolgirl.

"I cannot believe he made you wait around like that, then just took off after a couple minutes' talk," Jo continued, tearing off another bite of beignet with more force than the poor pastry deserved.

Maggie glanced at Erika, who smiled in silent agreement with Maggie's look. They both knew Jo was no longer discussing the musician. Jo had crawled out of bed after only a few hours' sleep to meet one of the sailors for breakfast at a place called Petunia's, but the guy had never shown. Jo was not pleased.

Apparently her irritation applied to all men at the moment.

Maggie took another bite of her beignet, chewing thoughtfully. She had to admit she wasn't upset with Ren. After all, she didn't even know him. But she was upset with herself—for several reasons. Primarily because she'd actually thought he might be interested, and for wanting him to be interested.

Thank goodness she hadn't flirted back. If she was mortified now, imagine how she'd feel if she'd attempted flirting and then he'd fled.

Of course, maybe if she had, he might have become interested. She was hopeless, eternally doomed to be devoid of feminine wiles.

"I was thinking we should get our fortunes told today," Erika suggested, obviously trying to change the atmosphere around the table. "I saw a place over on Chartres that looks great. All new-agey and cool."

Jo shook her head, pushing her remaining beignets away from her. Hopeful pigeons landed on the backs of chairs at a nearby table, gauging their chances of swooping in to steal a beignet . . . the drawback of an open-air café. Maggie pulled her plate closer.

"All they are going to tell me is that I wasted my whole morning waiting for some guy to not show up. And I'm cranky from lack of sleep." Jo took a sip of her café au lait.

Erika laughed. "Actually, that's past and present. Fortune-tellers tell your future."

"Well, my future involves a nap," Jo said, pushing away from the table. The pigeons fluttered loudly into flight at the sudden movement. "I have to get some sleep or I'm going to be grumpy all night, too."

Maggie nodded sympathetically. She could use a nap, but she knew it wasn't going to happen. As tired as she was, the weird energy she'd felt since arriving still filled her. Last night, she'd gotten, maybe, three hours of sleep, then had finally given up.

She couldn't relax. She thought about Peter. She thought about Ren. She thought about that music. Now she wasn't sure if he'd been playing the song currently locked away in the safe in her office. But the melody of what he *had* been playing kept haunting her.

Several times during the night, she'd been sure her initial thoughts were right—but then, not. The strange energy of the city seemed to cloud everything. So far, everything had felt surreal, like living smack in the middle of a lucid dream. Of course, that could be the lack of sleep too.

"So what about you?" Erika asked Maggie. "Will you go with me? I want my tea leaves read."

Maggie nodded. "Sure." She brushed more sugar from her shirtfront. She might as well go find out what her future held; it had to be better than her recent past.

"So you want your tea leaves read?"

Maggie turned slightly in the rickety ladder-back chair as an older woman pushed aside the curtain that covered the doorway.

Maggie's first impression was *witch*. Long, coarse gray hair, streaked in places, vaguely hinted at what had once been its original color. She was easily in her sixties, maybe in her seventies.

She navigated through the space, which wasn't much more than a booth, really, dodging two small tables scattered with mystical bric-a-brac, and took a seat across from Maggie.

She waited, a look of patient anticipation on her face. Then Maggie realized she had asked her a question.

"Yes. Tea leaves. Thank you." Maggie considered herself polite, but she suddenly felt the need to be extra polite to this woman. After all, she was going to tell her the secrets of her future.

The older woman nodded and began preparing for the reading, placing down a paper towel, arranging a yellowed tea cup on a saucer on top of that.

"My name is Hattie," she said as she worked. "I've had my ability to see the future since I was a child."

Maggie nodded, not sure what she was supposed to say to that.

Hattie paused from pouring tea into the cup. "And I am very good, very in tune with the ether—but I think it would just be easier if you told me your name."

A laugh escaped Maggie. "I'm sorry. I'm Maggie."

"Hello, Maggie." Hattie didn't offer her hand, but did offer a smile that revealed slightly yellowed teeth, and a warmth in her blue eyes. The witch impression was immediately transformed into a grandmotherly one.

Maggie found herself relaxing her posture, just a bit.

"So are you visiting us from someplace else?"

Maggie realized that was always one of the first questions people asked here. First sign of a tourist town, she guessed.

"Yes. From D.C."

Hattie nodded. "I went there years ago. Weird aura there. Must be all the politicians."

Maggie smiled, and realized she actually agreed. She couldn't deny that while New Orleans had a strong energy, it was a nice feeling. An almost giddy feeling. Whereas D.C. felt oddly cold and . . . well, like Hattie said, weird. And she supposed the abundance of politicians was as good an explanation as any.

Maggie paused. When had she ever considered such things? She'd never thought about the energy of a place. She wasn't so cosmic—yet after two days of being in this city, she was starting to think there could be a certain mystic quality to a place.

Still, she didn't really believe a person could tell her future. First of all, why would this woman get a vision of her life from the other side? Maggie wasn't interesting enough to merit spirits or energies or whatever taking the time to send visions to Hattie. At best, Hattie would get images of her bent over a desk, studying crumbling sheet music for hours on end.

Maggie watched as Hattie finished pouring the tea and laying things out in a systematic order. A dozen bangles on her left arm jangled as she worked. But aside from the bangles and the long, graying hair, Maggie realized Hattie didn't look particularly like a fortune-teller. She wore a turtleneck and tweed trousers

"Relax, Maggie," she said offering another warm-eyed smile. "Just enjoy yourself. You don't have to believe what I tell you, anyway."

Apparently Maggie looked every bit the nervous skeptic.

"Okay," Hattie said, "think of a question or a concern and turn over the cup."

Maggie considered what she might want to know. For the briefest moment, the musician from last night popped into her head. She'd love to know what he'd thought about her. Then she pushed that thought aside. She suspected she did know—and it wasn't flattering.

She considered again and decided to go with work. Work was always safe. And maybe Hattie would tell her some exciting story. Like she'd discover something truly amazing. A composer long lost and recognized only by her.

"Okay," Maggie said. She carefully picked up the cup, and tipped it over so the teacup was facedown on the saucer. She flipped it back over, and watched as Hattie lifted the cup and peered inside.

Hattie's eyes lost some of their warmth as she focused, totally engrossed by what she saw in the cup. Her lips tugged down at the corners.

"You work a lot."

Maggie's own eyes widened. Okay, it was a little spooky that she went right to the topic of work. But then work was central to many people's lives. Plus she had no wedding ring—and what did woman her age who weren't married do? Work.

"You actually hide in your work. Use it to avoid things like past failures, lack of love life."

Maggie remained still. Okay, see, that was the line of thought she'd just followed herself. Safe deductions.

Hattie turned the cup slightly. "And I see that you were engaged. But that didn't work out."

Again, given her age, Maggie supposed that was a safe guess too.

She turned the cup again, as if she was reading the information like a book. "He was a liar. But his lies weren't the worst of it, were they? It was how he lied to you—and also how he revealed his lies. Very painful."

Maggie didn't answer. She couldn't.

Hattie nodded as if she was silently agreeing with Maggie's thoughts. She looked up from the cup. "You were lucky to escape him. Not a nice person. You are too sweet to have to deal with someone like him. Best to just let him go."

Hattie shook her head as if she couldn't quite believe how awful what she was seeing in the leaves had been. Maggie hadn't believed it either, and she had a hard time imagining a scattering of wet tea leaves could do the whole fiasco justice.

For her, it had made her realize that you couldn't know a person. Not totally.

"But that is definitely the past and you need to move on. You can't let it make you bitter, or take the blame. You didn't do anything to deserve what happened," Hattie said, looking up to give her a stern look. "You didn't deserve it. What happened was due to the type of person he was, not the type of person you are."

Somehow Hattie's emphatic words helped. The tightness Maggie didn't even realize she had in her chest lessened. It was good to hear, even from a perfect stranger.

Hattie peered back into the cup, then made an approving noise. "I see music. Lots of music. You work with music, don't you?"

Before Maggie could answer, Hattie added, "You don't play music. You study it."

Maggie nodded, even though Hattie didn't look up to see if she confirmed or denied the statement. Instead, the fortune-teller turned the cup, and made an appreciative sound in the back of her throat.

"Hmm, I see a man. A new man." Hattie glanced up at her. "Not the liar."

Maggie's breath caught for a second. Ren? Then she disregarded the idea. Of course she saw a man—didn't all fortune-tellers see love in the cards? Or in the leaves, as the case may be.

"There is a man. And more music."

Maggie froze, forgetting to breathe.

"He is surrounded by music too. He's very artistic and creative. Just like you. But just like you, he doesn't play . . . he did, but he doesn't now."

Disappointment washed over Maggie. It couldn't be Ren. Like the reading was real anyway. And why should she care one way or the other if it was Ren or not? Sheesh.

"Do you know this man?" Hattie asked suddenly. "Because I feel like you have already met him."

Maggie automatically shook her head.

"Well, he's definitely in here," Hattie said, peering into the cup, like the man was standing at the bottom, waving up at her. "Are you sure you haven't met anyone in, say, the last week or so? I get the feeling this relationship is very new."

Maggie nearly laughed. If it was Ren, the relationship was so new, it might as well have never happened.

"No," Maggie said. "No one."

"More music," Hattie shook her head, clearly amazed. "The music is very, very important. That much is clear. And I keep seeing one note in particular. B-flat."

The hair on Maggie's arms stood on end, a chill running through her.

That was the key of the sonata she'd thought she'd heard Ren play. But then, that was the key of thousands of songs. But it wasn't any key or any song. It was that song—and the exact right key.

Hattie shook her head again. "Well, if you haven't met this man, you will. And the attraction I see here is so strong. Very strong. But I also see that you will be inclined to run away from it. You are scared of it. It isn't clear, but I get the feeling you should be a little scared. This is very intense. Your feelings are so powerful."

Maggie found herself nodding. Part of her wanted to ask more. But she couldn't quite allow herself to believe what Hattie was saying.

"This man is like no other you have met. He's wounded in some way. And he's been alone a long time. That is a lot to handle."

Hattie looked up from the cup, meeting Maggie's eyes directly. "Just remember that you can't cut yourself off from life and love because one person hurt you. You need to take risks. You need to live."

Maggie nodded again.

"And it's very clear that music is so important to all this. And not just your work. Your whole world seems surrounded by music."

Then Hattie held the teacup out to her, tilting it so she could see the smattering of fine black leaves clinging to the sides. Maggie looked in, unsure what she was supposed to be looking at. She certainly didn't see any of the things Hattie had mentioned. Not even the musical notes.

With a pen, Hattie used the tip to point at a pattern just below the lip of the cup. "Do you see that?"

Maggie nodded, studying where she pointed.

"This is of great consequence too. The way it's separated from all the other patterns means it's very important. But I don't understand exactly what it means."

Maggie peered at it, trying to decipher what the shape could be. And just as dawning realization hit her, Hattie said her very thought out loud.

"It looks like a face with long hair. And an eye."

Immediately Ren's face was vividly clear in Maggie's head. Long hair and his eye with the white lashes.

"So, what did your psychic tell you?" Erika asked as soon as they stepped out onto the sidewalk.

Despite the bright sunlight and the ever-present humidity, a chill clung to Maggie's skin. That had all been too strange. And a little too accurate. A small face with long hair flashed in her mind. The arrangement of leaves could have looked like a dozen different things. But it hadn't. She and Hattie had seen the very same thing.

"Maggie? Are you okay?"

Maggie nodded, even as another chill prickled her skin. She couldn't talk about it. Not yet.

Instead she asked Erika what her reading said. She was relieved when Erika excitedly told her. She was going to have a great year. Her career, as an artist, a sculptor, was going to finally take off. She'd actually have several very successful shows. She'd also meet a new guy.

Maggie hung onto that last prediction, telling herself she was right. All fortune-tellers foretold new loves.

"A blond, dark-eyed prince," she told Maggie, wagging her eyebrows. "Overall, it sounds like everything is going to fall into place."

Maggie said something appropriate, although she couldn't have said what it was a minute later.

"Are you hungry?" Erika asked as they approached a restaurant. The smell of spicy food managed to penetrate Maggie's frazzled thoughts.

"Sure." Although she wasn't the least bit hungry, food would be a good grounding sort of distraction.

"So," Erika asked again once they settled at a table in a quaint courtyard. "What did your reading say?"

Maggie busied herself with the menu, still reluctant to talk about it. But she knew Erika wouldn't let it go. She'd have to spill eventually.

Maggie pushed the menu aside and said, "I think that musician from last night was in my cup."

Erika didn't look nearly as stunned by the announcement as Maggie was.

"Then I guess we know where we're going tonight," Erika said, then turned to place her order with the waiter.

Chapter 6

Ren's glance returned to the doorway yet again as another woman entered the bar. Platinum blonde.

Not her.

Today had seemed like an eternity. Quite a statement for a vampire. But he'd been anxious to get here tonight and see if Maggie showed up again.

His sleep should have been an escape from thoughts of her. Slumber was always black and empty. He never dreamed. But even with the relentless, drugging weight of the sun's rays overhead, dreams had still managed to penetrate the blackness. The enforced rest had been filled with images of a strawberry blonde with green-gray eyes and bow-shaped lips.

As he rose for the evening, surprised and confused by the images, he told himself his subconscious had managed to think of her because of the question she'd asked about the sonata.

How could she know that music? Any print version was long gone. Yet she said she was an authenticator. Of classical music. Was it possible she'd somehow seen it? And where?

He had to know.

It could be dangerous if she somehow tied the music of a composer known as Renaldo D'Antoni to him. Such a discovery would certainly require a lot of explaining on his part.

But in truth, he could handle that. He could manufacture some believable lie. After all, she was hardly likely to think, "Ah-ha, vampire!" That just wasn't the first explanation a person leapt to.

So if she wasn't going to piece together that Ren, the Bourbon Street rocker, and Renaldo, the classical composer, were the same person, then why not let all this go? There was no risk, no danger. He should just leave her alone.

His focus returned to the doorway to his left as another group entered. Two guys and a girl with a hairdo that went out of style in the eighties. Or should have.

Not even close to Maggie.

He ignored the sinking disappointment in his belly. Okay, he did wonder about whether she had indeed recognized the music. And he could argue that was the reason he hoped she would return. But did he care that much? Those days were far, far in his past and better forgotten.

His attention snapped back to the doorway as three women stepped into the dim barroom. His pulse jumped as he saw black hair—Maggie's friend. Then he realized all the arriving women had black hair, and they were Asian.

Another wash of disappointment deadened his hope.

Okay, maybe he also needed to admit that he wanted to see Maggie again too. Something about her—she just drew him.

"Dude," Drake said after they finished up the song, "you're doing it again. Josie only goes on a vacation far away once."

It took Ren a moment to figure out what his bandmate was talking about. Had he really repeated the first line of the Outfield song they were performing? Damn, he knew that song like he knew his own freakin' name. Better, maybe.

"I've been distracted."

Drake nodded. "I can see that."

Ren opened his mouth to ask what they should play next, when a prickling of awareness, like needles of both fire and ice, tattooed down his spine. He spun to see Maggie and her friends enter the bar from the left side door.

She glanced up at him, meeting his gaze for a fraction of a second, then she looked back to her friend. The tall, black-haired one. Erika?

He watched as they crossed the room and stood at the bar, facing away from the stage. Waiting for a drink. Pretending not to be back here to see him.

Ren moved to the mic, trying to ignore that he felt almost . . . euphoric? Euphoric was not an emotion he was familiar with but—he paused, curling his fingers around the mic—yep, it sure seemed like euphoric. Even if she was making a vain attempt to ignore him.

"How are you all doin' tonight?" He played up his learned southern accent, because people seemed to like it. He wondered if Maggie did.

"I gotta tell y'all, I have a friend here tonight. Hey there, Maggie."

He nearly chuckled as she spun from the bar to face him, her expression somewhere between stunned and annoyed.

But instead of laughing, he waved.

She didn't wave back. Instead her wide-eyed gape turned to a frown. She wasn't happy. And he supposed he couldn't blame her after the way he'd taken off so abruptly last night.

Damn, he should just leave well enough alone. He should just let her stand there and have a drink, while he ignored her. Then she'd realize he was the same ass from last night and lose interest.

He should do that, but he couldn't.

Just like he couldn't stop his eyes eating up the sight of her. Tonight she wore a simple pink blouse with a high seam that nipped in to accentuate her full breasts. She wore faded jeans and boots—with a heel, and he'd bet a hundred bucks that she'd borrowed the boots from one of her friends. Her slight concession to Bourbon Street fashion.

Still, her attire wasn't remotely risqué, but his body reacted all the same. Damn, she was pretty.

"Ah, now I know why you keep messing up the lyrics," Drake leaned in to say, wiggling his eyebrows as he followed Ren's gaze.

Ren didn't bother to reply. It was true: since laying eyes on this woman, he hadn't been able to focus on anything else. So what would it really hurt if he went for it and tried to seduce her?

Sure, he was a vampire. Sure, she might, by some weird twist of fate, know the music he composed nearly two centuries ago. In the end, she would be just like all the other women he slept with—a tourist going back to her normal life, leaving him behind on Bourbon Street.

Maggie could not believe her ears. Was Ren actually up there announcing to the whole bar that they were friends? This guy really took blowing hot and cold to a whole new level.

"What is he doing?" Jo asked, obviously as confused by the abrupt change in behavior as Maggie was. He really was impossible to understand.

"So this song is for Maggie." He smiled at her again, then said something to the guitarist on his right. The music started, but Maggie didn't immediately recognize the tune.

Maybe this was just his way of apologizing for asking her to wait around only to leave almost as soon as they began to chat. Maybe he realized she'd been embarrassed—which actually made her feel even more embarrassed now.

Then she heard the lyrics.

A violent blush burned her cheeks. She could *not* be hearing this right. He wanted her to want him? He needed her to need him?

This was a joke, right?

"Subtle," Jo murmured.

"I think it's sweet." Erika practically sighed.

Maggie shot Erika an amazed look, then realized that most of the patrons in the bar were looking at her with the same goofy smile Erika sported.

Maggie's cheeks burned even more. This was just cruel; a mean joke. It had to be. Nothing that happen between them last night could lead her to believe he could mean any of what he was singing.

Suddenly she was back in another place feeling just as stupid, then too the butt of some colossal joke.

Her cheeks still burned, but now with irritation. God, she was so stupid. To come back here—because a fortune-teller saw it in a bunch of wet tea leaves.

She didn't say a word to her friends as she strode past the stage and out the door.

She'd made it a block down the street, past the mechanical swinging legs protruding through the window of one of the many nudie bars, when she heard her name being called. But it wasn't Jo or Erika as she expected.

She spun, slipping on one of the many strands of Mardi Gras beads that littered the street—even though it wasn't close to Mardi Gras yet. Obviously another joke by the universe to make her feel stupid. But before she could fall, a strong hand reached out to catch her arm and steady her.

She regained her balance and stared up into hazel eyes, one fringed with white lashes.

"Maggie," Ren said, not releasing his hold on her, although he loosened his grip. Maybe to let her know he wasn't going to stop her if she really wanted to go.

She told herself to do just that. Go. But instead she remained still, staring at where his fingers touched her bare skin.

And darn it, her body reacted to him. Even as she felt the burn of humiliation, she also felt the hot tingle of attraction.

"I don't appreciate you making me the target of some private joke back there," she said, managing to keep her voice even, despite her embarrassment, despite her arousal.

"I wasn't," he said, his own voice sounding sincerely confused.

She stopped staring at his hand and met his gaze. "You'd have to be. There was no other reason to sing that song."

A small smile curled his lips. "Actually, I can think of one."

"What?"

"Um," he said, pretending to consider other motives, "maybe because I've never been very subtle. And I wanted you to know I'm interested in you."

She stared at him, hardly believing he'd just said that.

When she didn't speak after several seconds, he added, "Or I could have just thought you seemed like a Cheap Trick fan."

Still she didn't speak. Did he really mean what he'd said? He was interested in her?

"Really, you decide which one you're comfortable with," he said, looking decidedly awkward. "I'm okay with whichever one will get you back in the bar."

She studied him, trying to read whether he was toying with her. All she could see was sincerity.

"Please," he said as if to reinforce her thoughts. He gestured back to the bar.

He'd sung that song in honesty? The irritation, the humiliation, drained from her. She'd known what to do with those emotions, but what she was feeling now . . . she had no idea.

"Why?" she finally asked.

"Why? Because I feel bad that I embarrassed you. And I'd like you to hang around."

"No. Why are you interested in me?"

He frowned as if the question made no sense to him. "Why wouldn't I be? You're pretty. You seem nice and intelligent and interesting."

"But you don't know me."

"Ah, but that's why I want you to come back to the bar. So I can get the chance to know you."

Maggie realized she wanted that too. Very much. And frankly, the desire scared her. She shouldn't be interested in a guy like this. Maybe it wasn't an invitation to heartbreak, but it was definitely an invitation to more than she could handle.

Ren moved his hand from her arm, only to catch her fingers. "Come on back. I won't dedicate any more songs to you. I promise. I'll even admit that the sentiment of that one was a little presumptuous." His grin widened to full Cheshire cat glory. "Although sincere."

Maggie felt her cheeks burn even more, if possible.

"Okay," she heard herself say, and that seemed to be all the encouragement he needed as he began to tug her down the street. His abruptness stunned her for a second, but she managed to gather her wits and dig in her heels.

He halted, turning to give her an inquiring look.

"I am going back with you," she said. "But only because I left my friends there, and I don't want to be rude."

Ren's eyebrow raised, stating without words that he didn't totally buy that, but then he said, "Like I said, whatever will get you back there works for me."

Again she found herself being towed toward the bar. As they got closer, she noticed that Erika and Jo waited in the doorway. Jo started forward, but Erika stopped her with a hand on her arm.

Maggie looked at her own arm where Ren had touched her. The skin there still tingled, but the sensation was nothing when compared to how her fingers felt surrounded by his longer ones.

"Hey, Erika and Jo," Ren greeted her friends before Maggie could speak to them or they to her.

"I really need to make up for upsetting Maggie here," he said offering them an endearing smile. "Could you please make sure she stays so she can see that I'll be on my best behavior?"

Erika smiled back. "Sure."

"If she wants to stay," Jo added. She wasn't as impressed with his easy charm.

Maggie appreciated both her friends' attitudes. It was nice to be both defended and supported. And since her brain still wasn't functioning properly, she could possibly need either one.

They all entered the bar, and as soon as some of the patrons saw Maggie and Ren, they began to applaud.

Heat burned Maggie's cheeks once again, but Ren simply lifted a hand in greeting. He leaned toward her. "See, you've got to stay or everybody's going to think I'm some kind of monster, driving away a sweet person like you."

Maggie didn't respond, but the word sweet resonated with her. The fortune-teller, Hattie, had used that word to describe her too. Good Lord, now *that* was hardly a sign.

He squeezed her hand, then released her. With a quick curl of a smile, he bounded back onto the stage.

"Okay," he called out over the microphone, "who wants some rock and roll?"

The crowd cheered, and the band went right into a song. Maggie followed her friends to the bar, staring up at the stage, still not understanding everything that had just happened.

She still couldn't quite shake the feeling that the whole thing was some horrible trick.

She turned to the bar and the bartender with the antenna hair came over immediately. The antennae were in full working order, obviously.

"What can I get you?" She smiled widely, as if they were old friends.

"Do you have wine?" Maggie asked, surprised her voice sounded so normal.

"Really bad wine," the bartender answered honestly.

"I'll take it."

The bartender bounced away.

"So what did he say?" Jo asked.

Maggie took a deep breath. "That he was interested in me."

"Just like the psychic said." Erika grinned, then she glanced around the crowded room. "Maybe my blond-haired, dark-eyed prince is here too."

"What?" Jo asked, thoroughly confused. She hadn't gotten the whole scoop on the readings, because upon returning to the hotel for a nap, she discovered her sailor waiting in the lobby. That did a whole lot to make up for him missing breakfast, so Jo had spent the day with him.

"The psychic saw Ren in Maggie's cup."

Jo still looked confused.

Erika started to tell Jo about the reading Hattie had given, but Maggie cut her off. "The reading was just a fluke."

Erika gaped at her friend. "Having you look into the cup, pointing to a pattern in the leaves and saying 'That looks like a face with long hair and an eye' was a fluke?"

All three friends looked up at the stage. Ren stood at the mic, his head down. When he lifted his head, his hair fell over one side of his face, leaving only his eye with the white lashes visible. He looked directly at Maggie, almost as if could hear them and was presenting the image that had been described.

"And that happening, right this minute, that was a fluke too, right?" Erika said, still gaping up at the stage.

"Here's your wine," the bartender shouted from behind the bar to be heard over the guitar solo taking place on the stage.

Maggie gladly reached for the wine, taking a long gulp. Then she reached for her purse, but the bartender lifted a hand to stop her.

"You're Ren's girl," she called. "I'll just put it on his tab."

Maggie started to tell her that, no, she wasn't Ren's girl, but apparently the hair antennae went off and the bartender bounded away to help another customer.

"The psychic really said that?" Jo asked, seeming as stunned by the idea as Maggie had been—and still was. She took another swallow of the acrid wine, then nodded.

Ever-practical Jo considered that for a moment, then stated quite reasonably, "Maybe we should stick around and check all this out."

Maggie just stared at the stage, gulping her wine like it was juice.

Maggie now understood what the phrase "liquid courage" meant. She was sipping her third glass of the cheap, vinegary wine. It was tasting decidedly better with each glass.

"I think you should slow down," Jo warned her, leaning toward her to be heard over the loud notes of a Kansas song.

Maggie nodded, but she felt a lot better than she had. She suspected there was a fine line, however, and if she kept going she might get a little outrageous.

She looked back up at the stage, watching Ren's every move. Would that necessarily be a bad thing? She grimaced at her own train of thought and resisted taking another sip of her drink.

She really liked the way he moved, and his hair. Who knew hair could be so sensual? She swayed with the music. With him.

She really liked the fact that his eyes kept finding hers in the crowded room.

"I think I am going to have a fling with him," she suddenly announced. Then she looked down at her plastic tumbler of wine. Okay, she was really too late on this outrageous thing, wasn't she?

"I think you should," Erika said.

Jo didn't say anything, but Maggie didn't get the feeling she was opposed to the idea. She seemed to still be considering the pros and cons of the plan.

It was good someone was. Maggie considered asking her what she thought. After all, between the warm hum in her veins from the wine and watching Ren, she was now feeling pretty good. And she kept thinking the idea of touching him was pretty good too.

But before she could ask Jo what she thought, Ren announced that the band was taking a break. And unlike last night, as soon as he made the announcement, he stepped down from the stage and headed right to her.

"Hi," he said, and stopped an arm's length away from her. Which Maggie found very disappointing. She liked it when he touched her. Just remembering how close he'd been when they were out on the street made her skin tingle.

She stepped closer, even as she told herself not to; that he might not want her getting closer. He didn't move away, instead he leaned toward her, his mouth very close to her ear, his hair brushing hers.

"What are you drinking?" His breath was warm against her skin.

She closed her eyes briefly as a shot of desire ricocheted through her body.

"Wine," she managed.

He straightened, reaching for her hand. He lifted both her hand and glass to his mouth and took a sip, then grimaced.

"I know a place that serves much better drinks. Want to go there with me after this last set?"

"Sure," she said, both scared and thrilled with the idea of being alone with him. Funny how quickly her wine-fueled bravado could evaporate.

He grinned, obviously pleased she had agreed. "Good. I'll try to make this set a short one."

She nodded.

He reached for her hand again, and again lifted both her fingers and her glass to his mouth. He took a lingering sip of the cheap wine, watching her reaction over the rim of the cup.

She breathed in slowly through her nose, trying to calm her thundering heart. God, he was so sinfully sexy.

When he finished, he grinned again. "Oh yeah, the place

I'm going to take you is so much better." He gazed at her a moment longer, then nodded at Jo and Erika and turned to bound back up onto the stage.

"Yeah," Jo stated, her voice dead certain, "you are so going to have a fling with him."

Chapter 7

Ren rushed through the set, winding it up as soon as he could. There was no way he was going to risk Maggie changing her mind about going out with him tonight.

She hadn't moved from her spot at the bar, though, and that had to be a good sign. He knew that she wanted him. He could sense the desire in her energy when he touched her, but he also felt hesitation. Uncertainty.

There was no way he could let her pull away now. He hadn't wanted anyone this much since Annalise. And frankly, that should have scared the shit out of him. It should set off warning bells and raise giant signs that said, *Stop now*.

As he walked off the stage, he let his gaze stray out the door toward the hotel across the street. For a second, he saw the opera house as it had been. Annalise had performed there. The hotel and the memory of the long-gone opera house served as a reminder why he couldn't let anything beyond a brief affair occur between himself and any woman.

And still he kept walking toward Maggie. He knew more now, he rationalized. He knew things had to stay light and fun and satisfying for both of them. He couldn't let Maggie get too close to him, too involved. He wouldn't. She would walk away safe and sound.

Maggie offered him a small smile as he approached, the

sweet curve of her lips rocketing his desire for her as high as if she'd touched his bare skin.

He wanted this woman more than he'd ever wanted Annalise, he realized. Annalise had never made him ache with a mere smile. But he could handle this. And in the end, Maggie would leave and that would be that.

But he had to have her for now. Her energy called to him, drawing him to her. And helplessly, he was going.

"Are you ready?" he asked, unable to resist reaching out and touching her. Just a hand on her arm. Her skin was warm and smooth under his palm. His desire leapt, almost painful in its intensity.

"Yes." She nodded, her eyes straying to where he touched her, then back to his face.

Again he felt her desire too, strong but mixed heavily with uncertainty. Still, she rose from her barstool to go with him. Then she looked at her two friends, still seated there.

Ren paused. The polite thing to do would be to ask her friends to join them. But damn, he wanted Maggie to himself.

"Did you ladies want to join us?"

The black-haired one—Erika—immediately shook her head. "Thanks, but I'm really exhausted. I'm just going to head back to the hotel."

The one with the short brown hair also shook her head. "Me too. But thanks." She turned to Maggie. "You have your cell phone, right?"

Maggie patted the small purse she held.

Ren smiled, again appreciating her friends' protectiveness. Delicate butterflies needed to be looked out for.

"Okay," he said. "Ready?"

She took a deep breath. "Ready."

And Ren couldn't help feeling like they were both preparing for something much more powerful than drinks at his favorite bar.

* * *

Maggie wasn't exactly sure what she'd expected when Ren had asked her to join him for a drink. She supposed she imagined something a bit more elegant than the bar they'd just left. Instead they ended up in a back room of a small dive bar on one of the side streets off Bourbon.

"I know it doesn't look like much," Ren said as if he was reading her mind. "But it's quiet, it has good drinks, and Sheri doesn't mind the drunken ramblings of all the obnoxious old musicians who hang around here until the wee hours of the night."

"You're not old," Sheri said, offering Maggie a conspiratorial wink. She looked like a woman who'd heard a lot and wasn't shocked by much of anything.

Ren directed Maggie to a table and sat down beside her, without placing an order.

Maggie wasn't quite ready to go without a little liquid courage, now that she'd discovered it. But before she could ask if they were going to order, Sheri appeared and placed a drink in front of each of them.

"What's this?" Maggie peered into the glass as if she thought the deep red liquid inside was going to answer her.

"It's the official drink of the band. The Impaler," Ren told her, then took a sip.

"The Impaler?" Maggie frowned. "As in vampires and a stake through your heart impaling?"

"Exactly," Ren said with an oddly resolute nod. "The Impalers is also the name of the band."

Maggie realized she'd never heard them say their name while they were playing. The name did aptly fit with the whole vampire/New Orleans connection, thanks to Anne Rice. And now that she thought about it, even though they were encouraging the crowd to have a good time and party, they did exude a dark edginess, a latent danger, when they played.

They were hypnotic too. That was a big vampire trait, right? Okay, she had only noticed that Ren was hypnotic. She couldn't say what the rest of the band was really like.

Then she realized she was staring at him. Not that he seemed to mind. He met her gaze easily. Still, she blushed at her own blatant behavior.

"Taste it. It's to die for." He chuckled at his own lame joke—the husky sound reaching her like a brush of warm suede on her skin.

She again peered down into the highball glass.

"The color is a nice touch," she said.

Ren smiled again, and even just in her peripheral vision, it was breathtaking. Distracting.

She took a deep breath and lifted the drink to her lips. It was . . .

"This is good," she said with surprise after swallowing the tiny sip. A little tangy and nicely sweet. She took another drink.

"I wouldn't steer you wrong, darlin'."

Maggie smiled. She really liked his accent. A slow drawl. Southern, she supposed, although she couldn't say from where. Being a Northerner, she didn't know southern accents very well. But it was different. Nice.

Then again, she liked everything about this man. A wave of nerves stirred up the calm that the wine had done a decent job of creating. She liked him, but she didn't have any idea what to do with him.

God, what was she going to do with him? She wished she had even an ounce of Erika and Jo's flirting abilities. Another wave of nerves hit her, until her posture was stick-straight on the edge of her chair.

She glanced up from her drink; he was watching her. Those intense eyes, a shade somewhere between amber brown and moss green. Sitting this close, she noticed that the eye surrounded by white lashes appeared a shade lighter than the one surrounded by brown. An optical illusion created by the difference between the lashes. Amazing.

Her body reacted to the sight, arousal replacing some of her nervousness. Everything about this man had a way of making her feel aroused. He seemed to ooze sexuality.

And that promptly made her uneasy again.

What was she doing? She couldn't have a fling. Not with this guy. Maybe she should start out with a waiter, or even a bartender. Something about jumping right to musician seemed like too much. Like she was hitting the sexual big leagues before she even signed up for T-ball.

"So are you having fun in the Big Easy?" he asked, his voice a little husky yet smooth, reminding her of the lowest notes on a violin. An almost soothing sound, as if he was aware of her anxiety and trying to calm her.

Almost against her own volition, she began to relax against the back of her chair. Calm like that created by the cheap wine weakened her limbs—although his voice was much nicer than the wine.

"Are you doing the usual tourist stuff?" he asked, his smile curling up slightly in one corner, as if he knew she'd already forgotten he'd asked a question.

Maggie quickly swallowed the drink she'd just taken, nodding as she did. "Yes. We're having a great time."

"What have you done?"

Maggie took another sip of the tasty drink with the rather naughty and exciting name. At least it seemed naughty and exciting when sitting so close to this lovely man that her knee kept bumping his under the table. Why was she having so much trouble following his questions?

"We went to Café Du Monde." She slowly tried to recall some things she'd done. "And we went on a cemetery tour."

She paused to think about what else she'd done. Why did everything suddenly seem discombobulated? As if her thoughts, and the room for that matter, had become strangely scattered.

"How was the cemetery tour?" Ren asked.

Maggie focused on him, thankful that she could.

"That's one place I've never been," he added, and Maggie noticed wryness in his tone that she didn't understand.

"It was interesting," she said, relieved that she wasn't feeling quite so dizzy now that she was centering her own gaze on him. On his white-lashed eye. "I even made a wish at Marie Laveau's tomb."

Ren raised an eyebrow. "Did you? What did you wish for?"

"A wild fling," she said, then snapped her mouth shut. Oh, dear. Had she really announced that to him? Judging from the slow unfurling of his Cheshire cat smile, she had indeed. Maybe she wasn't as centered as she thought.

"That's a good wish," he said. His knee bumped hers again under the table, and the brief contact shot need through her body as if he'd run his hand up her thigh. What would she do if he did? She took another sip of her drink. She needed to get this situation back on less . . . obvious terms.

"Have you enjoyed the band?" he asked, before her fuzzy mind could find a new topic.

She nodded. "Yes, you're all so good. Do you like playing with them?"

Ren seemed to consider that for a moment. "I guess. It pays the bills and keeps me fed."

Maggie frowned, surprised by his words. He was such an obvious showman, so good at working the crowd, encouraging them to have a good time. She just assumed he'd have to love it to be so at ease up there. But his words didn't reveal that.

"I've been playing a long time," he said by way of explanation. "I guess I'm a little burnt-out."

"Well, it doesn't show."

"That's good, I guess."

She looked at him, realizing he was the one who was now uncomfortable with the topic of conversation. She tried to think of something that would be neutral for both of them.

"I had a woman read my tea leaves today, too." As soon as the words were out of her mouth, she knew that wasn't it.

And unfortunately, Ren's interest was piqued.

"Oh yeah. And what did you find out? Something about having a wild fling with a long-haired, white-eyelashed musician?"

From her violent blush, Ren realized his flirtatious joke had been dead-on. Well, damn. He had to find that tea-leaf reader and give her a big kiss.

He studied Maggie. Had she revealed she wanted him to the fortune-teller? There was something thrilling about the idea that she'd made it clear to someone else that she wanted him—even after his brush-off. He didn't deserve one, but he was damned glad he was getting a second chance with her.

And a wild fling was exactly what he wanted, too. Man, this all seemed to be falling into place so easily. There *were* brief times in his existence when he didn't feel quite so cursed. This was definitely one of them.

Of course, he still sensed some reservations in her that he would have to get around. Actually two distinct feelings swirled around her like a cocoon, one real and one manufactured.

Her announcement had her embarrassed, and she'd also had too much to drink. He could take care of her embarrassment; she had nothing to be ashamed of, period. But he did not want sex with this woman to be the drunken variety. He should have realized that alcohol would affect her more in his presence.

Humans always got more drunk, more tired, more overwhelmed in his presence. A side effect of his nature. Even when he wasn't trying, he still stole some of a human's energy, which brought their natural tolerance down. It was a part of being a lampir that he couldn't totally control.

He did not want Maggie drunk when he was with her. He

wanted her fully aware of him when he ran his hands over her soft skin, kissed her, and entered her curvy little body.

His cock pulsed against the material of his jeans as if cheering at that idea.

And Maggie was so worth cheering about. Her energy snapped between them. So alive, so powerful. She had a wholesomeness that radiated from her and filled him. He liked that feeling. Wholesomeness. When had he ever known that feeling?

He started to reach out to tuck one of her flyaway waves behind her ear, but stopped himself. She was too uncomfortable now. He needed to give her time to settle down again before touching her, even in the most innocent way.

Instead, he pushed away her drink. "I think you've had enough Impaler for tonight." God, no double entendre there.

She didn't argue. "I think you're right."

"Do you want to get out of here?" he asked, needing to take her somewhere where he could touch her. Not that Sheri would think twice if he decided to make out with Maggie right where they sat. Hell, he'd done more than that at this very table. But Maggie wasn't like the women he was used to. She needed seduction, not the usual inelegant groping he'd become accustomed to.

"I think that's a good idea," she said.

He noticed that her eyes tracked the features of his face as if they were moving. Oh yeah, she'd drunk too much—and he'd taken too much of her energy too. It was so damned hard not to.

"Fresh air might be good," she said, still looking a little disoriented.

Ren nodded, and immediately regretted the action as she nodded in response, trying to focus on him.

He waved to Sheri, thanking her. Maggie thanked her too, her voice sweet and only a little slurred.

"Maybe we should walk around for awhile," he suggested.

"I think that's a good idea." This time *that's* was only slightly slurred.

He took her elbow. She allowed the touch, even leaned into it. He liked the feeling of her against his side, warm and soft. He focused on giving some of his energy back to her. Another trick a lampir had. He constantly took energy from those around him, but he could also give it back. That made him less of a leech, right?

They stepped out of the bar and he headed left onto Bourbon, only to take the next side street off it. The smells of Bourbon did not even approximate fresh air. Between the smell of beer, trash, and other disgusting things, it was not the place to sober up someone who was a little tipsy.

He walked slowly, not pushing her into conversation, in case she didn't feel quite up to it. But once they were away from the music blaring from within the bars and the air was a little less aromatic, she spoke.

"I already feel better. Thanks."

"Sure. Not like I haven't been there." It took him a lot more than three tumblers of wine and half an Impaler to get there, but he did understand. And yes, he had been counting her drinks. He'd been aware of everything she'd done since she'd walked into the bar tonight.

They reached Jackson Square, and he gestured to benches lining the outside of the wrought-iron fence. "Want to sit?"

She nodded.

Once they were settled, she turned to him, her big gray-green eyes regarding him solemnly—and more focused.

"I'm sorry I told you about the—thing at the cemetery and the tea-leaf reading."

He wasn't. He liked both announcements, a lot.

"Well," he said slowly, "technically you didn't tell me anything about the tea leaf reading. And I really liked what you had to say about the cemetery tour."

The dim light couldn't hide Maggie's blush.

"That was a really good story," he added when her gaze dropped to her hands folded on her lap.

"I don't think blurting out that I wished to have a wild fling really constitutes a story."

Ren smiled at that. "Oh, I don't know, I think there's a story there. And frankly, I'm really hoping that I get to be an integral part of it."

Her head popped up, surprise clear in her wide-eyed expression. How could she possibly be surprised by that? Did she still doubt that he wanted her? Silly woman.

"Ren," she started, and the slow way she said his name didn't make him think he was going to like what she had to say after it. So he did the first thing that came into his mind.

He kissed her.

Chapter 8

Maggie froze at the pressure of Ren's mouth. This gorgeous man was kissing her. Her.

His lips teased, brushing against the curve of her mouth. Molding to hers. Surprise was promptly replaced by a violent rush of desire, so strong, so overpowering, all she could do was curl her hands into Ren's shirtfront and cling to him. His lips sampled hers, strong yet velvety soft. Wonderful.

In a fleeting sweep, his tongue tested the seam of her lips, and she instantly opened for him, not once considering denying him. He tasted her, her tongue sampled him in return. Brief, delicious touches.

Jolts of desire like electricity coursed directly from him into her. The sensation was almost too much. Too intense. Still she couldn't let go. She wanted more.

A small moan escaped her, and he responded by pulling her closer, deepening the kiss. Soon they were clutching each other, his arms holding her tight to the hardness of his chest. Her hands tangled in the silkiness of his hair.

Silk, steel, heat and desire—all she could comprehend.

She moaned again. And this time, Ren lifted his head to look down at her.

"Damn," he murmured, the word almost reverent, and Maggie pulled in a ragged breath. Yes, that about summed it up. She'd never, never experienced anything as intense as that kiss.

Desire sizzled in her limbs, in her very skin.

"Maggie." His voice sounded huskier. "Come back to my place."

She nodded. Yes. She wanted that desperately. She wanted to keep kissing him. She wanted to touch him. She wanted to feel him deep inside her.

As soon as the thought registered in her brain, it shocked her. She'd never had thoughts like that about a man. Not even Peter, and she'd been with him for over five years. She'd planned to marry him. But he'd left her.

"Come on," Ren said as he rose and held his hand out for her. "I only live a block from here."

She remained on the bench, all her certainty gone.

She couldn't do this. She didn't have the tools to deal with a fling. She'd dated Peter for nearly six months before they even got into heavy petting.

Her gaze moved from Ren's extended hand to his face. His hair was brushed back from his face in long waves, his cheeks and chin were starting to reveal hints of five o'clock shadow. The black shirt he wore strained against the muscles of his chest and shoulders. He was truly beautiful, and so far out of her realm of knowledge.

She was willing to bet big money that he'd never even used the phrase "heavy petting," much less waited six months to get to it. One-night stands were a way of life for him. She knew that as surely as she knew that they weren't for her, as much as she'd wanted to believe otherwise. Especially when she looked at him.

"Maggie?"

She pulled in a deep breath, trying desperately to calm the conflicting emotions churning inside her. Begging her to go back into his arms, and in the next breath telling her to run as far away as she could.

She couldn't go with him. She was too . . . scared.

"Ren, I can't." She pulled in another breath as her body, ached at her words. "I just don't think I'm a one-night stand kind of girl."

Ren didn't speak, and for some reason, his silence hurt. Even though she hadn't honestly expected him to offer her anything else. And what could he offer, really? She was here on vacation. He was a musician, who would have a new woman lusting after him tomorrow night, and the night after that.

That idea solidified her decision. She couldn't handle that. Other women. That would kill her.

He stepped toward her, his heat reaching out to encompass her. He took her hands, tugging her to her feet.

He leaned in and brushed his lips across hers. A brief fleeting touch that he didn't deepen. Instead he straightened, studying her in a way that made her feel as if he could see right into her soul. Into her heart.

"I know you aren't," he said, his voice resigned. She thought, hoped, that she heard disappointment.

"I'm sorry," she said. "I thought I could."

He stared at her for a moment longer, then looked away, his expression hidden in shadow. "I-I wish I had something different to offer you."

She wasn't sure if he meant that, but the words were bittersweet consolation anyway. He didn't have anything, and he wasn't going to pretend. She appreciated his telling her the truth. She just wished the truth didn't have that invariable habit of hurting like hell.

"Come on," he said after clearing his throat, "let me walk you back to your hotel."

Ren led Maggie down the street. He'd considered for half a second trying to persuade her to stay. He could. Easily. Vampires had that way about them. Especially the type he was.

But instead, he widened the space between them, trying

not to feel her energy. Trying not to crave it. Which was virtually impossible.

Damn, she had him shaken. When she'd made her disclosure, which he had to admit was hardly a surprise, it had been right on the tip of his tongue to tell her he *was* offering more than a one-night stand.

Why the hell would he even consider saying something like that? Okay, yes, he could feasibly offer her every night until the end of her trip. But that was the best he could do. It wasn't what she wanted or needed from a man. He'd known that the first moment he saw her. He just hadn't wanted to believe it.

Because, damn, he wanted her.

Kissing her, feeling her response, that was as close as he'd come to pure bliss in his long existence. He could only imagine what it would be like to make love to her.

See? There. That was exactly why she'd been wise to call all of this to a halt. He did *not* think of what he had in mind for her as *making love*. The act was sex. Pure and simple. No love involved. He knew exactly how very, very dangerous love was for him. And for her.

"Well, here we are," Maggie said, stopping on the sidewalk to look at him.

He blinked, surprised to see they'd reached her hotel already. He hadn't even registered the noise and crowds of Bourbon.

He stared at the building—again his solid, tangible proof that love was not an option for him. Remember Annalise. Remember what happened to her because of your love.

"Right," he said, glancing at the bright lights and the glass entrance to the hotel. "Right." He had no idea what else to say.

"Thank you for the drink," she said, her voice sweetly shy. "And the kiss."

He stared at her, loving the way her pale skin flushed. She really was too delicate and adorable for someone like him. Even for a night.

He forced a casual smile. "No, thank you."

She nodded, obviously not knowing what else to say, and realizing she wasn't going to get anything more from him anyway.

"Good night, then." She started toward the doors.

"Maggie," he called, needing to stop her, if just for a moment.

She turned to face him.

"It was really nice to meet you," he said, staring at her for a moment longer, then turning to head back down the street. Back to his life of endless parties, women, and rock and roll.

"God, I'm such a fool," Maggie said, staring down at her steaming cup of chicory coffee. She'd woken up with a raging headache, which she suspected the cheap wine hadn't helped. But she knew the main cause was that she'd again gotten little sleep.

Instead she'd tossed and turned, rehashing all the events of the night. Their kisses, her insecurities, their kisses, her uncertainty, then their kisses again, and finally the look on Ren's face as he'd said good-bye. She'd recalled that as many times as the kisses.

He'd looked . . .

"I wish you had been there," Maggie said to Jo and Erika. "Then you could verify what I saw. I just don't know. But it looked almost like . . . heartbreak." She made a groaning noise and covered her face with her hands. This was crazy.

"Yeah, he was heartbroken because he didn't get any action," Jo said, buffering the words with a teasing tone.

Maggie knew Jo was probably right. Still, she just kept seeing his face. His haunted eyes. His eyes looking so much like they had when he'd been playing the keyboard that first night.

"Maybe he does want more, but he knows you're leaving. And he doesn't want to get hurt." Erika shrugged as if even she found her words a tad implausible.

"It doesn't matter," Maggie said, deciding what was done was done. It was for the best, so she might as well let it go. She took a sip of her coffee. Strong, just as she liked it.

The memory of Ren's lips against hers returned. Strong, smooth. Perfect.

She set down her cup with more force than necessary, and some of the hot liquid sloshed onto the tablecloth. She ignored the spill and forced a cheery smile. "So what's the plan for today?"

"What do you wish you'd done differently?" Jo asked her, ignoring Maggie's valiant attempt to get on with their vacation.

Maggie's posture drooped as she groaned again. "Oh, I don't know. I guess . . . I guess I wish I'd been daring enough to spend the night with him. Even if it was just the one night."

Both Jo and Erika considered her words.

"You know, this is a novel twist. Most people beat themselves up for having a one-night stand. Not for *not* having one." Jo took a drink of her coffee, then held the cup between her two hands as she pondered this interesting slant on a guilty conscience.

"I mean it's not like I really think he could or should offer me something more than a fling. And I think I *do* want a fling. I think I need one." Maggie shifted her eyes back and forth between her two friends, trying to read their thoughts. For once, they were both wearing poker faces. Of course.

"I didn't want to stop after we kissed. Not until Peter popped into my head. And then I suddenly got scared."

"Well, Peter has done a number on you. Your fear is understandable," Jo said.

"And that's why I'm even more annoyed for stopping. It's like Peter is still there, judging me. Making me unsure of myself. I don't want him to have that kind of control over me. He's gone, and I want my life back. I want Ren, and if it's just a fling, all the better," Maggie said. "Do you think I'm horrible?" she finally asked them.

"No," they both said in unison, and with conviction.

That made Maggie feel better.

"Wasn't it us who wanted you to wish for a wild fling at Marie Laveau's tomb? Of course we support you wanting something fun and sexy for yourself," Erika said.

"So what should I do?"

"Let me ask you this," Jo said. "Are you sure you said no because of your doubts about yourself and Peter? Or is there a real risk that a fling is going to mess you up more?"

Those were the very questions that had kept her awake most of the night. She wasn't sure.

"Maybe it's a combination of both of those things. I mean, I've never been with a man that I haven't considered myself in love with."

"*Considered* being the operative word," Jo said.

Maggie shrugged. "True. And I'm also scared that I'll be very underwhelming to a guy like Ren."

"No, you won't," Jo stated, as if she'd already seen the whole moment go down, and Maggie had performed brilliantly.

Maggie smiled, the first real smile of the morning.

"That's your fear because of Peter," Erika said gently.

"I agree." Jo nodded.

Maggie agreed too. She knew everything that had happened with Peter was haunting her. Coloring her opinions of herself, and how attractive she could be to another man.

"I really think being with Ren could be good for you," Erika said. "You need to remember that you are an attractive, interesting, sensual woman."

Maggie smiled at that. "Remember? When did I know that?"

"And that's why you should go for it." Jo took a sip of her coffee, then held the cup out in her best sophisticated pose. "After all, you are a modern woman. You can take exactly what you want."

Erika laughed, but nodded. "Jo's right. There is nothing

wrong with being a little naughty and having fun. You are a grown woman. And you are both consenting adults. He doesn't have to be Mr. Right—he can be Mr. Right Now."

Maggie laughed. She liked that. And she wasn't going to let her insecurities hold her back. She did want this. Maggie needed to get her groove back. Or maybe just get her groove—finally.

"So." Jo set down her cup and rested her chin on her upraised, folded hands. "How does he kiss?"

"Amazing. Freaking amazing."

All three women laughed, and Maggie felt happier than she had in the past six months.

Chapter 9

Maggie tugged at the neckline of the wraparound kimono-style shirt that her friends had convinced her to buy at a small boutique on Royal. It plunged low between her breasts. A tad too low. She tugged at it again.

"Stop that," Jo said, moving to adjust the shirt back to where it had been.

Maggie frowned down at the swells of chest peeking out of the neckline. "I don't know."

"It looks fabulous," Erika said, poking her head out from the bathroom, where she was putting on makeup. "You've got great breasts. I say flaunt them."

"Not to mention, that shirt is hardly revealing," Jo said, moving to the mirrors on the closet doors. She adjusted her own shirt, a vintage-style T-shirt tucked into faded jeans. Maggie was tempted to point out that, while flattering, Jo's outfit was the one that was hardly revealing. But she didn't.

Instead Maggie joined her at the mirror. She had to admit that the shirt—black, with flowers in shades of deep and light pink—did flatter her figure, giving her generous curves an hourglass effect. And while the neckline seemed low to her, it was hardly scandalous. She just wasn't used to wearing anything that showed off her—assets.

She wasn't used to caring about her assets. When she'd

first started dating Peter, he'd told her that she shouldn't bother with things like makeup and the latest fashions. At the time, she'd taken his comment to mean that she was fine the way she was. She now realized he'd meant any efforts would just be a waste of time.

Now looking in the mirror, she didn't think this attempt was a wasted effort. She liked the look. Erika had helped her with her makeup, and while it was still subtle, she liked how the mascara made her eyes look bigger and the lip gloss made her lips look a little pouty. And her new top was pretty sexy. She liked the look. She really hoped Ren did as well.

Tonight she didn't plan to say no. She just hoped the offer was still on.

"Okay," Drake said, fiddling with the tuning pegs of his guitar, "you haven't screwed up a single lyric tonight, and your little girly isn't here. Could there be a correlation?"

Ren glanced at his guitarist, resisting the urge to scan the crowd, even though Drake had just told him Maggie wasn't there.

"'Livin' on a Prayer' next?" he said, ignoring the question altogether.

Drake nodded, grinning broadly in the slightly crazy way he had.

Ren focused on the song rather than Drake's words or the crowd. He refused to look for her tonight. There wasn't much point; he knew she wouldn't show again. And if she did, he planned to ignore her. He couldn't risk getting involved with her. She wasn't his type. He had to remember that.

Of course, his usually void-like sleep had again been filled with images of her, except now he also knew what she tasted like, how she felt in his arms. That had replayed in the blackness like snippets of an erotic movie.

God, he'd never considered kissing so damned sexual. It

was fun, nice, a good starter to bigger and better things, but with Maggie . . .

Okay, he wasn't going there. His decision was made. He knew he was doing the right thing. Had done the right thing. It was done. He'd never see her again.

That knowledge seemed to bring everything in his world into glaring, stark reality. The bar with its smoke-steeped walls, the stale scent of beer and body odor.

He glanced at the band. He worked with these guys five nights a week, yet he didn't really know much about them. Occasionally they would go out for a drink after work, but they didn't talk about anything real. And he realized he didn't care.

He surveyed the crowd. A group of three girls danced at the foot of the stage. Two of them smiled widely, invitingly, as he made eye contact. He offered an automatic smile back, but he felt nothing. They were the usual women who tried to attract his attention—women who were out for one thing, just like he was. Nothing emotional, nothing real, just a business arrangement of sorts.

Maybe that was what drew him to Maggie in the first place. He knew she wasn't that type. She did expect something real, something beyond meaningless sex.

He couldn't give that. This was his world: dingy, dark, and desolate. He needed to just forget the strawberry blonde with huge gray-green eyes.

He focused on the feeling of the room. The energy vibrating in the air, radiating from every human in the bar. Their life force, their essence. His body absorbed it like a sponge, and none of them even noticed. Maybe they got a little drunker in his presence, maybe they woke the next day feeling a little more hungover than they thought they should. But none of them knew he had contributed to that. None of them knew he was standing up here, stealing their energy to keep himself alive.

Disgust filled him, making it hard to shout out the last note of the song. The audience applauded anyway, not noticing his strain. They applauded and cheered, oblivious to the fact that he was really there, not to entertain them, but to use them.

Yes, this was his life. He was a self-centered, disinterested leech, and the sooner he committed that to memory and stuck to his rules, the better off he'd be.

He took the microphone off the stand and leaned over the railing that surrounded the stage.

"How are you ladies tonight?" he asked the women with whom he'd just shared a smile. He held the mic out to them.

The busty redhead grabbed his hand. "I'm doin' fine, baby. How are you?"

Her voice was loud and nasal over the speakers. Ren forced his wince into a smile.

"I'm doing great," he said into the mic. Yeah, he was doing just fuckin' great. Damn.

He straightened up, moving back to the microphone stand. "Any requests?"

People started shouting out songs. "Freebird." "Carry On Wayward Son." "Brown-Eyed Girl." The usual. As much the staples of his life as the nameless women and the theft of their energy.

Then below all the thundering voices was a softer, sweeter one: "I Want You To Want Me."

Ren spun toward the voice and the energy that he couldn't believe he hadn't sensed sooner. Maggie stood in the doorway to the right of the stage. She openly watched him, something she hadn't ever done. Normally she'd look at him for a moment, then glance away, embarrassed or unsure. But not tonight. Tonight her eyes locked with his, her desire for him written all over her face.

Ren stared at her for a moment, then returned his gaze to the crowd on the dance floor, not really seeing them.

"Let's go with 'Brown-Eyed Girl,'" he said, also just reaching into his jumbled thoughts for any song. Any song but the one she requested. What was she doing here? He'd been so sure their good-bye last night had been final.

The music started and he missed his intro. Drake played a little solo to disguise the fact that Ren hadn't started when he was supposed to, but not before he pulled a face at him, then gave a pointed look in Maggie's direction.

Ren refused to let his eyes stray along that same path, even though he could feel her gaze on him. Her energy intensified, building around him like a rising storm, and he didn't have to look to know she was moving closer.

This time he did hit his mark and started the song, managing to sound like he wasn't thinking about anything other than some brown-eyed girl. Certainly not a girl with gray-green eyes.

Not an easy feat, when all he could think about was Maggie's closeness. And the fact that he wanted to look at her, to talk to her. To kiss her.

He fumbled, losing the words for a moment. But then he got them back, singing each word with renewed fervor.

Then he spotted her in his peripheral vision, up against the stage. He couldn't stop his eyes from darting toward her. She stood practically at his feet. Right there.

God, what was she doing? Didn't she know that last night she'd done the right thing by turning him down? She wasn't the one-night stand type. He'd known that. But in his desire for her, he'd let himself believe otherwise. He couldn't forget again. He couldn't risk her getting hurt. They weren't talking about something as simple as a broken heart here.

He walked to the other side of the stage and, leaning down, sang the lyrics—the ones he could remember—directly to the redhead with the nasal voice. He'd make himself want nasal over sweet, bright red over warm strawberry blond.

* * *

Maggie didn't move away from the stage, even as Ren blatantly ignored her, even as everything in her body told her to slink off. She had to keep believing what she'd seen in his eyes last night. What she'd felt in his kiss. Ren did want her. She needed to believe that.

She wouldn't behave like she had with Peter. If Ren didn't want her anymore, he was going to tell her so face-to-face. And until then, she was going to believe in herself. Believe that he did want her.

Even if he did lean over the railing surrounding the stage to serenade a tall, willowy redhead in a skintight dress.

Jealousy snaked through Maggie, but she remained by the stage, dancing with the crowd. She wished Erika and Jo were there for moral support, but they'd gone to meet their sailor boys for a drink at Pat O'Brien's, figuring tonight Maggie would want to handle her seduction on her own.

That was laughable now. Like she had any idea how to seduce anyone. Although she'd really thought Ren would still be amenable to the idea, which she was counting on to make her novice attempts somewhat easier. Apparently not. She was sure he'd seen her when she arrived, but since then, not even a single glance. He was far too busy with the redhead.

Apparently Maggie had missed her chance.

Maggie stared at the redhead, who beamed at Ren, flirting with him outrageously. Maggie couldn't blame him; the redhead was stunning. If a little bit garish, Maggie amended, eyeing the leopard-print spandex of her dress. Which actually looked great, she had to admit, feeling deflated about her own attempt to look sexy. And it was easy to see that the redhead was not going to turn down any move Ren made.

No, dammit, she wasn't going to think like that. That was exactly how she'd thought when Peter left her. She'd been polite. She calmly accepted what he'd done, behaving as if the whole fiasco was her fault. She wasn't going to take the blame tonight.

She did look as good as the redhead. She had dibs on Ren, and she was taking him. He was hers. This was the new and improved Maggie. Gutsy and not afraid of taking what she wanted.

And if Ren really didn't want her?

She pulled in a deep breath. She'd deal with that when she got there.

"Okay, y'all," Ren announced. "The band is going to take a little break, but don't leave. We will be right back."

Maggie noticed that the redhead was moving toward the steps at the side of the stage. She couldn't let her get there first. Maggie had to talk to Ren. To tell him she'd made a mistake.

Ren came down off the stage just as both she and the redhead reached him.

"Hi," Maggie said to him before the redhead could speak. She noted the irritated look the other woman shot her.

Ren glanced at her. "Hey, Maggie." Then he nodded to the other woman.

"Listen," he said to both of them, "I've got to go talk to the sound guy. I'll be back."

The redhead simpered appropriately, asking him to return quickly. Maggie just nodded. Ren zigzagged through the crowd to the booth in the back, and disappeared inside.

Maggie released a deep breath. That hadn't been the reception she'd hoped for, but it hadn't been terrible either. It was Saturday night, and the bar was crowded and he was working. She glanced at the redhead and realized she was just making excuses. Ren was blowing her off.

She wandered to the bar. She needed to get away from Ren's newest girl, who remained right near the entrance to the stage like an Amazon sentry.

As soon as Stacy of the antennae saw Maggie, she bounced down the bar toward her. She smiled broadly.

"How are you tonight?" she greeted. At least *she* seemed pleased to see Maggie again.

"Fine." Maggie managed a smile of her own, although she had the feeling it wasn't quite as genuine as Stacy's.

"Could I get a diet soda?"

"No wine tonight?"

Maggie shook her head. "Not tonight." Somehow alcohol seemed like a bad idea. God only knew what she might say. She glanced over to the redhead—even without liquor she could think of a few things she'd like to say to her. Not that she had any right to say anything, really.

The bartender grabbed a plastic cup, spun it in the air and then used the spigot to fill it to the brim.

"There you go."

Maggie placed a five on the bar.

"I'll just put it on Ren's tab."

"No," Maggie pushed the money toward her. She wasn't Ren's girl. She looked over her shoulder and saw that Ren had returned as he promised, but not to her. He and the redhead stood close together, she with her mouth near his ear, talking animatedly. Ren's back was to her, his long hair cascading down over his broad shoulders; she couldn't see his expression, but she could picture his flirty, curling grin.

"Why don't you let me get that?" a male voice said from close beside her. Maggie turned to see a guy she recognized vaguely from the dance floor. He'd been dancing next to her. She'd only noticed him because he'd bumped into her.

He was nice looking with thick black hair and brown eyes. And now that they weren't jostling on the dance floor, she noticed that he was also quite young. Maybe twenty-two.

He waved to the bartender, who with her usual radar noticed and came right over.

"I want to pay for this lady's beverage," he said gallantly, and Maggie noticed that not only was he young, he was also a little drunk. With a grand flourish, he materialized a—dollar bill. Then he gave Maggie a goofy look and tried again, digging around in his pocket until he found more bills. Finally he handed the bartender a twenty.

Maggie laughed. He was like a giant, good-natured teddy bear.

"Thank you," Maggie said, picking up her own money and sticking it back in her purse.

"Sure. What's your name?"

Maggie told him, and he said that his was Mark.

Behind her, she heard the band tuning up.

"Well thanks, Mark," she said, raising her cup toward him. "Nice talking to you."

Mark raised his bottle of beer in return.

Maggie wound back through the crowd, getting closer to the stage. She was determined to talk to Ren. Maybe she was just being a masochist—chances *were* that she was just being a masochist.

As before, Ren didn't seem to notice her. He focused on the crowd as a whole, with the occasional break to flirt with the redhead, who practically preened under his attention.

She should just leave, Maggie told herself as Ren moved on from one song to another. It had become clear that he didn't intend to pay her any attention. None. This was torture.

This was goddamned torture. Ren gritted his teeth as he tried desperately to ignore Maggie swaying down on the dance floor among the sea of others. Of course, she might as well have been out there alone. She was the only one he was aware of, try as he might not to be.

Coming down from that stage and only saying hello to her before disappearing into the sound booth under the pretext of some work-related mission, that had been pure hell. All he'd wanted to do was stop and talk to her so he could hear her soft voice. He'd wanted to pull her against him so he could feel her smooth skin and soft curves.

But he'd done the right thing and dismissed her. Then he'd

spent the remainder of the break talking to the redhead. And that had been another test in torture.

Still, he'd done it, certain that Maggie would leave. He knew she could be easily hurt, he'd sensed that in her.

But now he wasn't even sure Maggie had noticed his dismissal, because when he'd cast a quick look in her direction, she'd been talking to some guy who looked as if he'd just stumbled out of a frat house, and probably had.

Ren had noticed the guy earlier. He had been circling around Maggie all night, moving through the crowd like a shark sizing up its prey. Even now, he was standing right behind her, his eyes locked on her ass as she swayed to the music.

Ren's jaw clenched. He wanted to jump down off the stage and blacken both of the bastard's wandering eyes.

But he didn't. He wouldn't. Maggie was not his woman to defend. And frankly, the college kid wasn't doing anything wrong. And showing his jealousy was not the sign he was trying to give Maggie. Jealousy was not disinterest.

Maggie sighed. She *was* wasting her time, that was painfully obvious. Ren could not be more uninterested in her if he tried. It was time to admit she'd missed her chance. Ren was so over her. And really, did she want a one-night stand with someone who could forget about her that easily? She knew she couldn't expect a grand romance, but she didn't want to be just another notch on the bedpost either. She had believed she was special to him, even in that short a time. She'd seen it in the way he looked at her. Or least she thought she had.

Wasn't she the strangest combination of ego and insecurity?

She sighed. She should just go. She couldn't take watching him not watching her any longer.

She took the last sip of her soda, then turned to go toss the empty cup in the trash can near the bar, but instead she ran smack into a wall of chest.

"Oh," she said, startled. "Sorry." Then she realized it was Mark. He smiled down at her.

"Not a problem."

His words were said easily, but something about the way his eyes roamed over her stirred a ripple of wariness. She started to walk around him, but he sidestepped, blocking her.

"Are you leaving?"

Chapter 10

Maggie nodded. "Yeah. It's getting late."

"No, it's not. The party's just getting started."

She jumped as he grabbed her waist, pulling her tight against him. She struggled slightly, then realized she wasn't going to easily break his strong hold. Suddenly she realized the boy she'd considered a teddy bear was more like a grizzly. Apprehension snaked up her spine.

"Come on, Maggie, let's dance." Mark's words were slurred and she smelled the beer on his breath.

She pushed at his chest. "You know, Mark, I really am tired."

"One dance." From the way his hand was squeezing her bottom, she didn't think dancing was at all what he had in mind.

She squirmed, trying to slip out of his hold, but that only made him grip her tighter. Tight enough that her ribs ached. But it wasn't pain that made her panicked. No, it was what he was shoving up against her. The distinct hardness of his erection poked against her belly.

"I've been watching you all night. And I've got to say you are the prettiest little thing in this place."

Maggie blinked. She would have thought hearing a man say those words would have made her feel good, but given her current position, she just felt sickened. And nervous.

"Mark," she said slowly, trying to reason with him. "I'm flattered, but I think—"

Before she could finish, his head came down and his mouth covered hers. Wetness and the stale, sour tang of beer filled her mouth. His teeth ground against her lips, rough, painful.

She turned her head, breaking the disgusting kiss, and shoved at his chest, but couldn't get any leverage.

"Let her go."

Ren's voice echoed all around Maggie, and it took her disoriented and appalled brain a moment to realize that he'd said the words over the microphone.

She struggled against Mark's hold to look over her shoulder at Ren. He stood on the stage, glaring down at them. Although his hard stare wasn't directed at her, but at Mark.

Mark hadn't noticed the command at all. He still gripped Maggie tight, tight enough that she couldn't pull in a full breath. She struggled against his grasp, panic rising.

"Let her go," Ren repeated, and this time his words did capture Mark's attention, because they weren't being said over the music. The band had stopped playing, and now they all glared down at him.

Mark frowned up at Ren, blinking. "Mind your own business, buddy."

"I am," Ren said, his voice calm but hard. "Let her go."

Maggie attempted to use Mark's distraction to escape, again shoving at his chest, but despite his obvious drunkenness, he was quick. Quick and strong. She was pinned against him, his fingers digging into her rib cage. She made a small gasp, pain shooting from her ribs.

Discordant reverberations pierced the air as Ren threw down the microphone and jumped off the stage. He was instantly at Maggie's side, moving so fast through the crowd that she barely registered his movement.

He was just suddenly there. And he was furious.

"Get your fucking hands off her," Ren growled. "She's mine."

Obviously the speed of his movement unnerved Mark as well, because he loosened his grip on her waist. Despite Maggie's shock at Ren's possessive words, she used Mark's stunned reaction to jerk free, stumbling backwards away from him.

Ren took a step closer to her, his gaze darting to her, just long enough for Mark to lunge forward and throw a punch.

His fist caught Ren in the cheek.

Maggie screamed, but Ren barely seemed to notice the powerful blow, and caught Mark with a right to the stomach. Mark stumbled backwards but managed to keep his footing, then charged forward again. This time he missed Ren completely.

Ren landed a fist directly in Mark's face. Blood spurted from Mark's nose, and he staggered as if he wasn't quite sure where he was or what had happened. He stumbled backwards, leaning heavily on a table.

Two other college students, apparently Mark's friends, approached him. They didn't even cast a look in Ren's direction as they gathered up their bloodied friend and half carried, half dragged him from the bar. Going by their apathetic reactions, this wasn't an uncommon end to the night for them or Mark.

Ren followed them to the door, watching them disappear into the crowds on Bourbon. Then he turned back to Maggie, striding towards her. He absently pushed his tangled hair away from his face as his eyes roamed over her.

"Did he hurt you?"

Maggie shook her head, fighting the urge to rub a hand over her mouth. "No. I'm fine."

Instead she reached out and touched his cheek. A purplish bruise was appearing on his cheekbone. "But he hurt you."

He caught her hand, pressing her fingers to his cheek. "I'm fine too." Then he moved her hand away, releasing it.

She stared at him, not finding any words. Finally she offered him a small smile and admitted, "I don't know what to say. This is kind of out of my sphere of knowledge. What's the appropriate thing to say or do when a person gets in a fistfight for you?"

Ren stared at her for a moment, then a lopsided smile touched his lips. "I think you say thanks, then you throw yourself into said person's arms."

Maggie laughed. But she moved toward him, putting her arms around his neck, hugging him. His arms came around her, pulling her close. Maggie breathed in the clean scent of his hair, loving the solid feel of his body against hers.

"And," he said, his lips close to her ear, his breath warm, "I think you kiss said person's poor battered face."

She pulled back slightly, offering him another small smile. "Really? Even if they ignored you all night?"

Ren pretended to consider that. Then he nodded decisively. "In this case, yeah, I think so."

She smiled. Then surprising even herself with her boldness, she pressed a light kiss onto his bruised cheek. But before she could press more than one to the battered flesh, Ren turned his head and caught her mouth with his. Then there was nothing light about the touch.

His hand cupped the back of her head as he moved his lips over hers. Deep, devouring. Maggie moaned, her arms tightening around him. They remained that way, lost in their own desire for each other, until finally the strains of what the band was playing permeated both their minds. Slow, drum-heavy chic-a-boom-type music, the kind used for a striptease.

Ren pulled back from Maggie without totally releasing her, so he could glare up at his bandmates.

They all grinned back like naughty schoolboys.

Ren shook his head, then turned back to Maggie. "So should we stop pretending to ignore each other?"

Maggie smiled, pleased he'd admitted that he'd just been pretending.

"I wasn't pretending to ignore you," she pointed out. Then added, "Not tonight anyway."

That made Ren grin. Maggie's heart, which was already

soaring like a particularly daring trapeze artist, did another midair flip.

"So are you going to go out with me after I get off work?"

It was Maggie's turn to pretend to consider the idea. "Okay."

Ren swooped in and stole another kiss, then he strode back to the stage.

But before he could reach the steps, the guitarist with the goatee called down to him. "Dude, you're actually coming back to work after all that? And with her waiting for you?"

The musician cast a wide-eyed look of disbelief at Maggie. Maggie laughed at his exaggerated expression.

The guitar player turned his comical look back on Ren. "She's waiting to thank you," he said pointedly. Then he shrugged, as if to say the choice was up to Ren, but he added, "I'm just sayin'."

Ren laughed, glancing between Maggie and the stage. Then his eyes returned to Maggie. He still grinned, but Maggie could see his decision was made.

He walked back over to her. "Let's go."

"Are you sure?" She wanted to leave with him, but she also didn't want him to get in trouble over her. He already sported a bruised cheek for her, and the bar still hadn't recovered from the spectacle. People stood in groups watching them.

Then the band started to play, the bass player already at the mic, getting ready to sing.

"It's fine." Ren caught her hand. He directed her to the door.

"Where are we going?" she asked, not really caring as long as she got to be with him.

Ren slowed his pace. "We could go get a drink, or something to eat, if you like."

Maggie deliberated. Now that she'd made up her mind that she wanted him—well, she didn't know if she should wait. Part of her was worried the same fears she'd had last night might return, and she didn't want that.

"Can we go to your place?"

Ren wasn't quite sure what he expected, but it hadn't been that. After last night, he knew her words were downright brazen for her. He was stunned.

In a good way.

He was also stunned at how quickly he was giving up his own plan to leave Maggie alone. To let her go her merry way, while he stayed right where he was. But when he'd seen that guy's hands all over her, his mouth on hers, he'd snapped. He wanted to kill the bastard. Suck out all of his energy until he was a lifeless shell.

He'd managed not to go that far. But he'd wanted to, and that was unusual. Normally, he didn't lose control of himself, or his hunger. Sexually or preternaturally. He wasn't doing well on either count with Maggie.

So much for being gallant. Nobility had lost out to possessiveness and fury. Well, he'd never quite fit the bill for nobility anyway.

But he had to admit, while his lack of gallantry didn't surprise him, his possessiveness did. He'd like to say his reaction had been based on the fact that Maggie clearly didn't want the stupid giant touching her. And that did factor in, to be sure, but he knew that he'd have been even angrier if she had actually liked the guy.

Truth be told, he'd been so jealous he wouldn't be shocked if his eyes were permanently jade green. And jealousy was a new sensation for him. Normally, women were easy come, easy go. In every sense of the phrase. They were replaceable. All the same, all predictable.

Maggie was none of those things.

Of course, he hadn't always had this cavalier attitude about women. He hadn't wanted Nancy or Annalise to be replaceable either. But he'd had to learn not to get attached to women. Because of those two ladies.

He couldn't let himself get attached to this one either. Her life depended on that. He needed to remember that, when he was feeling possessive or jealous. He needed to try to be noble.

She walked beside him now, not speaking, her intelligent green eyes taking in the many sights of Bourbon. Sometimes she smiled, like when a group of college boys staggered by arm in arm singing the theme to *Cheers*. Then her smile turned to intrigued confusion as she watched a transvestite strike provocative poses outside one of the drag clubs.

He found her amazement at all the oddities of Bourbon fascinating to watch. It also made him realize he should walk away—she wasn't suited to what he had to offer. He was one of the oddities.

But the thing that made her vulnerable and dangerous at the same time, her pure aura, was the very thing that made his body go haywire. That alone was dangerous. His lampir side craved her life force. Her energy called out to him, and while he could control himself, especially when surrounded by so many other human life forces, he wanted some of her energy for himself. And then there was the purely male part of him, who wanted her body for himself, too.

Wanting a woman, body *and* soul. Definitely dangerous.

Tell her that you aren't interested. Tell her now, because if you take her back to your place, you won't be able to let her go without being with her.

He told himself the same words over and over, but they never reached his lips.

He was too greedy. Too hungry for her.

Maggie touched his arm, startling him out of his thoughts. She pointed toward a man wearing nothing but Mardi Gras beads, woven into a thong. Sort of.

Ren shook his head. "Another reason not to allow those damned beads to be thrown except on Mardi Gras."

Maggie laughed, glancing over her shoulder to watch the nearly nude man pass.

Another wave of jealousy washed over him—not quite as intense as when that jackass frat boy had been touching her, but still, it was there. Jealous over a man who thought it was a good idea to wander around New Orleans in nothing but green, purple, and gold beads—that was pathetic.

But more than that, the jealousy was a very real concern. He had no idea what to do with jealousy. It was a new emotion for him. He never even felt it over Annalise or Nancy— the only two women he ever felt any real emotion for. He needed to find the strength to do the right thing. He couldn't bring Maggie back to his place.

"You know, I'm actually kind of hungry."

Which was true—but not for food. His eyes darted down her body. She wore a blouse that crisscrossed over her chest, creating a V of pale skin, showing just the slightest swell of her full breasts. Sweetly sexy, if there was such a thing.

He couldn't be alone with her and not touch her. And he couldn't allow that.

"Okay," she said easily, seeming almost relieved that he'd pushed the idea. "What are you in the mood for?"

As if of their own volition, his eyes moved down her body, and this time she noticed his look. Her cheeks colored, but she didn't look away from him.

She was definitely different tonight. More confident. Strange, since he spent most of the night acting as if he hadn't noticed her, which he would have thought would upset her, make her unsure. And then he'd gone to the other extreme, getting in a fistfight, and declaring her his. A point he was glad she hadn't asked about. How would he explain that declaration?

He pointed down Toulouse Street. "There's a good place down this way. Great Creole cooking."

"That sounds good," she said, falling into step with him.

Because of the time, they didn't have to wait for a table.

"Why did you come back tonight?" he asked after they ordered drinks—she, an iced tea; he, a bourbon, straight up. He immediately wondered why he asked. He didn't want to know that. But it was too late, the inquiry was out.

She stopped perusing the menu, meeting his gaze.

"I wanted to see you." She smiled at him as if he was a total dolt.

"Why?"

Maggie smiled again. "I feel kind of like we've had this conversation before."

He frowned, not following.

"Because I'm interested in you. And I decided if you aren't subtle, I probably can't be either."

She really was different tonight. And not just in her clothing choices. He saw directness in her eyes. He could tell she was still shy, still a little uncertain, but she was suppressing those emotions, letting her bravery show through.

"Maggie," he said, feeling the need for the whole truth to be out in the open. "I can't offer anything more than a fling. My life just isn't conducive to romance."

She straightened slightly, but that was the only sign that his words had affected her.

"I know. And I don't expect anything more. After all, I have a life to go back to in D.C."

Ren regarded her for a moment. "You said you weren't comfortable with a one-night stand. And I believe that. And it is honestly all I have to offer you."

Maggie's first inclination was to break away from Ren's intense gaze and busy herself with the menu. But she forced her eyes to stay with him. She wanted this. In part to finally move on from Peter, but to also finally take something for herself.

She studied Ren's face. The hint of stubble on his strong jaw. His long hair framing his face, shiny and soft and so sexy. And his eyes—that color between amber and green with their ability to look haunted. Like they did now.

That look, haunted and a little sad, made her want him all

the more. And she wasn't going to let her fears stop her. Hadn't the fortune-teller said she had to no longer be scared? She trusted him, she realized, in a way that she'd never trusted another man.

It was strange but true. Maybe because he'd protected her. Maybe because he'd made her feel attractive as no one else ever had. Maybe because he was telling her that he couldn't offer her more than a night. Peter had told her he wanted forever, and then he'd left her looking like the fool.

She studied Ren again. She'd take Ren's cool honesty over pretty lies any day.

"I know what you are offering," she told him. "And I'm okay with that."

Ren's lips firmed into a straight line. Then he took a deep breath. "Maggie, I just don't believe this is right for you. And I don't want you to get hurt."

"I appreciate your concern, but I am a big girl. I'm totally capable of making my own decisions."

He opened his mouth as if to argue further, so she cut him off. "So what's good here?"

Ren didn't answer for a minute, and when she looked back up at him, she saw him studying her. That haunted look still there—but then, slowly, he smiled.

"I never would have believed that I'd be trying to talk a beautiful woman *out* of having sex with me."

She laughed. "And I never thought there'd be a time when I'd be trying to talk a beautiful man into having sex with me."

His smile broadened. "And I never would have guessed that you could be so stubborn."

God, she loved that smile. It made her feel a little powerful.

"I can be very stubborn," she informed him. "So you might as well accept that I'm going to have my way with you sometime soon."

Ren laughed, the sound throaty and warm. "I love that you just said that."

She grinned, rather pleased with herself, too. He really did make her feel so powerful. The sensation was heady.

"The ahi tuna."

Maggie frowned, completely confused by his sudden announcement. "What?"

"You asked what's good here. The ahi tuna. If you like fish."

"I do." She set aside her menu. "I'll get that." She trusted him.

Chapter 11

"Did you like the tuna?" Ren asked as they left the restaurant.

Maggie nodded. "It was delicious. But you didn't eat much of yours. You were the one who was hungry."

She still didn't seem to get that the dinner was just a diversion. A last-ditch attempt to stop this thing that was happening between them. A thing that was becoming more and more inevitable.

"I guess I wasn't in the mood for food."

"Are you okay?"

Ren smiled slightly. She really was sweetly naïve. Hadn't she noticed him watching her through the whole meal, devouring her with his eyes?

"So are you going to take me to see your place?"

Damn, who was this woman? He'd never have imagined that Maggie of the shy blushes could be so determined. Of course, a blush stained her cheek even now. Determined but still shy. He liked that.

"Come on." What was the point of telling himself he wasn't going to let this happen? He was, and they both knew it.

He caught her hand and led her down the street in the direction of his apartment. Neither spoke as they walked, not until they reached his door.

"Here we are." He didn't look at her as he released her

hand and unlocked what looked like a large wooden barn door. He shoved it open, and then caught her hand again. He led her through a little alleyway that opened into a square courtyard.

"This is amazing," she said, letting go of his fingers and walking further into the space. She slowly turned, her expression rapt as she took in everything.

Two stories of building surrounded them. Balconies overlooked the courtyard, the scrolled wrought-iron railings cascading with flowers and greenery. Stones paved the ground, and the perimeter was fringed with lush greenery. Small ground lights illuminated benches and a wrought-iron table and chairs in the far corner under a sprawling magnolia. Water bubbled merrily in a fountain at the center of the green oasis.

"This is your home?"

He owned the whole building, but he didn't say that. Instead, he gestured to the building at the end of the courtyard. "That is mine. There are four other apartments in the side buildings. But they are vacant—since Katrina."

Maggie continued to spin. "I feel like I stepped back into the 1800s."

"Well, it wasn't as nice in the 1800s."

Maggie paused, smiling at him, obviously amused at his certainty.

"My place was a carriage house," he added, "and the rest were slave quarters."

"Really?" She stared at the building, clearly trying to picture how it must have looked all those years ago. A frown pulled down her lips at the thought.

Ren didn't want that. He liked watching her amazement, not her disquiet. Maggie strolled around the courtyard, stopping by the fountain. Lights shone through the bubbling water, dappling her skin in light and shadows.

She was breathtaking.

He couldn't believe this. He was nervous. When had he

ever been nervous about the prospect of having sex? Hell, he didn't think he'd even been particularly nervous when he lost his virginity.

Of course, the older prostitute had expected very little of a mere boy—so he'd considered skill very little at that time. And while he felt confident he'd gotten considerably better at the whole enterprise since he was fourteen, for some reason, Maggie had him keyed up like a green schoolboy.

She watched him, still standing by the fountain. Lights created a kaleidoscope over her pale skin and shone on her loose, chin-length curls. She'd made the comment that the courtyard was like stepping back in time. She looked like she was a part of the time warp. Beautiful and warm, with an inherent innocence surrounding her.

More warning flares flashed. Not that he was going to heed them. Maggie was too much temptation, and he'd never been good at willpower. Not at all.

She didn't move. She simply waited, as if she knew he wouldn't be able to resist for long. She smiled, though. Small and inviting.

"Are you going to show me inside?" she asked, glancing at the carriage house. For the first time, he could sense her nervousness too. She'd done well most of the night to suppress it, but now that they were here, alone, it was back.

"Of course." But instead of approaching the house, he approached her.

"You do know what will happen if you go in the house with me, right?" He did feel the need to offer her one more chance to stop this.

Maggie nodded. "Yes." She smiled shyly.

God, she was so sweet, so adorable.

He caught her hand and pulled her close to him, feeling the lush softness of her breasts against his chest. She stared up at him, wide-eyed, waiting.

Again, a wave of doubt made him pause—for a fraction of a second. Then he was kissing her.

She responded immediately, but not with the practiced, self-indulgent ardor he was accustomed to. No, Maggie responded as if her whole being needed him, as if he was the most important thing in her world. Her hands touched his jaw, his hair. Her mouth was pliable and sweet under his. Her body leaned against his as if she couldn't get close enough to him. She was giving herself to him.

He pulled back. She gazed up at him, her eyes slightly dazed, heavy-lidded with desire.

God, she was beautiful. Passion, intense, swirling like a rising tornado, coursed through him. The sensation was foreign, and more than a little shocking. He'd never wanted a woman this intensely. Never.

Again warning bells sounded, just a faint jingle over the rush of desire. He ignored them.

Taking her hand, he led her to the steps rising up to his portion of the building. He unlocked the door, then pushed it open, allowing her to move past him inside.

He felt another wave of uncertainty radiate from her, but she walked into the room. Another sign, another chance to halt this. Again the warning fell on deaf ears.

As she had in the courtyard, Maggie slowly took in everything. Admiring the polished hardwood floors, the original restored brick walls. She trailed fingers over the back of the brown leather sofa and paused to study the artwork on the walls.

For the first time in a long time, Ren really looked at the place he'd called home on and off for over a hundred years.

The place was nice, he supposed. Maybe a little run-down. Maybe a little cluttered with books and CDs and magazines. Seeing the room through her eyes, he realized it was a bit of a mess.

But Maggie didn't seem to notice. Instead she smiled at him over her shoulder. "This is wonderful."

He didn't react except to take in that lovely smile. He had no idea why her opinion was so important, but it was.

She wandered over to peek into the galley-style kitchen. The one room that was spotless. He could eat, if necessary, to appear human, but it wasn't something he craved or particularly enjoyed. Needless to say, he didn't cook.

"How long have you lived here?"

"A few years," he answered vaguely. He bought the building in 1861, although he did move out for extended periods of time. It was hard to explain to his other tenants why he still looked exactly the same after several decades. So he moved when necessary, but he always came back. This particular building was one of his favorite homes.

"It's really beautiful." She smiled, then stood in the center of the room as if she wasn't quite sure what to do next.

Another wave of nervousness radiated from her across the room, washing over him. He realized anxiety flared in him as well, in response to her. Strange.

"Did you want to see the upstairs?"

She nodded, and her cheeks grew pink again. She glanced at the staircase that curved up to the loft above. Hesitation was clear on her face and in the air. Another perfect opportunity to stop this.

Instead he walked to the stairs, waiting for her to join him. She hesitated just a moment longer, then followed.

The loft was one huge room, a portion open to look down into the living room below. He had the large room sectioned off into a bedroom and a sitting area. Most of the bedroom was taken up by a huge canopied bed. The other corner of the room was filled by a baby grand piano and a worn sofa and a small fireplace.

Maggie strolled to the piano, running her fingers over the dark wood.

"You said that you don't really play."

He stared at her pale fingers, stroking the instrument. He swallowed, finding the action intensely erotic. "I don't. Not anymore."

For a moment, she seemed surprised by his response. Her

gaze left him to stare at the piano a moment longer, then her gaze flitted to the bed.

He followed her look. The piece of furniture was enormous, made of dark, ornately carved wood. It was draped in dark red velvet, with golden tassels fringing the canopy. Thick curtains were pulled back around the mattress, and could be untied to close the bed off from drafts or, in his case, light.

Strangely, the bed had been his before he'd become a vampire, purchased when he'd sold his first opera. An indulgence at the time, but now a necessity.

"The bed looks like an antique," Maggie said.

"Yes. It is." Like me.

She wandered toward the piece of furniture in question without getting too near it. She probably thought he'd throw her down onto the mattress and have his way with her if she got too close. The idea had merit.

"I have to admit, I'm a little nervous," she said, eyeing the bed, rather than him.

Ren smiled. She had the most interesting way of surprising him. Not that he didn't know she was nervous—he just didn't expect her to admit it.

"Well, I'll admit I'm a little nervous too." He hadn't expected to confess that either. Apparently she brought out surprises in him as well.

He walked up to her, taking his time with his approach, gauging her expressions. Trying to read every nuance of her features. He stopped right in front of her. The clearest emotion he read on her face, in her eyes, was disbelief.

"Why on earth would I make you nervous?"

"Why not?" he asked, reaching out to finger an unruly lock of her hair.

She pulled in a shuddering breath as if his fingers were stroking her skin rather than just her hair. "Because you feel comfortable doing things like this."

"Doing things like what?" His fingers paused in her hair.

"Initiating an affair. Touching a virtual stranger. Kissing a stranger."

He tilted his head to get a better look at her face. "I don't think we are exactly strangers now, are we? And don't you want to kiss and touch me?"

Her eyes remained focused on the floor between them. "Of course I want to touch you," she admitted, again surprising him with her candor. "But I'm . . . not sure."

"Not sure? About what?"

"It's just not . . . something I've done."

His frown deepened, not following what she was trying to say. Then he froze.

"You are a virgin?"

She gaped at him, then laughed. "No. I've done *that*. I just haven't really initiated the whole process much. Or only rarely. Or well," she pulled in a deep breath, her face turning pinker by the moment. "Ever, really."

Ren stared at her for a moment, not sure what one said to that sort of admission. Finally he smiled rather lamely. "Well, you've been doing a good job tonight of letting me know what you want. That should carry over to this, too."

She met his eyes a moment longer, then looked down. Her uncertainty still thickened the air.

His fingers moved from her hair to her face, cupping her cheeks between both his palms, making her eyes meet his again.

"I want you, Maggie. Very, very much. And I can assure you that I want you to touch me. I want you to do whatever you want to me."

"Really?"

He grinned widely. "Oh yeah. Initiate away, darling."

He waited for her to make the first move, sensing that she needed that in some way. She needed to be the one to start this, though he didn't quite understand why he felt this way. He just *knew* it.

She still hesitated, but then touched her fingertips lightly to his jaw. She leaned up and pressed her mouth to his, kissing him, her touch sweet, unsure. She pulled back, her cheeks scarlet.

"Darling, you don't have a thing in the world to be nervous about. I want you," he said, his forehead resting against hers. "I've thought of little else since the moment I saw you near the stage that first night."

She met his gaze, her eyes moving over his face as if trying to read his feelings, his thoughts. Then her hand came up, stroking his hair, pushing it back to tuck it behind his ear. He tilted his head, closing his eyes at the almost innocent touch. Desire, not innocent at all, rippled through him.

She rose on her tiptoes and pressed her mouth to his. This kiss was less unsure, more passionate. Desire rocketed through his veins, propelling his whole body to painful awareness. Damn.

He made a noise in the back of his throat, then broke the kiss. "I really have no idea what you are nervous about. You are good at this."

He wiggled his eyebrows, and she laughed, pleased with his response.

She kissed him again with more force, more confidence, but this time he couldn't resist taking control of the embrace. He cupped the back of her head, slanting his head to deepen the kiss. More need pulsed through him, sharp, painful, and so delicious.

All other thoughts were gone, nothing existed but Maggie and his need. And all the things he wanted to do with her. To her.

But to his surprise, it was Maggie who started to undress him. He broke the kiss to watch as her fingers, only shaking slightly, worked on the buttons of his shirt. Soon it was open and parted and her small hands brushed over his bare chest.

He groaned as her hands slid around under his shirt, kneading the muscles of his back. She pressed a kiss to his collar-bone.

"Maggie," he murmured, his own hands tugging at the sides of her shirt, pulling up the satiny material until he made contact with her silkier, smoother skin.

The briefest touches of skin had ignited them both into a frenzy, and soon they were tugging at each other's clothing. All the while their mouths devoured each other, only parting long enough to yank off another article of clothing.

When they were both undressed, Maggie to just her panties, Ren in his boxers, he stepped back from her.

"Maggie," he murmured, taking in all of her pale, flawless skin and lush curves. Her breasts were perfect, round and full with small, tight nipples.

She stood with her arms down at her side, but he could tell by her tight fists she longed to cover herself.

Good Lord, why? Didn't she have any idea how gorgeous she was?

Maggie watched Ren, trying to read the look on his face as he stepped slightly back from her and scanned slowly down her body. Her first inclination was to cover herself. To hide her abundance of curves. Curves she'd always considered bordering on chubby. Curves that Peter hadn't considered bordering on chubby. Curves he'd considered outright fat.

But Ren's expression didn't show disgust. If anything, as his gaze moved over her in excruciatingly slow perusal, she only saw approval and desire darkening his eyes.

"Maggie." The roughly muttered word said more than any pretty compliment.

Her muscles relaxed. The tension, the fear, drained from her, allowing her own gaze to move over him. All his long limbs and lean muscles. Her fingers twitched as she studied his bared chest, muscled and covered in a light thatch of dark hair that narrowed to a strip that trailed down his stomach, whorled around his belly button and disappeared inside the waistband of his boxers.

"You are beautiful," she murmured, then came forward to touch him. His chest hair was springy and tickling under her palms. His muscles hard, his skin hot.

He took a sharp breath as her hands stroked him, teasing his nipples.

Suddenly, her world tipped on its axis and she found herself scooped up in his arms. She wrapped her arms around his neck, letting out a small squeal.

"Ren! You'll drop me."

His response was a chuckle, then he kissed her. His lips, nibbling and hot. He placed her on the bed, the velvet of the covers rubbing the skin of her back, the soft mattress and covers swelling up around her.

He followed her down, his hard length covering her. The hair of his chest rubbed against her swollen nipples. His muscles flexed and relaxed. She gasped, the sensation too good.

She wrapped her arms around his neck, desperate for him to be as close as possible, mouth to mouth, skin to skin. He allowed himself to be directed to her, his hair falling in a curtain around them, as he pressed his lips to her. Her fingers tangled in the long locks pulling him closer still. She deepened the kiss. Her tongue found his, touching him in small licks.

He groaned, his weight pushing her down into the mattress.

"I never knew kissing could be like this," she admitted against his lips. Kissing Peter had always been nice. This was something altogether different.

"I know," Ren agreed, his voice low and husky, filled with a tone close to reverence. More arousal shot through her, the hoarse quality of his voice like velvety fingers stroking her.

He pressed another kiss to her mouth. "Let's see what happens when I kiss other parts of your body."

His mouth moved to her neck, nibbling the sensitive skin just below her ear. She shivered, desire curling through her.

Then he kissed her chest, pressing opened mouth kisses over her skin. He stopped to lever himself up so his gaze could roam down her.

"You have the prettiest breasts." He leaned forward and ran the tip of his tongue over the pebbled nipple. She gasped, arching her back, wanting more of his moist heat on her sensitive skin.

He smiled at her reaction, again straightening to admire his handiwork. The nipple shone pink and glistening in the lamplight.

"So beautiful," he murmured, leaning in to capture the whole peak in his mouth. She cried out at the intense pull, an electric shock of need zapping throughout her.

He sucked and licked and teased her, until she was wiggling against him, her body demanding more. She wanted him all.

But Ren didn't seem in quite the rush she was. He left that breast to show the same excruciatingly arousing attention to the other one. All the while, Maggie knotted her hands in his hair, constantly pulling him closer.

She wouldn't be satisfied until he was deep inside her. Until their bodies were one. That was the only coherent thought in her mind. She need all of him.

"Ren, please, please make love to me."

She felt the curve of his lips against her breast—even that touch so erotic she nearly cried out.

"That's what I'm doing, darling."

She slid a hand out of his hair to stroke the smooth skin of his back. His muscles undulated under her palms, the movement thrilling, arousing.

Ren's hand stroked down her side, shaping the span of her ribs, the curve of her hip, trailing over the swell of her stomach to find the edge of her panties. Her breath caught in her throat as he toyed with the waistband. His fingers slid inside only to slip back out.

She growled, the sound causing Ren to lift his head. He raised an eyebrow.

"Something wrong?"

Maggie was thoroughly and utterly dazed with need, but still she did manage to notice the pull of a smile at his lips.

"You're driving me crazy." The words came out ragged and desperate.

"You don't like this?" He licked her nipple again, his tongue a quick rasp across the hardened flesh.

She made a small noise. "No, I like it," she managed.

"Or this?" He nipped the tender flesh of the underside of her breast.

She nodded her head, when he gave her an innocently inquiring look.

"What about this?" He trailed kisses down her belly.

She nodded again, a shuddering breath escaping her lips.

"And this?" His tongue delved into her belly button.

She wriggled, a small laugh escaping her already parted lips. She shook her head at that one.

Again she felt his smile on her skin.

He tugged at her panties, easing them down her hips and thighs until he had them off and had cast them onto the floor. Then he pressed his lips to the top of the curls covering her sex.

She gasped, her hips reflexively rising up to push herself against his mouth. Again she felt his smile against her. Then he ran his tongue up the slit of her sex, his tongue just grazing the tender damp flesh beyond.

Her hips bucked, her legs falling apart to expose herself to him.

Ren intended to take it slow, to make sure this was perfect for her, but at the sight of her pink flesh spread open for him— hot, wet, and so damned lovely—he only stared for a moment.

Maggie rose up on her elbows, her cheeks flushed, her eyes heavy-lidded with desire. But even in her haze of arousal, she still frowned, concern marring her flushed, desirous look.

"What's wrong?" She started to close her legs, but he caught them, keeping her knees apart so he could look at her.

She nibbled her bottom lip, already red and swollen from their kisses.

"Do you have any idea how breathtaking you are?" His voice sounded raspy, low with awe.

She shook her head.

He shook his in return, although his action was filled with disbelief and awe.

"I've never wanted anyone the way that I want you."

Again she nibbled her bottom lip, and he knew she was warring with the decision of whether to believe him or not.

Why wouldn't she? She was truly stunning. Lovely full breasts, curved lush hips, pale thighs and tight curls like spun gold and copper creating a small triangle between her thighs. She was the perfect vision of female beauty. Soft, curved, stunning.

"I want to keep kissing you, to keep tasting you," he told her, his voice little more than a rough mutter. "But I can't wait to feel you all around me. Your tight heat. The vibration of your release."

Maggie released a hitched breath. "I don't want to wait either."

Her breathy words were all the invitation he needed. He positioned himself between her thighs. Her curls teased his erection, her heat called out to him.

But he did manage to control himself long enough to kiss her again. Her hands tangled in his hair, her finger stroking him, raising his desire to the point of pain.

He balanced himself on his elbow, positioning himself, the head of his penis just breaching the fiery moisture of her sex.

"Wait," she said, her voice ragged.

He froze, something akin to pure fear solidifying his very

marrow. She couldn't say no, not now. He had to have her. His body ached for her.

"We need a condom," she whispered. Her cheeks reddened.

He tried not to sag against her with relief. Hallelujah! She didn't want to stop. She just wanted to be safe. Smart woman.

His relief quickly fled. He didn't have a condom. Firstly, he couldn't pass on human diseases. Secondly, he didn't bring women back here. But he couldn't expect her to accept either of those excuses.

"Darling, I don't have any."

She looked slightly surprised. Her cheeks grew even pinker. He immediately calculated how long it would take for him to get to the store on the corner of St. Ann and back. Damn.

"I have some in my purse."

Ren stared down at her again, blushing and beautiful underneath him.

He groaned, then kissed her. "Thank God. Damn, I adore you."

Maggie actually laughed. "Thank Erika and Jo. They insisted."

"Thank you, Erika and Jo!" he shouted as he crawled off the end of the bed, spotting Maggie's purse on the floor near their strewn clothes.

He quickly found the silver packets, made a show of grabbing a couple of them, and then practically launched himself back to the bed. She laughed again as he returned to her, crawling up her body until he was back where he so longed to be, between those pale thighs.

He kissed her then, taking his time, to taste her, arouse her, make sure she was still ready for this. For him.

Soon she was back to wriggling against him, her soft smooth skin a delicious torment against him. He pulled back long enough to roll on the condom, then he positioned himself. His penis entered her, just barely, and already his muscles tightened with pure bliss. God, she felt good.

She lifted up against him, pushing him just a little farther inside. And with that tease of heaven, he seemed to lose his mind. He thrust into her fully.

She cried out, and he immediately stilled, remaining motionless as her tight, searing flesh strained around his length.

God, so much for finesse.

"Darling, I'm so sorry," he murmured in her hair, holding her tight, trying to gain some measure of control.

"For what?" she whispered back, her hands moving from his hair, to his shoulders, down over his back.

"I didn't mean to hurt you." He met her eyes, trying to see her emotions there.

"You didn't," she assured him. "You feel wonderful. Big," she added with a small, shy grin. "In a good way."

"Are you sure?" She felt so delicate under him, so small around him.

"I'm very sure." As if to prove her point, she moved, shifting her hips to slide up and down him, as much as his weight and angle would allow.

But that was all he needed. His desire, which he'd managed to keep in check with his concern, spiraled through his body again. It was damned near impossible to think about anything but moving inside her, feeling her fiery heat stroke him.

He braced himself on the mattress, pivoting his hips in steady strokes. Underneath him, Maggie followed his rhythm, anchoring her legs around his hips.

Their movements quickly became more frantic, more driving, until he was thrusting into her, hard and deep.

Then he felt her strain against him, her legs clamping around him, her heels digging into the small of his back as her body tightened, then her release jolted through her.

"Ren!"

He buried his face in her neck as he thrust into her to the hilt, feeling his own release shudder through him. His body trembling as she continued to spasm around him.

He remained on top of her, his body now limp, as if all the energy he had inside him had drained into her. As if she was the vampire, and he the helpless mortal.

Finally, he became aware of her fingers toying with his hair, stroking him, the action oddly sweet and caring.

He lifted his head to look at her face. She lay beneath him, her eyes closed until he shifted. Her hand paused, still in his hair, her eyes slightly dazed by her release.

"Thank you," she said offering him the most beatific smile. A smile that literally took his breath away.

"I'm not sure you should be thanking me." He meant it. He'd had nearly two centuries of sex, and he'd never experienced anything like this. It was . . . he didn't know how to give it words.

"I didn't know sex could be like that." She brushed strands of hair from his face, tucking it behind his ear.

Ren fought the urge to nuzzle against her hand like a cat. But her fingers felt so good touching him.

His cock began to harden inside her.

Her fingers stilled and her eyes widened as the swell pressed against her fiery walls.

His first inclination was to rock against her, inside her. To restart what they just finished. But he remained still, watching her.

"You can do this again?" Amazement clear on her face.

He nodded. "Apparently." This wasn't the norm for him. Usually he did his thing and that was it. Often he didn't want a second time. But if things were different and he didn't have to end things with Maggie, he'd never be done. He could be with her over and over and still never have enough.

But he remained motionless. He could tell from her tightness and her shyness, this wasn't the kind of sexual interaction she was used to. He didn't want to overwhelm her.

But instead of looking dismayed by his reaction, she smiled and pulled his head down to her, kissing his lips sweetly. "I guess I'd better make sure you are satisfied this time."

He made a noise somewhere between a laugh and a groan. "Oh believe me, darling, you satisfied me very, very well. I just suspect you make any man insatiable."

He expected her to laugh at that. But instead the sparkle faded from her eyes.

"No. This is a rarity for me, too."

Ren wanted to ask her more, but somehow this didn't seem the time or the place. Not when he was filling her with his body. So instead of talking, he kissed her again, and began to move his hips. Thankfully, the lost sparkle was replaced by an aroused glitter. A sight he liked much, much more.

He took his time with her. Teasing her, bringing her to the point of orgasm only to pull back. Until finally, she begged him for release, pleading with him in breathless, broken words. Beseeching him with the desperate gyrations of her body. Her heels digging into his back, her fingers squeezing his muscles, her body straining against him. In response, he deepened his thrusts, filling her over and over. His lips locked with hers, his hands stroking her skin.

He tasted her orgasm as she tightened around him. The sweet, honeyed release prompted his own as he followed her into the abyss of spiraling, drowning climax.

Again it was countless moments before he mustered the strength to roll off of her. But this time, her eyes were closed and her breathing even.

She'd fallen asleep, curled into the blankets, her hair a wild cascade around her delicate features.

He considered waking her, but she looked too comfortable, too peaceful, to rouse. Not to mention, the dawn would be here soon. He glanced at the clock on his nightstand. He had a couple hours before the sun rose, more than enough time to see her back to her hotel. He could even let her sleep for a while and then wake her.

But instead he eased her limp body up to the pillows, then pulled the covers up over her—only stopping occasionally to note how lovely she was.

He settled in beside her, watching her as she slept. Not only did women rarely come here, they never spent the night. And he never spent the night with them. It was too dangerous.

He reached for her, his hand hovering over her as if to shake her awake. Instead he tucked the blankets around her pale shoulders, and then he got up to pull the heavy velvet curtains around the bed.

He crawled back in beside her, moving so he could feel her soft, feminine body warm at his side, and listen to the steady rhythm of her breathing.

Just for tonight. Surely one night couldn't hurt anything.

Chapter 12

Maggie awoke, disoriented. She tried to focus her eyes, but the blackness surrounding her was so complete that, for a moment, she wasn't even sure she had opened her eyes. She blinked, but still couldn't see.

The thorough darkness was perplexing but not concerning, especially when she registered the hard warmth at her back and the arm flung over her waist. Ren.

Her body hummed with the delicious memory of what he'd done to her with that body of his. She rolled toward him, touching his arm, his shoulder, his hair spread over the pillow.

She repeated the touch, memorizing the feel of him in the darkness. Denied the use of her eyes, she focused on the texture of him. His skin was cool where no blankets covered him, warm where he made contact with her. The skin of his upper arms and shoulders was smooth like a perfect sculpture, his powerful muscles relaxed with his slumber, but still hard under the silkiness. The tiny hairs on his forearms tickled her fingers. She lightly stroked his chest, more hard muscle and bone covered in more tickling hair. Her fingers moved to his head and the long hair there, silk twining through her fingers.

She wanted to explore him more, take her time and memorize every detail of him. But she didn't want to disturb his sleep—not to mention she felt a little shy exploring any further.

Although this could be the last time she was offered the chance, and she did want to remember everything about him. About her first fling. About the man who'd managed to make her feel sexy and desirable when she believed she never would again.

Idly, she toyed with a strand of his hair, recalling everything he'd done to her. With his hands, his mouth, and his tongue. She wriggled slightly—Lord, that tongue! Her body reacted just to the thought.

She remained beside him, reluctant to move even though nature called. If she ended this moment, if she left this bed, the night would officially be over. And Ren had only offered a night.

She didn't want to give this up. This closeness, this attraction. She wanted to remain right here in the cocooning dark.

She played with his hair, letting the locks fall through her fingers. She listened for his even breathing, but the darkness was silent. If she couldn't feel him, his warmth, his relaxed strength, she'd believe herself alone.

She touched his chest, her fingers brushing the whorls of hair. She held her fingers to him, attempting to feel the beating of his heart. He was totally still. She couldn't even feel the steady thump of his heart.

She levered herself up, peering ineffectively into the blackness. For some reason, even as she told herself she was overreacting, she patted gently around until she found his lips. She held her fingertips to the petal-soft skin there.

"Ren?" she whispered.

He didn't respond, and again she was filled with fear. Was he okay? His skin was warm under her fingers. Yet . . .

"Ren?" she said, this time a little louder.

He didn't respond for a moment, then he made a gruff noise and moved the arm still at her waist to pull her tighter to him.

She sagged back against the pillows, relief making her

weak. Then she laughed slightly at her own foolishness. Had she really believed he was . . . What? Dead?

She was obviously overwrought. And rightly so, she supposed. She had made the monumental leap of sleeping with a man she'd only known for three days. That was huge. Of course, why it would lead her to the idea that Ren was dead . . . well, that was a little melodramatic, wasn't it?

She frowned into the darkness, then realized that between her overactive mind and her very full bladder, rest wasn't going to be possible.

She curled her hands around Ren's arm, surprised at the dead weight of the appendage. This man was a very sound sleeper, she'd give him that.

She wriggled away from him and pushed back the covers. She put her feet over the edge of the bed, and realized that the room was shrouded in such complete darkness because the thick velvet drapes had been pulled closed around the bed. Dim light peeked in from the bottom of the curtain and the split where they met.

She pushed the material back, just enough to slip out into the room, then let the heavy velvet fall back into place behind her. She crossed her arms over her chest, embarrassed despite the fact there was no one there to see her nudity.

She blinked and squinted. Even the dim, watery light was blinding after such complete blackness. When her eyes adjusted, she scanned the floor, trying to find her clothes. She couldn't find her own shirt, but did spot Ren's balled up by the foot of the bed. She snatched it up and tugged it on. Then she started toward the door on her side of the bed. She did a little desperate dance as she pulled the door open, silently praying it was the bathroom.

Thankfully it was. She rushed inside, closing the door behind her. Once finished with her poor overfilled bladder, she moved to the sink to wash her hands.

The mirror over the old pedestal sink was cloudy, revealing its age. She leaned in to look at herself. Tousled hair, puffy lips, skin bright pink on her neck and chest.

She smiled. She looked like a well-satisfied woman. She tilted her head, studying herself a little more. Yep, definitely well-satisfied. She giggled.

Who'd have thunk it, the best sex of her life with a virtual stranger. Except Ren didn't feel like a stranger to her. In many ways, she felt like she'd known him forever. Like he was a part of her. Like he understood her, knew her fears and concerns and how to calm them.

That couldn't really be true, of course. But he did have this uncanny way of reading her. And that was sexy too.

She left the bathroom, pausing in the middle of the bedroom, trying to decide what to do. She glanced at the curtained bed, but immediately dismissed the idea of waking Ren. Given the deepness of his sleep, he was obviously exhausted. And frankly, he'd earned his rest.

She smiled again, her body humming with satisfaction. Satisfaction and an almost electrical sense of energy. She felt alive and vibrant and happy.

She looked around her again, wondering what to do. Now that she was up and awake, she realized she was also hungry. And thirsty.

She searched for her panties and found them under the bed, but her jeans seemed to be missing. Had they really been that frantic when they'd undressed each other? She located her shirt, flung onto his piano bench, but without pants, Ren's shirt was a better option for now, since it was long enough to almost cover her bottom. She also grabbed her purse. She'd have to call Erika and Jo. They might be worried about her.

She smiled again at the image she must make, climbing down Ren's stairs in his shirt, her butt in imminent danger of hanging out.

She didn't really care. She liked this feeling. She'd never worn Peter's clothes. He was very particular about his stuff.

And there was something very intimate about wearing a man's clothing.

Of course, it wouldn't do to think about that too much. She had to keep in mind this was just a one-night stand. Maybe two, if she could finagle it.

She headed straight to the kitchen, and opened the fridge. The wire racks were empty, except for two beers. She closed the door, then moved to the cupboards. Those were empty, except for some mismatched dishes and an ancient-looking box of teabags.

She supposed that Ren's lifestyle didn't lend itself to cooking much. But didn't he even have cereal or bread or something? She shrugged, taking down the box of tea. Lifting the lid, she sniffed the contents. It smelled like tea. She turned, pleased to see a kettle on the stovetop. Well, a cup of tea was going to have to tide her over.

She filled the kettle and turned on the gas range. The flame flared blue. She then wandered into the living room. Picking up a magazine, she flipped through the pages. Strange that he kept insisting he didn't play piano and keyboards, yet she'd heard him do so—very well. And he had a gorgeous piano—in his bedroom no less. Plus he had—she glanced at the pile of periodicals on the end table—at least twenty magazines on the subject of keyboards and pianos.

I used to play. I don't anymore.

Wasn't that practically verbatim what the tea-leaf reader said? She shivered slightly, wrapping her arms around herself. She had to admit that was weird. Another shiver washed over her.

She reached for another of the magazines when she heard a faint buzzing sound. She glanced around, trying to figure out what the sound was and where it was coming from. After searching around the room, she realized the noise was emanating from her purse. Her cell phone.

She pulled it out. Thirteen missed calls.

She frowned. They had to be from Erika and Jo. They'd be the only ones who would call. Her mother was on a trip to Bermuda with her Aunt Agatha—and her mother never called her cell anyway. And no one from work would possibly call her.

She checked the numbers. Sure enough, all were from either Jo or Erika. Concern tightened Maggie's chest. She expected her friends might be worried about her being out all night, but thirteen calls seemed rather excessive. She quickly called Jo back.

"Where are you?" was the greeting she received.

"I'm at Ren's. What's wrong?"

"What's wrong?" Jo sounded thoroughly irritated. "The fact that our friend has disappeared for the entire night and the entire next day, that's what's wrong."

Maggie frowned, confused. "What?"

"We knew you might be gone all night, but when it hit evening and we still hadn't heard anything, of course Erika and I got worried."

Maggie shook her head, still not understanding. She glanced at the windows, realizing the gray light wasn't getting brighter—it was actually getting darker.

"It's evening?"

There was silence on the other end of the line. "It's after six."

Maggie stared at the window, then glanced around for a clock. There was none to be found. Not that she thought Jo would be lying—she just couldn't quite wrap her mind around the idea. She knew they'd been up late, but to sleep the whole day away . . .

"Well, I'm fine," she reassured her friend. "I had my phone on vibrate, so I didn't hear it."

"Thank God," Jo said, relief now replacing irritation. "So? How was it? How was he?"

Maggie smiled, shaking her head at her friend's sudden

shift. Leave it to Jo to be her usual straightforward self about this particular topic, too.

"It was . . . good."

Jo made a disbelieving noise. "Just good, huh?"

"Okay, pretty freakin' great."

Behind her, the teapot started to whistle, the high-pitched noise echoing through the room, made louder by the complete silence of the house.

"Listen," Maggie said as she rushed to the stove, removing the kettle from the heat. "I'll fill you in later."

"Is he there?"

Maggie glanced at the stairs, really hoping the teapot hadn't woken him. "No, he's still sleeping."

"Wow. You must have been good too."

Maggie laughed. "I hope so."

"Okay. Fill us in later. We know where to find you if you don't make it back to the hotel before he has to go to work."

"Okay. Bye." Maggie hit the end key, smiling down at the phone for a moment. Last night had been amazing. Astounding. Wonderful.

She opened the cupboard and took down a teacup. The yellowed china reminded her of the fortune-teller, and of the things she'd said: That she'd meet a new man. That there would be intense passion. What she'd said about the music.

She smiled to herself as she dropped a teabag into the cup and added steaming water. She watched the steam curl through the air, matching the curl of warmth inside herself. She still didn't know if she believed Hattie and her loose tea, but she couldn't deny that what she'd experienced last night had definitely been passion. Overwhelming, intense, crazy passion. And the most thrilling moment of her life.

She picked up her cup, cradling it in both hands as she wandered over to the sofa. She sat down, curling her legs under her. She took a tentative sip of the pale amber liquid.

Not too bad. She relaxed back against the soft leather

cushions, letting her mind wander. God, she felt good. Better than she had felt in, well—forever.

Another smiled tugged at her lips.

Ren snapped awake as he always did. No easing into the day for a vampire. He touched the other side of the mattress, not finding Maggie's warm body still cuddled down under the covers. Not even sensing lingering heat.

Had she left? Did she sneak away before the rays of the sun disappeared from the sky and allowed him to awaken?

He could still feel remnants of her energy in the air, like a particularly heady perfume, a lingering reminder. But he couldn't tell if she'd left. He listened. The apartment was quiet.

Pushing back the curtains, he looked toward the windows. The sky was a deep, steely gray. He couldn't quite guess the time. Maybe seven-thirty or so. Plenty of time for Maggie to rise and leave.

He considered the idea, trying to decipher how he felt about that. He should be relieved, right? After all, he knew this could only be a one-night stand, and if she snuck away that was all the better, wasn't it?

But it definitely wasn't relief that weighted his limbs as he got out of bed and hauled on his jeans.

He glanced back at the bed. The twisted bedding, the indentation on the pillow where her head had been. He breathed deeply, sensing the pureness she'd radiated, although it was fainter now than when he'd first woken up, disappearing quickly.

Somehow he didn't think the memory of their night was going to fade nearly as quickly. Or ever, really.

He glanced one more time at the bed, then headed down the stairs. He'd have to be at work in a little over an hour, but he wasn't prepared to get ready yet.

When he reached the bottom step, he could sense her energy even more strongly. She'd been down here, and from the residual vibration in the air, not so long ago.

He wandered to the kitchen, picking up the vibe there. Then he followed it to the living room, touching the sofa as if he could touch her.

This was foolish. He didn't act like this. Hell, he always knew the score. He always knew what he had to do, how he had to live, and he'd learned to accept it. He certainly didn't pine for women, no matter how great the sex had been.

He pulled in a deep breath, widening his eyes at the understatement of that thought. Amazingly great sex. Fantastic sex. Perfect.

Okay, he was disappointed she was likely gone. But it was for the best.

He wandered over to the windows, looking out into the twilight. Watching the slight breeze stir the magnolias in the courtyard. For a moment, he didn't see her, even though his eyes could easily see in the waning light.

Then he spotted her. Maggie sat on one of the benches, legs curled under her. Perfectly still, like a beautiful statue. The swaying of the magnolia branches played peekaboo with him, making her appear and nearly disappear, like a figment of his imagination.

His muscles tightened with anticipation, with excitement. She was still here. He was nearly giddy with the idea.

He reached for the doorknob, then stopped.

Damn it. He had to get himself under control here. He had no right to be feeling this excited. After all, he was going to have to do the right thing and send her away.

He opened the door and stepped outside. Maggie noticed his appearance immediately, uncurling her legs from under her, revealing their bare, shapely lengths.

Ren gritted his teeth as his body reacted to the sight. He needed to get this situation under control, and fast. Things would have been easier if she'd just been gone. Then he wouldn't have to be the one to handle it.

"Good morning," she said, leaning forward to see him better through the magnolia leaves. His shirt gapped slightly, hinting at the pale, lovely breasts underneath. "Or rather, good evening."

Her greeting froze his aroused thoughts. Another stark reminder of why this had to end as they had agreed, with last night being the only night.

"You are still here?" The comment came out gruffer than he intended, but he didn't temper it. His only thought was that he had to make her leave. If he didn't now, he might never.

Chapter 13

Her own smile slipped and some of the sparkle left her eyes. "I was just out here enjoying the courtyard and the warm breeze."

He nodded, trying not to look at the way his shirt parted again as she shifted uncomfortably under his gaze. He got another hint of cleavage. He also tried not to notice her pale thighs, only partly covered by the hemline. Or her tousled hair that reminded him of how it had looked spread across his pillow.

"I don't want to be rude"—but wasn't that exactly what he was doing?—"but I have to get ready for work."

She straightened as if she'd been slapped. But that's what he'd intended, to wound with his words, with his aloof indifference.

"Oh, okay." She tried to cover her hurt, but didn't manage it in the least. She rose, tugging his shirt down to cover herself, trying to somehow make the shirttails longer.

He swallowed, wishing she could do just that. God, she was distracting.

Possessiveness filled him again. Who knew that seeing a woman in his clothing could make him feel that way? No, not a woman. Only Maggie. Maggie made him feel that way.

He had to get her out of here.

"I'll just go up and get my clothes." She didn't even meet his eyes as she walked past him.

He didn't follow her, knowing it would be too hard to watch her gather her things and leave. And far too tempting to stop her.

He waited outside a few moments, but couldn't stay completely away. He moved to the living room. He could hear her rushing around above him, searching for her discarded clothes. He imagined her dressing. Unbuttoning his shirt and peeling it off to put on her own.

He groaned. What was he doing? He had to stop this nonsense. He had to stick to their deal. She knew the arrangement going in. He'd made it very clear. He didn't need to beat himself up over simply following the established plan. And he certainly didn't need to torture himself with thoughts of her up in his room in various states of undress.

Realizing he was pacing, he forced himself to stop. He leaned on the back of the sofa and waited.

Shortly, she came down the stairs, fully clad, yet still looking adorably tousled. His finger itched to touch her hair, her flushed skin.

Instead he crossed his arms over his chest, trying to keep his expression dispassionate, even as crippling yearning raged inside him.

"I think I have everything," she said after she located her purse on one of the kitchen chairs.

He nodded.

She waited for a moment, not quite meeting his eyes, but not leaving either. Torture. Absolute torture.

"Okay," she said again and nodded as if to affirm to herself that this was indeed over. "Good-bye, then."

He nodded, unable to speak. Afraid of what he might say if he did.

His silence seemed to be the final blow. She looked deflated, as if all her pure energy had been drained away. His gut twisted with disgust. He'd taken a beautiful butterfly and plucked off her wings. Crushed her.

She didn't say a word as she turned and walked to the door, her shoulders slumped slightly. Then, just as she would have stepped outside, she looked back to him.

"I know you weren't offering a romance, but I didn't think the arrangement had to preclude friendship. I didn't know it would be something truly wonderful and then end like this."

Ren didn't speak. He didn't know what to say. Yes, he did, but he couldn't say it. He had to let her go.

"I guess I *was* naïve, wasn't I?" The emotions he read in her eyes were so clearly pained, so heartbreaking, he had to look away.

"Right," she said again, and this time he heard the door close.

The latch had barely clicked into place before he was moving, his stride eating up the floor to get to her. When he opened the door, she was already disappearing into the unlit alley leading to the courtyard doors.

"Maggie," he called, and half expected her to ignore him. The crunch of her rushed steps on the pavement came to a halt. She didn't turn to look at him, she just waited.

He jumped off the steps, striding to her, even as he told himself to stop. His body wasn't listening to his head. His head wasn't particularly convincing. Not when losing this woman was at stake.

He stopped close behind her, but didn't touch her. He didn't feel as if he had the right to—not at the moment. Not after his callous dismissal.

"I'm sorry," he finally said, his voice sounding oddly hoarse. "Last night really freaked me out."

She still didn't turn to him. "Why?"

He almost didn't hear the softly asked question. And then he didn't answer immediately. He had no idea how to tell her the effect she had on him. He, who'd managed to turn indifference into an art form, or at the very least a way of life, was feeling altogether too much. Emotions roiled though him, one tumbling over the other. Hell, he didn't even understand half of them.

"I'm not used to liking a woman so much." That seemed so inadequate to express what had been going on inside him—from the moment he saw her.

She spun to face him, her eyes glittering, and definitely not with warmth. "I get that you are a musician on Bourbon Street, and that women are a dime a dozen for you. But quantity doesn't make them any less real, any less human."

He nodded, knowing that was absolutely true. "You're right. And honestly, I've never treated any of them the way I just treated you."

Her brows drew together. "That doesn't really make me feel any better."

"I know." Damn, he was floundering here. He, who usually knew the right thing to say without thinking. She was having the same effect on his charm that she'd had on his lyric memorization; he was fumbling everything. All he knew was he couldn't let her leave hating him. He just couldn't, even though that was the surest way to protect her. Being a vampire was the least of the problems he had.

He sifted through his mind, trying to find a way to fix everything—to keep her from hating him and to keep her safe.

"Maggie, you aren't the same as the other women, because I like you. I like you a lot. And that scares the shit out of me. And frankly, it should scare you too."

Maggie stared at Ren, trying to decipher what the heck he was talking about. "I don't find you scary at all. I do find you moody and more than a little hard to understand at times."

He considered that, then made a face that said he could accept that. "That's a start, I guess."

Maggie frowned. A start to what? He was doing it again. Being very difficult to understand. Hadn't he basically told her to leave? Now he was talking about a start? God, this man was confusing.

"Why should I be scared of you?" she couldn't help asking, even though that was the least of what confused her.

Ren pulled in a deep breath, his expression showing his struggle to find the right words.

"Maggie, I can't ever love you. And I can't let you love me."

She gaped at him. Was he serious? All she'd expected was that he would be nice the morning after. She hadn't even worked her way up to love, for heaven's sake.

"Well, I'm not sure I would want to be in love with someone like you anyway."

He opened his mouth as if to speak, then he snapped it shut, only to say, "Okay."

She took a step toward him, bringing them practically chest to chest. "Believe it or not, I really just want a fling, too. I'm attracted to you. I like you—sometimes. And I'm on vacation." She stopped, realizing her voice had risen into a yell. Good God, what was she doing?

He stared at her as if he didn't know quite what to make of her outburst either. Then slowly a smile uncurled across his lips.

"Maybe we need to discuss all this a little more."

She blinked. This man really was mad.

Before she could respond, he took her hand and dragged her back toward his place.

"Ren, what are we doing?"

He glanced at her over his shoulder. "We are going to discuss exactly what we want from this arrangement of ours."

"What arrangement?"

"The arrangement we started last night."

"I thought that was a one-night stand."

"Well, it was a one-night stand," he said as he opened the door and pulled her inside. "Now it's an arrangement."

Ren knew he'd lost it, but he just couldn't let her go. After all, if it truly was just a fling she wanted, then a fling could last longer than just one night, and that still made him just the man for that position. Far be it from him not to share with her the one thing he'd been perfecting for over a hundred years.

She seemed pretty adamant that she wanted nothing more from him. Maybe a little too adamant when she'd mentioned that she wasn't sure she would want to be in love with someone like him.

That actually stung a bit—as if he had any right to feel bad about it. He'd essentially said the same thing to her. Not to mention that he should be viewing her announcement as a good thing. She didn't even think she would want to love him. That was perfect, really.

He stopped by the sofa and waited for her to sit. Instead, she walked around behind it, as if she needed to have something tangible between them.

He let her go and remained standing too. He shifted from one leg to the other. Now that he had her back in his house, he didn't know what to say. What would the arrangement be?

Maggie appeared just as uncertain, crossing her arms over her chest, another unconscious attempt to put up a barrier. But she did regard him directly, not shying away from his gaze as she sometimes did.

Just when the room had become almost unbearably quiet, she spoke. "So why are relationships so hard for you?"

That question wasn't what he expected and certainly didn't lessen the tension, at least not inside him.

"I . . ." What did he say about that? "Would you believe I'm cursed?"

Maggie frowned, indicating that she didn't appreciate his attempt at humor. Of course, he hadn't actually been trying to be funny.

So much for the truth.

"Do you feel that way?" she finally asked. "Cursed?"

Oh, yeah. No feeling involved. It was just a fact.

When he didn't answer, she said, "I actually get that."

It was his turn to frown. He didn't ask her why. He just waited.

She strolled around the sofa, heading away from him, still keeping that distance between them established.

"I definitely feel a little cursed when it comes to love. Or when it comes to men in general."

Her admission didn't exactly surprise him. Although he hadn't realized it until she said the words, that was the vibe she gave off. He'd only sensed it as uncertainty, insecurity. But it had been more than that. Maggie was wary of men. All men. That truth seemed so obvious now.

Except that the vibe had definitely lessened last night. Lessened by being with him. There was something humbling about that.

"I've never had good luck with the men in my life," she admitted. "Starting with my dad. He left when I was seven. He simply walked away from me and my mother. He married another woman and had three children with her. And by all accounts, he is a fabulous father to them. So for years, I wondered what was wrong with me." She sighed. "It's easy to feel that way. It's easy to keep feeling that way."

Ren remained still. Oh yeah, he understood that feeling. His father hadn't wanted him either. Dismissed him in much the same way. And there was no harder rejection than that. Denied by a parent.

"My life was much the same," he heard himself saying, suddenly unable to not share some of his past with her. "Now add a mother who was self-centered, petty, and cruel, and you have . . ."

What was he doing? He shouldn't tell her any of this. All she needed to understand was that he couldn't get romantically involved. Physically, yes. That he could do, but anything else had to be off limits.

Maggie stepped closer to him. Still several feet away, but at least the sofa wasn't like the Great Wall of China between them.

"I understand that can really mess you up." He saw sympathy in her eyes. Her reaction unwound something twisted painfully tight inside him. Something that he hadn't even realized was coiled so damned tight.

She took another step toward him. "So we are both rather messed up."

He nodded. "So it would appear." Although what with his being a vampire and cursed to boot, he sort of felt that he was ahead in the messed-up department. If he left her alone, Maggie would be fine. She'd find the right guy. She'd settle down. She'd have kids and a happy life.

But of course he wasn't going to let her look for that just yet.

"So let's discuss this arrangement," he said.

That made Maggie smile. "What arrangement?"

"The one we are going to set up," he stated, businesslike, determined. After all, that's what this deal had to be. Like a business. No emotion.

"Okay, so what exactly do you want?" he asked. "The best-case scenario."

She stared at him, her brows pulled nearly together. From her perplexed look, it was clear that she thought he'd lost his mind completely. And he sort of felt the same way.

She'd called him moody. He'd give her that. But the way he'd swayed back and forth on this particular topic—it was damned near bipolar.

"Okay," she said slowly, as if she was mentally setting herself up for some serious negotiation. She glanced toward the ceiling, thinking about the question. "Best-case scenario."

She was quiet for a moment.

"I'd like to have fun with you. Hang out. Laugh. Listen to your band." She paused, her cheeks reddening, as if she was ready to say more, but embarrassment stopped her.

"I want to keep hanging out with you, too," he admitted.

She nodded.

"And I want to keep having sex with you."

Her cheeks turned pink, but she maintained eye contact. "I want that, too."

For some reason, even though he was relatively sure that was what she was going to say, he felt a rush of relief at hearing it.

This was where it got tricky. Tricky and still very dangerous. "But we do have to keep this fun and light, and not take it anywhere beyond a good time."

Maggie pulled in a breath. That small hesitation worried him. But then she smiled. "Agreed."

"And when next Sunday arrives, and you head back to D.C., we just let it end. A holiday fling."

Again, Ren sensed hesitation in Maggie, but then she nodded. "Right. Sunday is where this story ends."

This time, he stepped forward. She shifted slightly, but she didn't back away. Instead she surprised him by offering her hand.

When he just stared at her outstretched palm, she said, "Shouldn't we shake on it? Or something?"

He smiled, then took her hand, pulling her against him. "Oh, I think we should seal the deal, but I had something a little more binding than a handshake in mind."

Maggie watched as Ren's mouth came down to catch hers. Definitely sealing their bargain. And even as her rational mind told her that this whole situation was nuts, she reacted to him, her lips pressing against his, her arms coming up to encircle his neck.

And then her rational mind no longer had any say in things.

Her fingers tangled in his hair. His knotted into hers.

They stood twined together, kissing for several seconds. Maybe minutes. She wasn't sure; she was simply lost in Ren.

"Can you really do this?" he asked against her lips, his husky voice vibrating through her body. The sensation was too good, too inviting. She couldn't let this go.

Not yet. She wanted whatever time she could have with him, and she was willing to abide by his terms. After all, she hadn't been lying when she'd told him that she didn't think she would want to be in love with someone like him.

He was definitely fling material. He wasn't love material. But that wasn't going to stop her from going with this and enjoying every minute of it. Last night had shown her what sex could be like, and she felt like a kid with a new toy.

"Yes. I can do this. Can you?" she asked, even though she knew the answer.

To her surprise, Ren pulled away from her, staring into her eyes, his own eyes taking on that haunted quality.

"Yeah, I can." His words sounded determined, as if he was trying to convince himself. Which made no sense to her, since he was the one who was unlikely to fall in love.

Least of all with her.

She caught herself. She wasn't going to think like that. This wasn't about being hard on herself. This was about enjoying her time with Ren.

"Come on," he said suddenly.

"Where?" Maggie allowed him to take her hand.

"I need to get ready for work."

"And you need me to help you with that?"

He glanced over his shoulder at her, revealing one of his Cheshire cat smiles.

"I need someone to help me wash my back."

Chapter 14

How was it that Maggie could tell him what she wanted from him—a fling with good sex and fun—yet now she stood in his bathroom looking for all the world as if she wanted to run?

Ren smiled slightly as she glanced at the closed door for the fourth time in half as many minutes.

He turned away from her, testing the warmth of the shower spray before he spoke. "I can't believe I still have the ability to make you nervous."

There was quiet behind him, and he half expected to glance over his shoulder and see the bathroom door open and Maggie gone. But when he did look, she remained right where she'd been, her arms still tightly crossed over her chest.

"I . . ." She pulled in a deep breath, something she did whenever she was agitated. He wondered if it was a natural coping mechanism or one that had been taught to her. He tried to picture her in yoga or therapy. He couldn't quite see either one.

He opened his mouth to ask, then stopped. Asking about potential therapy of some sort wasn't a good idea. That would be heading into "too much sharing" territory.

But then, they had already talked about their deficient fathers. That was definitely sharing.

"I've never showered with a man," she blurted out, dragging all his attention back to her. Well, now that was sharing too.

"Never?"

She shook her head, looking embarrassed and miserable. Ren moved across the small bathroom, needing to disperse the energy around her. Her self-doubt tainted the wonderful quality of her aura. He didn't want that.

"You have no reason to be nervous about this. After last night, you can't doubt my attraction to you."

She pulled in another breath, this one slowly, through her nose. He doubted she even knew she did it. It just happened he noticed everything about her.

"Somehow it seemed a little easier happening in the horizontal." She cast a quick look up to the ceiling light, domed in opaque glass and illuminating the white tiles brightly. "And without so much light."

Ren frowned. Light was good. He wanted to see all of her. Vertical was good too. But she obviously didn't agree. And he didn't want her so tense. That took away all the fun. He wanted wanton Maggie—or at least shyly wanton Maggie. He didn't want her to hold anything back from him.

He reached for her, his hand touching the smooth skin of her face. He wanted all of her with no reservations. His fingers paused on the side of her neck.

No. He wanted everything she was willing to give him physically. He couldn't want everything she had to give. Their relationship had to remain on a physical level.

Could they have friendship too?

He looked into her eyes. They already had that. Hell, he'd told her more than he'd told anyone in the last century about his family life. And while what he'd said was hardly an epic tale, he *had* talked about his parents. He tried not to think about them, much less talk about them.

So they were friends. That was allowable. Just like building up Maggie's ego when it came to men was allowable. He was doing her a service, really, because she should believe that she was attractive and interesting to the opposite sex.

Hell, she'd had his full attention at first sight.

He was helping her get over her past. Well, maybe a little. Assuming that he, emotionally broken himself, could ever heal her completely was conceited to the max.

But he could assure her that he found her amazingly beautiful and sexy and fascinating.

His hand moved on her cheek again, brushing the velvety swell of her cheek with his thumb. She leaned into the touch, seeming to take strength from him. He allowed her to, allowing some of his life force, or rather, his stolen life force, into her.

She shivered at the sensation, desire flaring in her sea-green eyes. He shuddered too. There was something strangely intimate about sharing himself with her this way. Almost as intimate as being deep inside her. Almost.

"You know how attractive I find you. Surely last night showed you that?"

She nodded, closing her eyes, nuzzling his hand. The sight fired up his desire even more. She had to know what she did to him. He felt as if his need for her snapped in the air around them. Alive, perceptible.

Her hand came up to cup his, pressing his palm closer to her. She opened her eyes, their depths filled with her own longing.

"I do," she said, although there was still an uncertainty in her voice. "I-I just feel different doing all this outside of a bed. And you know . . . vertical."

He laughed, pulling her tight to him, kissing her hair. "You'll like it. And believe me, before this week is over we'll do it in a lot more places than just the bed."

"Really?" Now she sounded more intrigued than worried.

He didn't answer her, but instead kissed her.

Soon their clothes were coming off, although, much to his dismay, she had far more on than he did.

"I shouldn't have even pretended that I was going to let you go."

"No," she agreed, "you shouldn't have. Maybe we should both stop pretending things, like ignoring each other, like not wanting to be together."

"Good point," he murmured, nipping her ear. She shuddered, her fingers digging into his bare shoulders.

He continued to nibble her earlobe and the sensitive skin below, loving every shiver and shudder of her body against his. His fingers worked on her bra. He wanted that same reaction, but with no barriers between them.

The hooks unfastened, he moved back to peel the pink lace from her body. Then he just studied her. Steam now swirled around them, making the whole situation feel a tad surreal, like the best dream he'd ever had.

She didn't cover herself. She didn't even knot her fists. She just let him look. They were making headway.

He moved back to her, but this time, he didn't just touch her. He picked her up. Like the last time, a squeal escaped her. Actually it was more a small squeak—they were making headway with this too.

"Why do you feel the need to pick me up?" she asked as he stopped by the shower, balancing her against his chest so he could test the water.

"I don't know. I just like to."

"It's your seduction style, huh? Making the woman feel tiny and protected?" Her tone was teasing, but the humor didn't quite reach her eyes.

For a moment, unease nearly made him set her down. Why should she care what his seduction style was, as long as it worked for her? Why think about what he did with other women? Her train of thoughts could reveal something dangerous.

But then he disregarded the idea. She just wanted to be special—that was human nature, which had nothing to do with love.

"No, it isn't," he answered, realizing it was true. He couldn't recall carrying any other woman. Well, he'd carried Nancy. But only when she'd been too sick to walk on her own.

Why did he feel the need to pick up Maggie? He did feel the need to be strong for her, protective of her. Weird.

"Well, you picked the wrong woman to start this with."

He frowned at her, not understanding.

She glanced down at herself. "You should have gone for willowy to start this whole Rhett Butler thing."

He frowned, further confused.

"Chubby," she said, giving him a look that stated she thought he was slow.

But it was his turn to give her an incredulous look. Was she calling herself chubby?

He stepped into the shower, the warm water raining down on both of their heads. She started to make another startled noise, but he caught the sound in his own mouth.

After they devoured each other with the water pouring over them, he broke the kiss and set her down, letting her wet, silky body slide down his.

"Let's get one thing straight, right now. You are gorgeous. You are sexy. You have curves that are exactly where they should be. And you drive me mad."

Maggie couldn't deny the resolute tone of his voice or the look of blatant desire in his eyes. Her gaze drifted down—to the lust evident in other parts of his body.

He did want her. She didn't doubt it. And she had to learn to let herself revel in his desire for her, instead of looking for there to be a flaw.

She had a week. She wasn't blowing this with her own self-doubt.

She reached up and touched his chest, testing the texture of his chest hair, wet on hard muscle. He hissed as she leaned in to lick his nipple, catching the steamy water on the tip of her tongue.

"And you say I run hot and cold," he muttered roughly. "Vertical seems to be agreeing with you."

She smiled against his skin, then licked him again.

He only allowed that for a few moments, then he caught her tight to him, his lips finding hers, his hands stroking the wet skin of her back and bottom.

Then he was walking her backwards, her back connecting with the cool tiles. The combination of cool and hot, the rub of his damp skin against her aroused body was heaven. Absolute bliss.

Her head fell back against the wall as his lips left hers, moving down her body. He suckled her breast, tugging at the sensitive point with his lips, grazing her with his teeth.

Her hands tangled in his wet hair, the long strands sticking to her fingers, creating a web around her, mimicking the desire surrounding her, pulling her tighter into its grasp.

She watched, her body boneless against the wall, as he slid down her body, pressing nibbling kisses over her stomach, her thighs.

Then his amazing tongue was parting her, finding the sensitive nubbin of her sex. His tongue flicked and swirled as hot water ran over her aroused skin.

She gripped his hair tighter, feeling like that was the only thing keeping her anchored to her body. Ecstasy snapped in her veins, alive, vivid, pulling at her until she wasn't aware where his tongue ended and she began.

"Ren," she moaned, her fingers clutching him.

He groaned in response, and continued laving her aroused flesh, licking her in long, slow sweeps only to speed up, his tongue flicking over her in rapid, darting swirls.

Just as her orgasm rushed through every fiber of her body, tensing her muscles, making her cry out, he rose, lifting her. In one powerful movement, he pinioned her to the wall and thrust himself into her, filling her totally, intensifying the release to the point that she screamed.

He didn't give her overwhelmed body time to adjust. He began to move, hands anchored to her bottom, holding her as he filled her again and again. The spread of her legs, the angle of his hips made each stroke full and complete, his pelvis grinding wonderfully against her.

His body dominated hers. Filled her totally. She stretched and strained against him as another violent orgasm shook her.

She cried out, arching into him, impaling herself over and over. Her body convulsed around him, squeezing him, taking all he had to give.

Vaguely, she was aware of Ren's own orgasm, his taut strain of muscles as he released deep inside her. His own ragged breaths were clear over the rush of water all around them.

Then they were both limp against the wall, her body still trapped between the wall and his tall, hard body. She realized she still clutched his hair, the locks twined through her fingers. She released them, stroking out the knotted tangles.

He moaned against her neck, then kissed her. "I love it when you touch my hair."

"I love your hair," she admitted. Then they stared at each other for a moment, as if they both realized they'd used the word love. The off-limits emotion. But surely not when applied to body parts.

He eased her down, holding her as she found her bearings, her muscles like jelly. When she was stable, he turned and reached for the soap.

He began to suds up his chest, and Maggie couldn't help feeling like he was pulling back. She didn't want that. She would leave when the week was over, and she knew he'd let her go. But for now, he was hers. Totally.

She picked up the white bottle of shampoo in the corner of the shower stall. She opened it, immediately recognizing the scent. Squirting a dollop into her palm, she stepped behind Ren. She set aside the bottle, then she massaged the shampoo into his hair.

At the first touch, he froze, then as she worked the lather into his scalp, then down the long strands, he let his head fall back. He groaned as she continued to wash him.

"That feels so good," he murmured, his voice low and husky with pleasure.

She smiled and kissed his shoulder. As she moved his hair aside, she noticed for the first time a tattoo centered between his shoulder blades. In vivid black and red ink, the image depicted a dealt hand of cards, fanned over his spine.

She pressed a finger to the lines, tracing the cards.

"What does this mean?"

Ren glanced over his shoulder at her. "It's aces and eights. The deadman's hand."

Maggie frowned. Is that what he'd felt he'd been dealt in life? The idea bothered her, even as she continued to trace the tattoo.

Then he reached behind him and caught her arm, pulling it around his front, his stomach hard and slick under her fingers. She rested her cheek against his wet back.

"It was just an impulsive decision on a drunken night," he said as if he knew the tattoo, or rather the potential meaning behind it, was bothering her.

She nodded, her cheek pressed against the somehow heartbreaking image. There was more to the story.

They remained still for a few moments, the water cascading over them.

Then Ren turned in her arms. He walked her backwards until the water fell over their heads like a torrential downpour. His lips sought hers.

For a moment, Maggie tasted the same heartbreak on his lips but quickly the kiss changed, filling with intensity, with desperate need. And she was swept away on the tide of the need—all feelings of sadness gone.

Maybe it was never there to begin with.

Suds glossed her lips, and she didn't care.

Chapter 15

Ren strolled into the bar nearly an hour late for work. Both Dave and Johnny had called his cell phone, trying to locate him. But he'd been just a little busy.

He glanced over to Maggie. She wore one of his shirts, a white one with faint white embroidery on the front, knotted at the waist of her jeans. Jeans which, he happened to know, she wore with no panties.

He stared at her ass, imagining her bare skin underneath. He pulled in a breath. Hadn't the two amazing bouts of sex in the shower been enough?

He looked at her curvy rear end again. Obviously not.

Tonight she wore no makeup, because she'd come with him directly from his place—also the reason for no panties. And her strawberry blonde hair framed her face in a tousled sexy bob. He couldn't resist giving her a quick kiss before he headed up on the stage.

"Nice of you to make it, buddy," Drake said as Ren took his place on the stage.

Ren didn't apologize; he just slid the mic back to his height from where Dave, the bass player, had it. Hell, there was no way he was going to apologize for being late. Not when it was because he had been with Maggie.

He only had a week. He planned to use as much of that time as he could.

The band went into Boston's "Foreplay/Long Time"; Ren didn't miss the not-so-subtle innuendo. Of course, the band would claim they chose that particular song because it had a long intro, to give him time to get prepared. And of course, they all knew otherwise.

He started to sing, watching Maggie find a spot in the back of the bar. Since it was Sunday night, the bar wasn't as crowded as the previous nights. She took a stool at one of the round high-top tables in the back.

She sat down, then turned her attention back to him. Swaying with the music, watching him.

He couldn't remember the last time he'd found work this interesting, this exciting for him. It was like she was the only one there, his own private audience, and he found himself wanting to perform for her. Exhilaration filled him, as it once had when he'd performed an original piece of his work. As if he was sharing something special and private with her. Even if it was someone else's song.

He remembered what he'd once loved about music. He saw it on Maggie's face. He found himself wishing he could play some of his compositions for her. Just the two of them and his piano.

But for tonight, Journey, Boston, and Kansas were going to have to be enough. Then he caught himself. No. Not just for tonight. He was never going to be able to play his songs for her. She was too clever—and she knew classical music.

Maybe even his.

So instead, he jumped off the stage and walked slowly toward her, singing out the lyrics of Journey's "Lovin', Touchin', Squeezin'," enjoying the way she blushed prettily as he approached. That was until he thought about the actual sentiment of the song. About how she would have another affair beyond the one with him.

Was that true? Of course it was. It wasn't as if she'd remain alone the rest of her days, pining for him. And did he want that, anyway? Even he wasn't that selfish.

Still, some of his high faded. But he forced the sentiment of the song out of his mind and moved around to hold her, his arm around her from behind. His head next to hers. The waves of her hair brushing his cheek. Her body leaning back against his chest.

Then he was just pleased to be performing for her again. But more than that, he was glad he was holding her. That he could hold her. For now.

Just as he was getting ready to release her and head back up to the stage, her friends came into the bar. From their identical amused looks, they were obviously pleased for their friend; happy she'd found her holiday fling.

Again his happiness flickered. Then he reprimanded himself. That was all he was going to get out of this relationship. He knew that, so there was no point wishing for more.

He was fling boy. And frankly, he should just embrace that role. It wasn't as if he'd ever seen any relationships, once past the rosy glow of newness, that lasted anyway. And if the relationship did last, it didn't remain happy.

He hugged Maggie against him before releasing her. Her hand came up to squeeze his arm. The exchange seemed oddly intimate. But he did let her go and headed back to the stage, waving to her friends as he bounded up the steps.

When he looked back to Maggie, she was greeting them. A big pleased smile curved her small bow lips. A smile he'd put there. He could take satisfaction in that.

Then Erika asked her something which made Maggie blush. He could guess what. He smiled. Then Maggie looked up at him, her smile still wide and beautiful, and solely for him.

Yeah, he just needed to have fun with this. Just enjoy Maggie and what he could have. Hadn't he learned a long time ago that there was no point longing for things that could never be? Live in the here and now. Or rather, exist in the here and now.

*   *   *

"Look at him." Erika sighed. "He adores you."

Maggie's cheeks grew even hotter at her friend's pronouncement. Ren had been watching her most of the night, and in truth, she did see desire there. Adoration seemed like a stretch, but she knew he wanted her. And that felt pretty good. Almost as good as adoration.

"He really is smitten." Jo nodded, taking a sip of her drink.

"I wouldn't say that." In truth, Maggie didn't even want to hear things like that. She and Ren had a deal and she needed to keep everything in perspective. Hearing words like "adoration" and "smitten" made it altogether too tempting to hope for more than a fling.

She'd told him that she wasn't sure she would want to be in love with someone like him, and that was true. He was still too far out of her realm of experience to know if she could handle being in love with him. But there was a small part of her, a little kernel deep inside, that would like to take a shot at it. And she was afraid that if the idea was encouraged, it just might grow.

She didn't want that. She couldn't let it happen. Her battered heart didn't need any more abuse. This whole fling idea was intended to make her feel better, not worse.

So she needed to focus on what was good. The way Ren looked at her was good—but she needed to remember it was lust she saw in his eyes, not adoration.

"Well, you can believe whatever you want, but I know what I see," Erika said, not realizing her words weren't helping.

Maggie didn't bother to argue. Erika was a romantic, which was a huge part of her artistic nature, so Maggie would let her see whatever she wanted. But Maggie wasn't going to believe the same thing.

"We're going to take a short break," Ren announced. "Visit the bar and we'll be right back."

He came down off the stage, making a beeline right to Maggie. He stopped close to her, but didn't touch her.

"This is the longest night of my life," he said. Then he smiled at Maggie's friends.

"You're doing a great job," Erika said.

"Thanks," Ren said. "Although I'd be happy if we didn't have to do another set." He gave Maggie a slow smile that he knew revealed everything he would rather be doing.

As expected, she blushed.

"So how long have you been with The Impalers?" Jo asked.

Ren had already realized that Erika was the more easygoing of Maggie's friends, whereas Jo was the more straightforward, no-nonsense type. Ren liked both women, and he did appreciate Jo's candor, but she would be the harder of the two to put off if questions became too candid. She seemed like someone who expected direct answers—which he couldn't always supply. Like now, for example.

"Quite a while."

"Have you always been a lead singer?" Again, a direct question from Jo.

"No," he heard himself saying. "I was a keyboard player for a while."

He felt Maggie's gaze on him. He didn't need to look at her to sense her curiosity. The whole keyboard and piano thing intrigued her, and understandably so. After all, she had seemed to know that piece he was playing, and she was an authenticator. Did she honestly know that sonata? He'd been so taken with her, he'd almost forgotten her reaction to his music.

"Maggie, you said you authenticate classical music. Do you often find long-lost compositions?"

Maggie seemed almost surprised that he mentioned her work—maybe because he'd shut her down so quickly last time she'd mentioned it.

"Quite often," she said. "I've discovered pieces by Friedrich

Kiel and Walter Rummel. I also verify whether pieces are indeed written by who they are attributed to."

Ren nodded, his mind whirling. Had she really seen that sonata? It certainly seemed possibile. She'd seemed sure of it.

"Have you always played rock and roll?"

This time Erika questioned him.

"No. I've played all sorts of music." Again, he felt the need to be truthful—even if vague.

"Maggie plays too," Erika offered, and it was Maggie's turn to be put on the spot.

Ren moved closer to her, putting an arm around her shoulder. "Is that so?"

She shook her head. "Not really."

Her response didn't stop his curiosity. "What do you play?"

"Piano," she admitted reluctantly. "But not very well. Hence my career as an authenticator."

"Piano? You will have to play for me." He grinned at her.

"If you play for me."

Ren's grin widened. She hadn't missed a beat with that one—and for a moment, he got the distinct feeling she was thinking about the piece he'd been playing when they'd met. Just as he had been.

"She plays great," Erika told him. "She just doubts herself because of Peter. Thank God, you are nothing like Peter."

Peter? Ren's smile faded. "Who's Peter?"

Maggie resisted the urge to kick Erika under the table. The last person she wanted to tell Ren about was Peter. Like she needed to reveal any of that embarrassment to him.

"Peter was my old boyfriend." Old made it sound like they'd been broken up for much longer than six months. And "boyfriend" certainly didn't imply the seriousness of being engaged. Hopefully that would satisfy his curiosity.

"Peter didn't think you were a good pianist?"

Maggie gritted her teeth. She really did not want to talk about this.

Luckily, Jo seemed to realize that, although Erika still seemed oblivious to the turmoil she'd stirred up in Maggie.

"Peter was a jerk. Not worth talking about. Maggie is a good pianist."

Maggie appreciated the finality in Jo's voice. Of course, Maggie also noted that Jo only said she was good. Not great. And that was true. Peter hadn't been wrong about that.

Ren's eyes roamed over Maggie's face as if he wanted to ask more, but he took Jo's hint and let the topic drop. Thankfully.

"So what are you working on now?" His tone was casual, but Maggie thought she sensed an undercurrent in his voice.

"I just received a large shipment of unsigned compositions, but I didn't get much chance to look at them before I left."

He nodded, his brows raised slightly with mild interest, mild enough that she felt he was masking the real level of his interest. Had he been playing a little known piece of music? That question still bothered Maggie.

"One of the pieces I did look at was very similar to—"

"Yo, Ren, get your ass up here," the guitarist with the goatee called over his mic.

Maggie saw relief wash over Ren's features.

"Back to work," he said with an easy smile, but she still felt as if he was hiding something.

As soon as he was back up on the stage, Maggie did give Erika a soft kick under the table.

"What?" Erika asked, confused.

"Why did you bring up Peter?"

"I didn't know it was a secret."

"Well, it's not sexy to look like a heartbroken ninny," Maggie pointed out.

"That's true," Jo agreed. "You should go for strong and mysterious."

Okay, she probably wasn't going to pull that off, but Maggie didn't want Ren feeling sorry for her. That was the last thing she wanted.

"Sorry," Erika said contritely. "I wasn't thinking. I was just happy that he isn't anything like Peter. That's a very good thing."

Maggie looked back up at the stage. Ren flipped his hair back as he sang out the lyrics to "You Shook Me All Night Long." No, he definitely wasn't anything like Peter. And that was indeed a good thing.

"I like your friends," Ren said as they headed toward his place after his last set.

Maggie smiled. That was another difference between Ren and Peter. Peter hadn't liked either Erika or Jo. Of course, the feeling had been mutual.

"They are very dear to me," she said, realizing how true that was—and how important it was for the one she loved to like all the people she cared about. Peter hadn't even given them a chance. But then, Peter had always acted like he was doing her a favor by liking her. Maggie had bought into that one, too. Now she didn't understand why.

Ren unlocked the large door that led into his courtyard, then waited for her to enter. She did, letting out another sigh at the lovely, lush garden. She did adore Ren's home. For a moment, she allowed herself to imagine living in a place like this. Then she quickly quashed the vision.

She wouldn't imagine what couldn't be. This was about the now. Acting on that very thought, she turned. Ren was directly behind her, and she wrapped her arms around him and kissed him with all the desire she'd felt all night watching him up on the stage—with all the passion she felt whenever she looked at him, period.

He made a pleased noise in the back of his throat and his arms came around her, pulling her tight against him. The kiss made time stop, until Ren pulled back to smile at her.

"You must have read my mind. I wanted to do that all night."

She smiled, pleased that he'd been thinking the very same way. "I've wanted to do a lot more than that all night."

Ren actually looked surprised by her audacious admission, then that Cheshire cat smile unfurled. "Maggie Gallagher, you are turning into a bad girl."

She laughed at that. "Hmm. Me, a bad girl? I doubt that. But I am going to get better at getting what I want. And I want you."

"I'm yours."

She grinned again, then released him, only to grab his hand and lead him toward his apartment.

Chapter 16

Ren followed quite happily as Maggie pulled him inside and straight up the stairs. Then they were in the middle of his bedroom, kissing as if they'd been denied each other for days and months, rather than a matter of hours.

"God, you feel so good," he murmured against her lips. Her curves were warm and soft under his roaming hands. Her own small hands moved over his shoulders, down his back.

"So do you." She kissed his jawline, then his neck.

Shivers snaked down his spine as her teeth grazed the sensitive skin just below his earlobe. Totally aroused, he pulled her tighter to him, grinding his erection against the curve of her belly.

Her smile curled against his skin, and he knew she was very pleased with the effect she had on him. And she should be. He was harder than nails, and damned near mad to be inside her.

His fingers moved to the buttons of her shirt, and then he remembered it was his shirt she wore. With that realization, he tugged at the knot at her waist, then pulled, the buttons bouncing to the ground around their feet.

"I hate when women rip the buttons off my shirts, but I have to admit I don't mind ripped buttons when it's me doing it to you."

Maggie blinked, apparently stunned both by his actions and his words. "Women rip the buttons off your shirts?"

"Mmm-hmm," he answered, his attention already off that topic and on to the way her breasts looked barely encased by the pink lace of her bra.

But obviously Maggie wasn't done with the idea. "Why?"

"They sometimes pull on my clothes when I lean over the stage to sing—or if I go out into the audience."

"Oh," Maggie said, still sounding baffled by the whole idea. "That's rude."

"Mmm-hmm," he agreed as he nudged the buttonless garment off her shoulders, then leaned down to kiss the swell of her breasts.

She made a small noise, and the topic of destroyed clothing was promptly left behind.

Her hands slid into his hair.

His fingers moved to the hook at the back of her bra, desperate to taste the rosy nipples hidden beneath. Her own fingers attempted to undo the buttons of his shirt, but she gave up and slid her hands underneath, smoothing up over his belly and chest.

"I can see where ripping would be easier . . ." she commented, trailing off as he pulled one of her nipples into his mouth, working the hardened flesh with his lips.

"Rip away," he said, his voice a rough vibrating against her skin as he moved to her other breast, teasing that nipple in the same fashion.

"No," she breathed. "I don't want to be like those women."

"You aren't. Not even close."

Her hands were still for a moment, then resumed touching him. Stroking his belly, then his back. Then they slipped out from underneath his shirt. He moaned, a sound of disappointment. He loved her hands on his bare skin. Small, deft hands arousing him to the point of sharp, intense longing.

But then they found the button of his jeans, working it

open. Her fingers moved to the zipper, the rasp of the metal echoing the rasp of his breathing. Her finger slipped inside his jeans, inside his boxers.

His erection seemed to leap, greeting her, welcoming her touch.

His own hands came up and cupped her full breasts, testing their weight.

He breathed in deeply, savoring the arousal-scented energy wafting from her skin like a delicate yet heady perfume. His own desire rose. He wanted to take from her, breathe in her essence, but he controlled his vampiric ways. Her desire, her satisfaction, meant more to him than his hunger.

He gasped as her delicate fingers began to move, stroking him. His thumbs mimicked her action, flicking her nipples.

Then he slipped down her belly to the waistband of her jeans. He popped the button open, then unzipped, the parted denim revealing the thatch of curls underneath. Damn, that was a gorgeous sight.

His mouth came down on hers, as his hand moved to the apex of her thighs, cupping her mound, feeling the moist heat radiating from her body.

Then he parted her, sliding the pad of his finger over her taut clitoris. At first, he only teased her, playing with her, listening to her small moans, her low hums.

She wiggled against him, demanding more with each shimmy of her hips.

He smiled against her lips, loving how incredibly responsive she was. Giving to him with her desire. Her hand still touched him, which made it a challenge to stay focused—a fun challenge.

She stroked his length, her thumb running up and down the sensitive ridge of his penis, each stroke spurring him to get her naked, and to get himself deep inside her. Slowly, he walked her backwards.

When her thighs hit the bed, he stopped kissing and touching her long enough to lift her onto the mattress, then he followed her down.

"You have the most beautiful breasts," he murmured as he took one of her tight little nipples into his mouth. Instead of the moan he expected, she giggled.

"You are breast obsessed."

He lifted his head, giving her an unapologetic smile. "Mmm-hmm."

This time her giggle did turn to a low moan as he teased her taut nipple—pulling it deep into his mouth. His hands worked on pushing down her jeans, then shoved at his own.

He sucked one of her nipples until she began to wriggle underneath him, all her silky skin stroking him. Belly to belly, thigh to thigh, his erection against her soft curls.

He couldn't wait. He'd thought about being inside her all night. He leaned over to snag a condom off the bedstand.

"Darling, I'll go slow next time."

She nodded, her gaze again unfocused, heavy-lidded with lust.

"Next time," she agreed. Her legs parted, her opened sex inviting him inside.

More temptation than his mere immortal body could take. He hurriedly rolled on the condom and positioned himself and thrust into her, filling her completely.

They both cried out.

"Are you okay?" His voice was a low, gravelly mutter.

"Oh, yes." She writhed under him, urging him without words to move.

He obeyed her, pulling out until only the head of his penis was inside her, then pushing in, until he was so deep he could swear he felt each of her breaths, each beat of her heart.

All too quickly, the lust spiraled up between them, and he was driving into her with wild abandon. She splayed herself below him, her arms flung wide, her fingers curled into the bedding, her legs anchored around his hips. Her body accepted each thrust, her hips rising to meet him, to take him deeper.

It was too much. He felt his orgasm coming, rising in him, tightening his muscles.

Just when he thought he'd fail her, that he couldn't stop his own release before she reached hers, she cried out, her outflung arms coming around him as her body shuddered, her vagina pulsing, squeezing.

He growled deep in his throat as he drove deep into her pulsating heat and felt himself explode inside her.

He collapsed onto her, his eyes closed, bright lights playing across his closed lids. He had to be seeing heaven—and even if he wasn't, he knew this was as close as he was ever going to come to it.

Maggie lay utterly boneless under Ren, reveling in the delicious aftershocks pulsing though her body, only made more pleasurable by his weight, and his penis still buried inside her.

Even with the intensity of his lovemaking and the drained feeling of her release, she felt giddy, almost high. Ren's reaction to her was so intense, so passionate. It was a heady feeling to know she incited a man to this kind of lust.

"I turn you on, don't I?" She knew it was a rather random and silly thing to ask, but she was simply so amazed that she had this kind of effect on him.

He lifted his head, his hair falling down in a veil around them. One brow lifted and he offered a lopsided smile.

"Hmm, I'm going to have to think about that."

She smiled, knowing her grin was wide and ridiculously pleased.

"Oh, yeah, darlin'," he said, his voice low and velvety, "you definitely turn me on." His lips brushed against hers as he kissed her slow and long.

"Am I too heavy?" he asked, moving to kiss the side of her neck.

"No, you feel nice."

He smiled, then kissed her again. But when he broke the kiss this time, he rolled off of her, and pulled her up against the pillows. He moved up beside her, until they were nestled together in the billowy softness of the covers, face-to-face.

He reached out and twirled a piece of her hair around his finger.

"So, who is Peter?"

Maggie blinked. She hadn't expected that question. She figured her answer at the bar had been good enough. Apparently not.

"I told you, he was an old boyfriend of mine," she reiterated, fiddling with the edge of the blanket. His hand left her hair, and caught her fingers, stopping them.

"Was he a serious boyfriend?"

She met his eyes, trying to find the right thing to say to dismiss the topic. Of course, the easiest way would be to just say no. But as she looked into his eyes, seeing the honest interest there, she heard herself saying, "Yes. We were engaged."

Something flickered in his hazel eyes, an emotion that she couldn't quite read.

"Then you were very serious."

She pulled in a breath, not sure how she wanted to handle this. She didn't want him to pity her; that ruined the sexiness of this whole situation.

"Is he the reason you're so uncertain with men?"

That question startled her. She'd thought she'd done a pretty good job of disguising her discomfort around men. She'd managed to go through with this last night, and tonight she hadn't even hesitated. She remained silent.

"What was Peter like? Why did he think you weren't a good pianist?"

"Because I'm not," she said, rolling onto her back, wanting to talk about her failed career as a pianist even less than she wanted to discuss Peter. Okay, maybe not less—but she would just as soon avoid that topic, too.

"Was Peter a musician?"

Maggie turned her head at his tone, the slow, southern drawl suddenly replaced by a different accent completely, clipped and proper.

The change was so disconcerting, she found herself nodding. "Yes. He was a violinist."

Ren rolled over onto his back, frowning up at the velvet canopy. "Violinists can be so damned pompous."

Again, she caught the change in his accent. "Do you know a lot of violinists?" she asked slowly, trying to understand the change in him and the adamancy of his statement. He sounded as if he knew many in his lifetime, which didn't seem likely to her. But then, what did she really know about him?

He glanced at her, and something akin to surprise flashed in his eyes, then disappeared as he said flatly, "Not a lot. But enough to know they can be real dicks."

She considered his words, and the fact that the slow, southern drawl was back.

Then she sighed. "Yeah, well, in this case you are right."

Ren rolled back toward her. "Did it end badly?"

She laughed humorlessly. Now it was her turn to stare up at the canopy. "Yeah, you could say that."

Ren was quiet for a moment, and she thought maybe he was letting the subject drop. She should have known better. She felt the bed shift, then his hand gently nudged her to face him.

"What happened?"

For a moment, she got lost in his eyes. Amber brown flecked with pale green. Hypnotic eyes. Again, she was amazed by how the mere difference in his lashes could make his eyes look so different.

His thumb traced her lower lip as he studied her in return. The combination of his gaze and his caress was comforting, so nice.

"He broke it off on our wedding day."

His thumb paused and she immediately wished she could take back the words. She so did not want his pity.

"On your wedding day?"

Maggie pulled in another breath, staring back at the velvet canopy. "Yeah. But I don't want you feeling bad for me. It was probably for the best."

Ren levered himself up on his elbow so he could see her face.

"Hell, yeah, it was for the best. The guy was obviously a stupid ass."

Maggie met Ren's gaze. His mouth was pulled down, his brows together. He was furious. For some reason, that made her laugh. Ren's glare of anger turned to one of confusion.

"What's so funny?"

"He didn't just jilt me on my wedding day. He announced in front of all the guests that he was in love with the caterer."

"Holy shit. This guy really was a stupid ass."

She giggled, actually feeling okay that she'd told Ren about the whole horrible experience. Somehow saying it aloud made her feel better. His reaction was making her feel better, too. He didn't pity her; he was furious on her behalf.

"At the time, I was really upset, and painfully embarrassed, but now,"—she rolled over to face him, touching his hair, then the strong muscles of his shoulder—"I definitely feel like it was a good thing."

He leaned over her, his gaze roaming over her face as if trying to read her real emotions. Trying to understand her.

"You're right," he said, some of the irritation leaving his face. "I know he did *me* a hell of a favor." He kissed her soundly.

"Do you still love him?"

Ren couldn't guess why he'd asked her that. What should it matter to him—aside from the fact that he did like Maggie, and he hated to think she was still pining for a man who did not deserve her affection.

Maggie didn't answer right away. Her silence created another strange sensation in him, something close to dread. Although again, he wondered why.

"I thought I did." One corner of her mouth pulled down as she considered the idea. "But now I see that he wasn't good for me. At all. And not just the cheating, which I will admit battered my ego, big time. He spent a lot of time chipping away at my confidence."

Images of Ren's parents flashed in his mind. The mother who only wanted him when she thought there was something for her to gain from him. The father who never wanted him at all.

He understood how others could wear away a person's confidence, leaving them doubting themselves. It was good she'd escaped the ass before the damage was irreparable.

He levered himself away from her. "Play for me."

She laughed, clearly not following his thought process. "What?"

He gestured toward his piano with his head. "Play the piano for me."

She immediately shook her head, still smiling, but reluctance clear in her eyes. "No."

"Come on," he said, sliding off the bed, grabbing her ankle as he went, pulling her toward the edge of the mattress.

She squealed, flinging out her arms to grab onto the sheets, the mattress, whatever she could to stop him.

He continued to tug until her bottom was at the edge of the bed, her naked body only half covered by rumpled covers.

"Ren." She wriggled a little more, laughing.

He grinned, loving the sound of her laughter, as musical as any piece he ever wrote. He loved how her pale skin grew flushed. He loved the tangle of her hair.

"Please," he murmured, his words low. "Play for me."

Her laughter faded away as she considered him. She sat up, taking the sheet with her as she did so, keeping her full, luscious breasts covered.

"You'll be thoroughly unimpressed."

He held out his hand. "Let me be the judge of that."

She hesitated, then with one hand still keeping the sheet pressed to her, she took his fingers with the other. He pulled her to her feet, then watched as she shuffled to the piano, swathed in white cotton. She looked adorable, mussed, and still unsure.

His chest tightened at the sight. God, she was beautiful.

She wrestled with the piano bench and the sheet until she was finally settled with the sheet firmly tucked around under her arms, leaving her covered from the chest down. Warm lamplight cast a golden glow on her bare shoulders. He moved behind her, almost touching her, the lure of her smooth skin a mighty temptation. But he didn't. He didn't want her to stop. He wanted to hear her play.

Her small, delicate fingers stroked the top of the piano. Not a pianist's hands, Ren thought. More the hands of a fey creature, small and shapely.

She pushed up the lid and touched the keys. It was an almost loving touch, the way he'd once stroked the keys himself, with a sort of reverence.

The way he no longer touched them, but the way he wanted to touch her.

She held her fingers over the keys, then started to play. "Moonlight Sonata." A standard piece. She played it competently. He heard the music, but he was lost in watching her. He stepped closer, his body nearly brushing against the sheet surrounding her. The warm scent of her body rose up to him. Sweet vanilla and the clean aroma of his shampoo.

He leaned closer, breathing in, both the scent and a bit of her energy.

Her fingers stumbled on the keys, as she became aware of him, so near. But she resumed, changing songs, surrounding them in beautiful music and sweet desire.

He couldn't stop himself; he had to touch her.

Maggie nearly gasped as Ren's big, strong hands touched her shoulders, driving shivers of need through her body. She'd been painfully aware of his presence behind her, wondering what he thought of her playing. But surprisingly, she was more focused on the fact that he wasn't wearing anything, and she could be admiring the lean muscles of his gorgeous body.

She was surprised that she even remembered the notes of the song she was playing. She was surprised her fingers could move now. His caress was too wonderful, too exciting.

He brushed her hair aside and kissed the nape of her neck, nibbling kisses that sent coiled heat straight to the core of her. She dropped her head forward, offering him better access. A violent shudder rippled through her as his tongue darted out, tasting her.

Her fingers grew still on the keys, the music replaced by the ragged sound of her breathing.

She turned on the bench, looping her arms around his neck, finding his mouth. He responded in kind to her passion, his lips holding hers.

Then she felt her world shift as he picked her up from the bench. She expected him to carry her back to the bed. Instead he moved around the piano, setting her on top of it.

Then she looked at him, standing before her, totally and utterly comfortable in his nudity. Her eyes roamed over his broad chest; she loved the smattering of dark hair there. His strong, muscled arms. Long legs narrowing down to feet with high arches and narrow toes—even they were works of masculine beauty.

Her eyes again rose upward, stopping at his groin. And then there was that part of him that she'd not yet allowed herself to study quite this openly. But now, maybe with Peter out in the open, maybe because she'd played for him, she felt more confident looking at him.

His erection was large and thick, as powerful and breathtaking as the rest of him. She knew that from the way he'd felt in her hand and when he was deep inside her, but she quite enjoyed getting to see it. Heavy and thrillingly imposing.

She felt her own sex pulse in response to the sight. She'd never seen a man so sexy, so perfect.

"I love the way you look at me," he said, his own eyes intent on her.

She smiled at that. "I love looking at you."

"The feeling is very mutual. In fact, let's lose the sheet."

He stepped toward her, her first reaction still to hold on to the white cotton shielding her from his gaze. But then she let him slowly unwrap her. He wanted her—she knew that, and she wasn't going to let insecurities stop her from losing herself in this amazing moment.

He dropped the sheet, allowing it to pool around her on the top of the piano.

"I'd like a painting of you just like this."

Maggie blushed, even as she found that sentiment a little strange. Why a painting?

But she only had a fraction of a second to wonder about that, because then he was kissing her And she was thinking of nothing but the feeling of his mouth on hers, his soft hair and hot skin rubbing against her electrified skin.

His hands played over her thighs, parting them as he moved between them. Cool air hit the moist, heated flesh of her sex, making her moan and instinctively move toward him.

His lips left hers, moving down her body, leaving a burning trail in their wake. Then he placed a spread hand on her stomach, gently pressing her back against the piano.

"What—" she started, confused by what he wanted.

But he hushed her, nudging her again, until she went back on her elbows, watching him between her legs.

He kissed the curve of her belly, stopping at the small triangle of curls. Then he pressed kisses to her thighs, moving inward until he was positioned right at the core of her. Strong hands at her waist slid her a little further onto the piano, so that his mouth was positioned directly over her sex.

Her pulse pounded, her breath hitched, watching him there. Then he lowered his head, running the tip of his tongue through her curls, the tip just breaching the ultrasensitive flesh beyond.

She gasped, her hips lifting at the fleeting touch.

He smiled, a supremely masculine and utterly sexy smile. Then he repeated the action, except this time his tongue went deeper, bringing pure bliss.

She made a noise deep in her throat. There was nothing more arousing than this man, positioned where he was, doing what he was doing to her.

He smiled at her, then flipped back his long hair. He pressed his tongue directly to the flesh that ached for his touch.

She cried out. Dear God—she'd died and gone to heaven.

Chapter 17

Ren watched Maggie's expression as he tasted her. Her eyes were half shut, her lips parted. She was the picture of ecstasy—and he was damned proud that he was the one making her feel that way, and fully aroused at the thought.

His tongue swirled around her clitoris, the taste of her desire like honey. Warm, slick, and sweet. He could taste her energy, just as sweet, but he didn't want to take that from her. Her passion was more than enough; the only thing she needed to share with him.

In fact, he wanted to breathe his life force into her. His fingers squeezed her thighs when he realized what he wanted to do to her. Being a vampire, and especially a lampir, he never willingly parted with the energy he collected. It was his sustenance, his air.

Not to mention that it wasn't in his nature to share anything that he so desperately needed. Yet he wanted to give it to her. Of course, he knew that if he passed his energy into her, she would experience pleasure as he did. The added life force would intensify all of her sensations, her reactions.

He wanted that. He wanted to give her mind-blowing sex. Sex she would never experience with anyone else, ever. Sex only he could give her. Sex she would remember long after he was gone from her life.

Then he realized there was something else behind his desire to share his essence with her. He wanted to obliterate any memory of Peter. Any satisfaction the mortal had given her would be insignificant in comparison to the gratification Ren could give her.

So truly, his reasons were selfish. He supposed there was some security in that. To know she hadn't changed him in that way.

His tongue began to move again, flicking over her, circling her until she was bucking under him, straining to gain her release.

He could give her the climax she begged for, but he enjoyed the way her body felt under him, the taste of her on his tongue, the noises she made, small moans pleading for him to satisfy her.

And he would. He was simply having too much fun.

Then her fingers sank into his hair. It was his turn to groan. Damn, he loved when she did that, the feeling of her hands tangled in his hair. Hell, whenever she touched him, period.

Suddenly his body was as desperate for release as hers was. He centered all his attention on that small nubbin that made her writhe and scream.

Quickly, he felt her orgasm building, and just as she tensed under him, her body arching with the power of her climax, he simply kissed her, pressing his lips to the moist flesh between her legs, and let his energy flow into her.

She screamed out his name, her fingers knotting in his hair. Her body arched again, this time higher and harder against his mouth.

And as she took his energy, he felt his own orgasm slam through him, his own muscles contracting, nearly seizing up with the ferocity of it.

It was his own cry that broke the kiss and ended the transfer between them. Still, it didn't seem to end immediately, as energy snapped in the air around them.

He collapsed on top of her, his head on her belly, her hands still tangled in her hair. The life force slowly dissipated from the air, like the aftereffects of their mutual climaxes.

Finally, he managed to lift his head, still stunned that sharing his life force with her had had that effect on him.

"Are you okay?"

She raised her head enough to look down her body at him. A dazed, adorable smile curved her bow lips. "That was amazing."

He had to agree. He'd wanted to give her the best sex of her life, and instead had been hit with an orgasm unlike any he'd ever experienced. And he hadn't even been inside her tight little body.

Oh, he was so going to do that again, but when he was deep enough inside her to feel every shudder of her body around him.

He rested his head on her stomach again, loving the silky softness of her skin under his cheek. He nuzzled her and she stroked his hair in response.

Damn, this was so good. So right.

As soon as the thought registered in his mind, he pushed himself upright, putting space between himself and Maggie.

"Where are you going?" she murmured, her lids half closed, her voice low with the beginnings of sleep. Even though he'd given her his energy, the extra had been used up in intensifying her response to him. She looked like a sleepy kitten, trying to focus on him.

"I think you need to get to bed."

She made a noise of disappointment, but then she yawned. "I think you are right."

She struggled to raise herself up, and he didn't touch her to help. He was too freaked out by how much he truly liked her. Liked her simply being here with him.

He'd shared his life force with her, for Christ's sake. This was all getting a little too dangerous.

She slipped down off the piano, using the edge of it to steady herself. She gave him another sleepy smile, and he couldn't stop himself from slipping his arm around her, leading her to the bed.

Once she was settled in under the covers, he left her to go into the bathroom. Not because of any physical need, of course, but to try to figure out what the hell he was doing.

After all, hadn't he been the one to lay down all the rules for this affair? Yet he was the one sharing a part of himself with her, a part of his vampire self, at that. He had never done so before.

And wasn't he the one enjoying her being here altogether too much? It wasn't wise. Yet, when he looked at her, wisdom tended to fly right off into space.

He paced the small room, his bare feet silent on the cold tiles.

In truth, it wasn't exactly uncharacteristic of him. He tended to be selfish, and he tended to want more than he could realistically have—traits he inherited from both of his parents. He shouldn't be surprised he was pushing the boundaries with Maggie. But he had to stop.

Or if he didn't stop—because, man, he really wanted to do the energy thing with her when he was inside her—he needed to keep this all in perspective.

He just got a little caught up tonight; the revelation about Peter brought his machismo out in full force.

Okay, he shouldn't be so freaked. Everything was good.

He stepped back into the bedroom and walked over to the bed. Maggie lay curled on her side, her breathing even and low. He touched her hair, pushing back a stray wave.

Realizing he was doing it again—"it" being something remarkably like mooning—he wandered over to the piano. The sheet was still crumpled on the top, a rather artistic-looking reminder of what had just happened there.

He stared at the instrument for a moment, then sat down on the piano bench. The hard wood felt oddly foreign underneath him. Strange, since he'd spent hours upon hours on that very bench—though he supposed it was so long ago now that the feeling had faded from memory.

He stared down at the black and white keys, his hands folded loosely on his lap. Then slowly, he reached out and laid a finger on one of the keys. He remained that way for a long time. Then he positioned all his fingers over keys, and pressed down lightly. The soft notes filled the room.

He played for a moment, not even concentrating on what he was playing. He just enjoyed the smoothness of the keys, the soft melody surrounding him.

Suddenly he stopped, the lovely tune abruptly ending as if he had lost his place, or the song just stopped because it had no ending. But it wasn't the abrupt finality that struck him as strange—it was the fact that he'd even wanted to play in the first place. He never felt the urge to play, as he once had. In fact, that desire was so distant now, he could barely recall what it felt like.

He preferred being the front man of the Impalers, staying away from the instruments altogether, if possible. He didn't even play his own pieces. Except for the other night, and just now.

He turned on his bench, studying Maggie, even though he could only make out the curve of her form under the velvet of his duvet.

What were the chances he'd play one of his compositions that night? And what were the chances she'd seem to recognize it?

He frowned. Something was very strange here—he just didn't know what.

Maggie woke, and again it was as dark as it had been the previous morning. Only this time she knew the darkness was created by the drapes surrounding the bed. She reached out, brushing her fingers against the soft material. Finding the spot where they met, she pushed it back enough for dim light to filter in, illuminating the bed just a little.

She could make out Ren, lying on his back, perfectly still, his features sculpted and beautiful. Especially with the white lashes facing her, he looked like a statue.

She settled back onto the pillow, her head resting on her arm. Last night had been beyond anything she'd ever experienced. She hadn't believed the sex they were having could get any better, but it had.

Sex with Peter had been enjoyable—which sounded so pallid and dull when compared to the words swirling through her mind now: thrilling, delicious, toe-curling, mind-blowing. Perfect.

She touched Ren's face gently, careful not to wake him. His skin was warm, his cheek and chin raspy with stubble. Gently, she touched his white lashes. His eye was unique, just like everything else about him.

Her fingers lingered for a moment longer. Then she drew back, as if she needed to restrain herself from waking him. She was comfortable enough lying next to him, basking in the warmth and her satisfaction.

She'd slept so deeply, as she had the night before. That seemed strange to her. She'd never been a deep sleeper; she always got up several times a night. But not since meeting Ren. Not that she should be that surprised—he'd certainly worn her out.

She smiled. And very nicely too.

Still, she could have sworn that she started to awaken at one point, her mind in that place between waking and dreaming. She'd heard the most beautiful music. It was over quickly, and she'd sunk right back into deep sleep, but she vaguely remembered piano notes swirling around her.

Just then, as if conjured by her thoughts, music began to play, startlingly loud in the quiet room.

After a moment, she realized it was her cell phone, the music "Für Elise," chosen more for her love of Schroeder in *Peanuts* than her love of the piece.

She hurried out of bed, only pausing momentarily over her

state of undress. Then she quickly tiptoed across the room and rummaged through her purse, amazed it could be so hard to locate the stupid phone when her pocketbook was so small.

Finally, she did.

"Hello?"

"Let me guess," Erika's voice greeted her. "You're still lounging in bed with rocker boy."

Maggie glanced back at the curtained, canopied bed and didn't detect any movement. She tiptoed into the bathroom before she answered, "Yes. I was."

"Sorry," Erika sounded truly contrite. "But I wanted to see if you were still planning to come with us on the ghost tour. You don't have to if you don't want to. Or we could pick up a ticket for Ren too."

"Isn't the tour at eight or something?" She did still want to go, but she hated to wake Ren to ask him about it. He'd played five sets last night with very little time for breaks. And then they'd come back here and . . .

He must be exhausted.

"It is. But it's nearly six now. So we figured we should go buy the tickets before it got much later. The tour guide sounded as if they had limited space."

Maggie frowned. "It's almost six?"

"Yeah."

She'd done it again. Managed to sleep a whole day away. Unheard of—until the past two days.

"Umm, yeah, get us two tickets. I think Ren will want to go. And if he doesn't, I'll just pay for it. He's still sleeping," she added, by way of explanation for why she didn't ask him.

"Mmm, I guess you plumb wore him out, too," Erika said, mimicking Ren's drawl.

Maggie laughed at the attempt.

"Okay, we'll get the tickets and then meet you down by Jackson Square. That's where the tour meets."

"Okay," Maggie agreed.

They said their good-byes, then Maggie hung up. She chuckled to herself at Erika's rather poor attempt to imitate Ren. Southern accents were not her friend's forte.

But then, sometimes Ren himself didn't sound quite as southern as he did other times. Last night, Maggie could have sworn he'd gone from laid-back good ole boy to almost sounding snooty.

She considered that, then decided he just sounded different when he was irritated. And she'd only ever noticed the change when he'd talked about Peter; he'd been upset.

She had to admit, she'd liked his anger at her ex. If he'd felt pity for her, she would have hated that, but indignation on her behalf . . . that was good.

"Maggie?"

She peeked out of the bathroom to see Ren sitting up in bed. She heard unease in his voice, and saw it on his face, too.

But as soon as he saw her, his face relaxed.

"I thought you might have sneaked away," he said.

She shook her head, still not stepping out from behind the door.

Ren gave her a quizzical smile. Ren was very comfortable being naked—she didn't think she'd ever get quite so relaxed. And the idea of walking across the room, while he watched . . . she needed a moment to build up her courage. It was different now than when she was caught up in passion and desire.

"What are you doing in there?" he finally asked, when she still hadn't moved.

She hated to admit her fit of modesty, since she knew he wouldn't understand.

She ducked her head back into the bathroom to look for a towel or something, but before she could locate anything, there was a light rap on the door.

She turned to see Ren's arm poking into the room, one of his shirts dangling from his finger.

"I thought you might want this."

She smiled, pleased he had understood her embarrassment and had done something to help her.

She accepted the shirt and wrapped it around herself, not taking the time to button it. She stepped out, offering him a wide, grateful smile. Then she walked up to him and pressed a kiss to his lips.

"You are a very sweet man."

Ren raised an eyebrow. "I guess I've officially blown my badass rocker image, haven't I?"

"Well, you can be the sweet rocker."

He grimaced. "How about I'm just sweet to you and bad ass to everyone else?"

Her heart fluttered in her chest. She liked that plan.

He put his arms around her, kissing her again.

"So," he murmured, resting his forehead against hers. "Since tonight is my night off, what do you think about staying in bed for most of the evening?"

She started to say it was a really good idea, her attention focused on the desire in his eyes. Then she remembered Erika's call.

"That does sound wonderful, but I was supposed to go on a ghost tour with Erika and Jo, and since this is their last night, I feel like I should go. But you don't have to go. I'd like you to, but—"

Ren placed a finger to her lips, silencing her sudden nervous rambling.

"I thought that you were here until next Sunday?" His brows drew together and his eyes darkened to a shade closer to brown than hazel.

She nodded. "I am, but Jo and Erika have to head back to D.C. for work."

Relief relaxed his frown. "Well, of course, you want to go be with your friends their last night here."

Maggie was relieved he understood. "I told them to buy you a ticket too. I mean, if you want to go. You don't have to."

Again his finger pressed against her lips. "I'd love to go. If Erika and Jo don't mind."

"They don't," she said, against his finger.

He smiled and dropped his hand.

Maggie smiled back.

"But I bet you'd like to go back to your hotel and get clean clothes. And then get something to eat?"

Maggie moaned at the idea of clean clothes. Food wasn't a bad idea either. "Yes. Please"

She moved to the bed, looking for her jeans.

"Maggie?"

She stopped her search to glance at him.

"You don't have to worry about telling me what you want to do."

She nodded, realizing that her concern that Ren would be annoyed with her was another holdover from her relationship with Peter. He'd been the one to call the shots, and made sure she knew it.

She nodded again, this time to herself. She wouldn't allow someone to control her like that again.

Chapter 18

Ren didn't reveal his annoyance as he watched Maggie find her clothes. He knew that if she sensed it, she'd think his feelings were aimed at her. They absolutely weren't. They were aimed solely at the jerk who'd made this beautiful, talented, sweet woman doubt herself so deeply.

Peter the violinist had better hope their paths never crossed. Ren would gladly show him what happened to men who demeaned women that way.

Ren might be selfish, but he never hurt a woman the way this guy had injured Maggie. If Maggie walked away from her time with Ren with nothing else but the knowledge that she was an amazing woman, he'd be satisfied.

"Okay, I'm ready," she said, adjusting his shirt over her full breasts.

He finished pushing his foot into his shoe, then nodded to her. "What time is the ghost tour?"

"Eight."

"Then we better get a move on."

"So are you planning to stay in this room after Erika and Jo leave?" Ren asked from the sitting area of the suite she and her friends had been staying in.

"No," she answered, "I can't afford the suite all on my own. I'll just move to a single."

She hurriedly applied a little mascara, then dabbed on some lipstick. The whole time she'd been getting ready, she'd heard Ren out in the sitting area, the old floor squeaking as he paced. As soon as they'd stepped inside, she sensed he was agitated. Unusual behavior for someone usually so laid-back.

The hotel room seemed to be bothering him, and she couldn't say why.

"Okay, ready," she announced, as she stepped out of the bathroom in another outfit Jo and Erika had talked her into. A peasant blouse, pink and gauzy, with a matching skirt. She knew in Ren's world the outfit hardly screamed "hottie," but she thought the look was flattering, and the flowy material made her feel feminine.

Ren stopped his pacing to face her. "You look beautiful," he said.

She suddenly felt even better about her decision to splurge on the new clothes.

"Thank you." He looked beautiful to her in his low-slung faded jeans and black-and-white flowered shirt—a shirt that might have looked feminine on another man, but with his broad shoulders, smoldering good looks, and musician's demeanor, he pulled the look off easily, and very well.

Oddly, they almost looked like they belonged together. Well, their clothes did anyway. Maggie still thought she looked much too ordinary to be an obvious fit with him.

"So did you want to squeeze in a bite to eat before we meet your friends?"

Before Maggie could decide how hungry she was, she became aware of Ren again. He stood in the center of the room, his arms crossed tightly over his chest. He looked beyond uncomfortable.

"Are you okay?"

He frowned, obviously surprised by her question.

"Sure. Why?"

"You look very tense. And I don't think you stopped pacing the whole time I was getting dressed."

He blinked, in what struck her as a feigned innocence. "Tense? No. I'm just—excited to go on this tour."

That didn't ring true to Maggie, but she let it go. If he didn't want to tell her what had him looking like he wanted to crawl out of his skin, then she couldn't make him. She'd gotten the message from their very first conversation that Ren didn't discuss things he didn't want to.

"Then let's just head to Jackson Square. We can get something to eat after the tour."

Ren hadn't expected to feel the way he did when he entered the Inn on Toulouse. God knew, he looked at the building nearly every night, a constant reminder of what could happen if he let things get out of control. But being in this hotel, the structure that had replaced the Opera House, was more overwhelming than he'd expected.

When they'd entered the lobby, he'd recalled how the entrance had once looked. Impressive, regal, done in beautiful Greek Revival architecture. His mind had suddenly been filled with memories of walking into the majestic building to work with the orchestra. He remembered everything about Annalise. Not that he'd ever forgotten her, but being there, where she'd performed, where she'd died—the images were overwhelming.

As he waited for Maggie to get ready, he could feel Annalise. He remembered her perfume, a heavy, musky scent. He even recalled her laughter, a husky, bawdy sound. He'd carried tremendous guilt over Annalise, as well as Nancy. And he'd felt deep bitterness about how he'd ended up hurting—ultimately killing—both women.

He glanced over at Maggie as she gathered up her purse. He wouldn't let that happen to her. He'd do whatever he had to and keep her from falling in love with him. He wouldn't let her die. Somehow he'd gone on after Nancy and Annalise, but he didn't think he could recover from Maggie's suffering a similar fate.

* * *

As soon as they were outside, the oppressive feeling that had hovered around him within the walls of the hotel lifted. The visceral reminder that he had to be careful with Maggie didn't lessen, but he did feel like he could breathe again.

And now he was going on a ghost tour. Like he needed to deal with any more ghosts tonight.

But to his surprise, once they got to Jackson Square and met with Jo and Erika, he found the good spirits of Maggie and her friends infectious. Maybe it was just Maggie herself, but he became more wrapped up in what she and her friends were saying than in the tragedies of his past.

"After falling to her death from one of the balconies, Caroline still haunts the Le Petite Theatre," the young, blond tour guide said, using her best eerie voice, which didn't tone down her obviously bubbly personality.

"Caroline didn't fall from a balcony," Ren said, with a disbelieving laugh. The chuckle died on his lips as he realized Maggie and her friends were staring at him,

"Well, that's not how I heard the story, anyway," he added quickly. Good going, he thought to himself. Nothing like bringing attention to the fact that he was a two-hundred-year-old vampire.

"What did you hear?" Erika asked, and he realized that at least they bought his excuse.

Ren tried to remember exactly what did happen. What did he remember about the rather unremarkable woman? "She was an actress, although not a great one." To say the least. "She had an affair with one of the directors at the theater, but he spurned her for another actress. A more renowned one, as I recall." He paused.

"As I recall the story," he clarified. Maggie and her friends didn't appear suspicious of his wording.

"And I believe she quit the theater shortly after that. To move somewhere near Lafayette."

The women stared at him, noticeably disappointed with his recollections.

"That's it?" Jo asked.

Ren nodded.

"Why would that story even be passed along from generation to generation? It's pretty uninteresting, really," Maggie said.

"It is," Ren agreed, thinking maybe he should have embellished a little.

"Who told you that version of the story?" Maggie asked.

No one—he'd known both her and the director, who, truth be told, she was better off without. Though it would spice up the tale, he couldn't tell them that.

"I don't remember," he said.

"So she didn't even die in the theater?" Erika gazed at the building, her lips turned down.

"I like the tour guide's version better," Jo stated.

Ren nodded. Sadly, in this case, the truth wasn't stranger than fiction. Which certainly didn't hold true for him.

The group moved on, and Ren made a mental note to keep his thoughts to himself for the remainder of the tour. Although he did think the women would be quite amazed at how many of these supposed ghosts he'd known when they were alive and kicking. Now, that was a story they'd be shocked by.

So much for avoiding ghosts from his past tonight.

"Are you absolutely starving now?" Ren asked. He kept forgetting that Maggie needed to eat—a problem with being a vampire. He'd actually fed as they walked the streets with the crowd of tourists. Being a lampir was so much easier than being a regular vampire, which tended to be a tad messy and require privacy. Ren could feed without ever being detected.

And in the case of this tour, his feeding habits had come in rather handy when a particularly loud and obnoxious tourist from New York kept interrupting and speaking over the guide. Ren had just siphoned off a little of his energy—and ta da! He'd been much calmer the second half of the tour.

"Yes, I am pretty hungry," she admitted, then turned to her friends. "Have you eaten?"

They had.

"Well, I know this place in Marigny that has good food, good drinks, and good jazz."

"Something for everyone," Jo said.

"That does sound good to me," Erika agreed, but then she seemed to reconsider the idea of joining them. "But maybe we should part here."

She gave Maggie a pointed look, asking with her eyes if they wanted to be alone.

But Ren responded before Maggie could. "Come along with us. This is your last night, and I know Maggie wants to hang out with you. Besides, she's all mine after you leave."

Both Erika and Jo grinned at the possessive tone in his voice, obviously approving—which would be good, if he had any right to that possessiveness.

Maggie didn't look at him, but he sensed his words excited her. They excited him too. Even as he told himself to lighten up, to keep this just about casual fun. No possessiveness, no claims.

He couldn't seem to keep that pact with himself. Which wasn't good.

But, he told himself, he realized what he was doing, so that had to make things safer, right?

Maggie stepped closer to him on the sidewalk as they headed in the direction of the restaurant. Without even thinking, he put his arm around her. Having her close just seemed natural.

They turned down a street that appeared mostly residential, but as they continued walking, Maggie could hear the rhythms of jazz filling the night air. Soon, the delicious aroma of spices joined the music. Ren led them to a building that looked as if it had once been a private house, but now the large front windows had been removed, giving the restaurant the feel of an open-air café.

"This is too cool," Erika commented, and Maggie nodded. She smiled at her friend, but she could see Erika was too busy admiring every detail of the architecture with her artist's eye.

They stepped inside and were immediately greeted by the host, a tall, thin man with skin the color of lightly creamed coffee and big, nearly black eyes. He grinned widely at Ren.

"Where have you been?" he said, making it clear Ren was a regular here.

"Working," Ren answered easily, moving forward to shake the man's hand.

"Well, it doesn't look like you're working now." The host smiled at each of the women. "This definitely looks an awful lot like pleasure, eh?"

Maggie found herself laughing at the animated man, as did Erika and Jo. He had a magnetic, charming quality, not unlike Ren.

"Emile, this is Erika and Jo. And Maggie." Maggie noted the pause before he said her name, as if unconsciously separating her from her friends, as if she were special. It made her feel good, just like his comment earlier about her being all his once her friends headed back to the East Coast.

She supposed she was reading too much into these things. It was going to be over by the end of the week, but they would be the things she remembered when she was back in her box of an apartment, watching reruns on cold winter nights.

"So do you want your usual table near the stage?"

Ren shook his head. "No. Somewhere where we can order food, and talk."

Emile raised an eyebrow, a gesture Maggie didn't quite understand, but then he grabbed four menus. Waving for them to follow, he headed to a darkened corner away from the music. After everyone was seated, Emile handed out the menus with a wide smile.

Then he leaned closer to Ren. "Try the filet special. Most palatable. No garlic." He winked at Ren and then drifted off with a satisfied laugh.

"Do you not like garlic?" Maggie asked, confused as to why Emile found the suggestion so funny.

"Not particularly," Ren said, then asked, "So what do you think?"

Maggie glanced around again. "Very nice. Much better than that little bar you took me to."

Ren looked offended, although the wounded look was obviously feigned. "That is a cool place."

Maggie couldn't keep up the pretense, not really wanting to offend him. "It was. And the drinks were good . . . from what I can recall."

Ren smiled.

"So what is this place called?" Jo asked, turning her attention from the stage to Ren. "I didn't see a sign."

"It doesn't really have a name. Locals call it Louis's."

"That's cool," Erika said, obviously in love with the place.

A waitress, dressed in bright colors, with a gold scarf around her head, appeared to take drink orders. Erika and Jo both ordered the house special—some extra-exotic version of a mojito. Ren ordered a bourbon on the rocks and Maggie a wine.

They all watched the band, which consisted of a guitarist, an upright bass, a saxophonist, and a drummer. Several of the patrons danced, their dances much more complicated and interesting than the dances that went on at Ren's bar.

But Ren's band created a totally different atmosphere. They got people up and dancing and partying. This was a festive atmosphere too, but different.

As could have been expected, two men approached their table to talk to Erika and Jo.

"See, it takes them less than ten minutes in a room to garner the attention of the male species," Maggie said with a fond smile.

"Well, you have them beat," Ren said, and when she gave him a quizzical look, he added, "You walked into the bar and I noticed you instantly."

Maggie smiled. Well, that had been the same for her, hadn't it?

"I can see why you like it here," Maggie said. "The band is great."

Ren nodded, appreciation for the musicians clear on his face. "They are."

"Have you ever considered playing at a place like this? You could start playing piano again."

Ren shook his head before she'd even finished speaking. "I don't enjoy playing like I once did."

"Why?" Maggie realized she probably shouldn't pry, but the question was out of her mouth before she could pull it back.

Ren didn't answer right away, and when she thought he might not answer at all, he said, "I just don't love it like I once did. I'm happier singing." He stopped and looked as if he wanted to say more, but instead he just shrugged. "Nothing more than that, I guess. What about you? Why don't you play?"

It was Maggie's turn to be silent for a moment. "I just knew I'd never be great."

"Is that you talking? Or Peter?"

"Both," she admitted. "I wanted to be a concert pianist. That's a tough career choice to begin with, but when you add that I'm just not brilliant, well, it was a lost cause."

"So why not do something else with music?" Ren asked.

"I do. I research and authenticate it."

Ren nodded. "But don't you want to perform?"

Maggie considered that question. She hadn't thought about it for so long, nearly four years. She supposed she did miss performing.

"I guess. But I like my work too."

"Can't you do both?"

Maggie gazed at him for a moment, surprised he was pushing the idea. The waiter appeared, placing a wine goblet in front of her.

"Why is my playing so important to you?"

Ren frowned at her question. Why was it? He hadn't really realized it until she pointed it out.

"I guess I hate to think of anyone giving up something they really love." As he said those words, he realized they should apply to him too. After all, he'd been composing his own pieces since he was ten—and then he'd just stopped. He still loved music; he just didn't seem to have any new music left inside him.

"I just don't want something that ass Peter said to stop you from doing what you want. I thought your playing was terrific."

Maggie reached out and took his hand.

The waitress returned for their orders. Erika and Jo didn't order any food, and were still involved in their conversation with the two men. Maggie ordered a shrimp dish and Ren ordered the filet, knowing he wouldn't touch it. But he also knew Maggie would feel self-conscious eating all by herself.

"So are you from New Orleans originally?" Maggie asked. Then she laughed.

"What?" He smiled, unaware of what was funny about the question.

"I feel like I've known you forever. And I've certainly done things with you that I've never done with anyone else and yet I don't even know where you grew up."

Ren realized that for Maggie, that must be strange. But to him, it was the norm. Of course, he did feel differently about her than about the average woman who came into his life.

Which had been baffling him since the moment they met. But then his attention was captured by something else. The comment about doing things with him she'd never done with anyone else.

"You've only ever had sex with Peter?"

Maggie's cheeks immediately darkened, the pinkness clear even in the dim light.

"So are you from here?" she asked again, ignoring the question, although that was answer enough.

He decided to let it go. "No. I've lived all over. I was born in Italy, and spent several years of my childhood in England."

He instantly wondered why he'd even admitted that much about his past.

"Really?"

He nodded.

"Well, that makes sense now. Because the other night I noticed your southern accent seemed to vanish for a moment. Then it was back."

It had. He took a sip of his bourbon. He couldn't recall a time when he'd had difficulty with his assumed persona. Hell, he'd lived in the South longer than he'd ever lived in England.

"When?" he couldn't help asking.

"When you were upset about Peter," she said, then took a bite of her rice.

Really? How odd.

"So is Ren short for something?"

Okay, this conversation wasn't going the way it should. He needed to keep things impersonal. Vague. And not about anything outside of the here and now.

"Would you believe my mother was a big *Footloose* fan?" he heard himself saying. He took another swallow of his drink.

She frowned, not following. Then understanding dawned on her face. "Oh, you were named after the Kevin Bacon character. Ren . . . what was it?"

"McCormack," he said.

"Right." Maggie smiled at that. Then her brows drew together again. "Wait, aren't you too old to be named after that character?"

"Way too old," he said wryly. Then he decided to take another tack to change the topic of conversation.

"What about you? Are you from D.C.?"

"No. From a small town in New Hampshire. My mom still lives there."

"Are you close to your mother?"

Maggie nodded. "Yes. We usually talk every other day or so. But she's in the Bahamas with my aunt." The animation suddenly left her face and she took a sip of wine.

"They are actually using the travel package I purchased for my honeymoon."

Ren hadn't expected that, and another wave of irritation hit him on her behalf. "Peter was such an idiot. I'd kill to see you lounging in the sun in a skimpy bathing suit."

There was no way she could understand how appealing that idea was—in part because of its impossibility.

His words seemed to help. She took a bite of her shrimp, chewing it quite merrily.

"You don't mind if we join Vince and Craig here for a dance, do you?" Jo asked them, which Ren found amusing, since he and Maggie hadn't been paying them any attention anyway.

"Go have fun," Maggie said, smiling at her friends.

Ren had to admit he was rather pleased to really have her to himself.

"So what about you? Do you ever see your family?" Maggie asked, mildly dulling Ren's thrill of having her alone.

Yet he answered her. To stop her questions, he told himself. Certainly not because he wanted to share any of his life with her.

"My father has been dead for many years." Many, many years. "And I don't see my mother. And I do have a half brother."

"Are you two close?"

Ren nodded. He loved his half brother. Vittorio was the only other being in existence who actually understood him. Understood the pain of growing up with Orabella D'Antoni, or in Vittorio's case, Lady Orabella Ridgewood, as a mother.

"Where is he?"

"Around," Ren said vaguely, vague because he had no idea where Vittorio made his home these days. He'd lived in New Orleans for a few years—even played in the Impalers. He was a great keyboardist himself. But then Vittorio had decided to leave.

Ren had never gotten an exact reason, although he suspected it had to do with a woman Vittorio had been seeing briefly. Well, that and moving around a lot kept their mother off his back. Orabella was much harder on her youngest son. Maybe because Vittorio accepted it more readily—or maybe because, even after hundreds of years, Orabella still lived by the old rules. And Vittorio was her legitimate son.

Or it could just be that Ren didn't disguise his hatred of their mother the way Vittorio did. Whatever the reason, Ren was just glad that Mumsie paid more attention to Vittorio. Poor guy.

"And do you see your mother?" Maggie asked, as if sensing his train of thought.

"Not if I can possibly help it."

Maggie seemed saddened by his bitterly muttered words. "Is she that bad?"

"Worse."

Maggie reached out and squeezed his hand. It was on the tip of his tongue to tell her that he was fine with his feelings about his wretched mother, but Maggie's sympathy and understanding did feel nice.

"What about you? Do you see your father?"

"I saw him once when I was ten, and I invited him to my wedding. He came—so I was spared no one missing my humiliation at Peter's announcement." She laughed, though the sound was a little brittle, without the melodic quality he loved.

He squeezed her hand in return. "That wasn't exactly how you wanted the reunion to go, I'm sure."

She nodded. "No. But it did. And actually, my dad seemed genuinely offended for me."

Ren didn't know quite what to say—how to make that pain go away. Just like he didn't know how to let his past go. It wasn't as if he hadn't had decade after decade to sort out all of his feelings about his mother's selfishness and cruelty, and his father's rejection. But it still hurt, all of it, like a wound that just wouldn't ever quite heal. Just when it all seemed to be scabbed over, something would rub it raw again.

Maggie was one of those things, he suddenly realized. She made him realize how not over his past he was.

He looked at her for a moment, suddenly hit by an overwhelming, almost breathtaking feeling of longing. But this time not a sexual longing—although that was there too. This longing was to be something other than who he was. Someone worthy of Maggie. Someone who could offer her more than a holiday fling.

Maggie looked up from pushing around the remainder of her steamed vegetables, catching his expression, before he could guard it or look away.

"What is it?" she asked, giving him a quizzical frown.

He told himself to stop looking at her like a forlorn puppy, but he couldn't stop drinking in her features. Big eyes that shifted from gray to green depending on her moods. Small bow lips. That wavy, disheveled hair that looked almost like a style from the twenties, like something Fay Wray would have worn.

Just tell her you're fine. Crack a joke. Something.

"Look who the cat dragged in," Emile called—acting as the distraction that Ren couldn't seem to create himself.

Ren tore his gaze from Maggie to look at his old friend.

Behind Emile was Vittorio, and although he'd just been talking about him, Ren didn't find his brother's arrival strange. Vittorio had a weird way of appearing whenever Ren thought about him. He supposed it was a bond they had because of being vampires. Of course, it only seemed to work in Ren's direction. Vittorio came to him. Ren never seemed to be able to sense when Vittorio thought about him. Maybe Vittorio didn't.

Ren rose, greeting his brother with a hug. "What are you doing here?"

"Just checking in with you," Vittorio said in his usual vague way.

"Were your ears burning?" Ren asked, gesturing to a chair at the table.

Vittorio smiled. Even his smiles were hard to read. "No. Should they have been?"

"I was just talking about you. To Maggie here." He nodded to Maggie.

Interest sparked in Vittorio's dark eyes and, for a moment, something like jealousy flashed inside Ren. But he quickly quashed the feeling. Vittorio wouldn't be interested in his woman. That wasn't Vittorio's style. Not that Ren had ever seen his brother be overly interested in women. In fact, when he'd played with the Impalers, he'd been the most sought-after member of the band by the ladies—because he was aloof.

Ren had no idea why Vittorio never showed interest in any of them, but he always felt it was because he was pining for someone.

"Maggie, this is my brother Vittorio."

Chapter 19

Maggie reached forward to shake Ren's brother's hand. "Hello," she said, immediately liking him. There was a sweetness to his face—an almost angelic quality. A broken quality, too.

That was the only real similarity to Ren. They both had a haunted quality in their eyes. But otherwise, Vittorio looked much different. His sun-streaked hair touched his shoulders, where Ren's was darker and longer. And while Ren had hazel eyes, a rich amber color specked with jade green, Vittorio had dark, dark eyes, a brown so deep it was nearly black.

"Hello, Maggie," he said, and she was surprised such a deep voice could come from such an angelic, boyish face. He held her fingers for a moment, looking at her speculatively, as if trying to decide what was going on between her and his brother.

Then he smiled. The curve of his lips made him look even sweeter and more heartbreakingly lovely. She could see hints of Ren in that smile.

"Maggie is here on vacation," Ren said, and Maggie got the feeling that was supposed to clarify their relationship.

Vittorio nodded as if it had. Somehow that didn't make Maggie feel particularly good. She wondered if Ren had actually set up these week-long affairs before. She'd believed their arrangement was unusual for Ren; now she wondered how she got that idea.

As Ren smiled at her, she noted that Vittorio gave him an appraising look, a look that said he found this situation interesting. That made Maggie feel better.

"Maggie," Erika said, appearing at the table, flushed and laughing. "Come out and learn this dance that Vince is teaching . . ." Her words trailed off as she spotted Vittorio seated beside Ren. Her wide, giddy smile faded.

"I'm sorry," she said. "I didn't realize someone else joined you."

"This is my brother, Vittorio," Ren said. "Vittorio, this is Maggie's friend, Erika."

Vittorio rose, regarding Erika for a long moment before extending his hand. Erika, who Maggie always considered the most touchy-feely of her friends, paused a moment before accepting it. And then their touch was so brief, it might as well have not happened.

"What dance are you learning?" Maggie asked when the silence at the table lingered.

"Umm." Erika blinked, then frowned at her, trying to recall. "It's called the Lindy Hop."

"I'll go try it," Maggie said, even though she noted that Erika didn't seem nearly as excited about the dance as she had when she approached the table. But she did gather her wits enough to ask Ren and Vittorio, "Want to join us?"

Ren gave her a self-deprecating smile. "I'm not much of a dancer. But I'll be happy to watch you."

"Chicken," Maggie teased.

"Yep," Ren agreed readily.

"How about you, Vittorio?" Maggie asked, although she knew the answer.

He shook his head. "I'll keep Ren company."

Maggie smiled. She also noticed that Vittorio seemed to be avoiding looking at Erika. Oddly, Erika seemed to be doing the same thing.

"Okay." Maggie stood and followed Erika back toward Jo and the waiting men.

"Are you okay?" Maggie asked Erika as soon as they were out of hearing range of the table.

Erika's fair complexion had paled to a near white. "I think that's my fair-haired, dark-eyed prince."

"So what was that reaction to Erika?" Ren asked, shocked at the strange interaction between his brother and Maggie's friend. He'd never seen Vittorio react with any particular interest to anyone. Well, with the exception of Maggie, and that reaction was in relation to him.

Vittorio shrugged, his usual poker face back in place.

He crossed his arms over his chest and then offered Ren a smug smirk.

"The more interesting question is who's this Maggie?"

It was Ren's turn to lean back in his chair and position his arms over his chest.

"Just a woman I met at the bar. The usual tourist."

Vittorio raised an eyebrow, disbelief clear on his face. "You are so full of shit."

Ren frowned. "Why?"

"I can tell you are crazy about her. I saw it on your face as soon as I walked up to the table."

Ren shook his head. "No, you didn't. I like her, sure, but it's just the usual thing. A bit of fun."

"Okay." Vittorio clearly didn't believe him.

Ren found his brother's disbelief annoying. He certainly wasn't helping Ren keep this all in perspective.

"Where is Maggie from?" Vittorio asked, at least taking the topic to a safer place.

"Washington, D.C."

"I have to admit that Maggie looks exactly like what you need."

Ren wanted to ask why, but he didn't want to give Vittorio more to read into this relationship—or whatever it was that he had with Maggie.

"She's a lovely woman." Ren tried to keep his tone objective, cool.

Vittorio nodded. His gaze moved back to the women on the dance floor as they attempted to follow the moves one of the men was demonstrating.

"And her friend?"

The question was asked offhandedly, but Ren smiled, realizing his brother was feigning casual conversation.

"What about her?"

"Where is she from?"

"I'm not sure. D.C., I would guess."

Vittorio nodded. Then he waved to the waitress. "I'll take a beer." He glanced at Ren.

"And I'll have a bourbon on the rocks." Ren suddenly felt like he needed a little more liquor to calm him. Vittorio's observations felt a little too accurate. A little too good. And it was always dangerous for him to want something. No good had ever come of it.

When the drinks arrived, Vittorio raised his glass. "To you and Maggie. It's about time you found a woman who can care for you the way you deserve."

Ren raised his glass, but didn't allow Vittorio's words to fill him with . . . hope. Yeah, that was the emotion that *was not* filling his chest right at this moment. Not at all.

After all, he had to keep this in perspective.

Maggie walked beside Ren down the sidewalk, realizing now that he'd been silent for most of the remainder of the evening. When they'd been around his brother and her friends and the loud jazz, she hadn't really noticed. But since they'd left Vittorio at the restaurant and dropped her friends at the hotel, he'd said very little.

She wasn't bothered by companionable silence, but this quiet didn't seem like that. And with each step, she was growing more nervous—although she couldn't read anything in his expression that told her she should be.

"I really liked Vittorio."

Ren blinked at her as if remembering that she was still beside him. "Oh. Yeah, he is a good guy."

She nodded, not knowing what else to say. Something was wrong, and she had the feeling it was something wrong between the two of them. Not something that he and his brother had discussed. Something she wasn't sure how to fix, since she didn't even know when or how it went wrong.

They reached Ren's place, and he unlocked the front doors and stepped aside to let her in the courtyard as he always did. Now, though, she felt he was reluctant to even have her there.

She could have sworn earlier that he was looking at her with longing, but now he seemed so distant she thought she must have imagined it.

He followed, walking slightly behind her. Trying to find a way to tell her to go? She paused near the fountain, watching the water bubbling and splashing, the liquid churning like the worry churning in her chest.

"Are you coming?" Ren stood on the steps to his place, waiting for her.

She pulled in a deep breath, trying to decide if she should say anything. He was inviting her in. Maybe she was reading too much into the silence. After all, this was an affair. Did you try to understand what was troubling your lover when it was going to be over in five days anyway?

But she liked Ren. She considered him a friend. He'd been more of a boyfriend to her in five days than Peter had been in five years. She wasn't sure what that meant exactly, but she did like him. So very much.

"Are you all right? Because I get the feeling something is bothering you."

Ren didn't respond for a moment. Then he came down off the steps, walking straight for her.

He didn't say a word as he pulled her against him, kissing her as if he'd die if he didn't. She responded, even though she still wanted to understand what was going on in his head. She responded with all her heart, her fingers tangling in his hair.

As he seemed to like to do, he rested his forehead against hers, his breath ragged, his body tense. "Can we really keep this just a fling?"

The question seemed rhetorical, asked of himself more than her. But she answered.

"What else could it be?" Even as she said it, she found herself wondering. Could they have a long-distance relationship? Could she move here? Would he come to her?

She immediately dismissed the ideas. Why even go there? He must be feeling like he should offer her more. She knew she gave off the good-girl vibe. Not to mention she had pretty much admitted that Peter had been her one and only. Maybe that's what had him shaken. Maybe that tugged at his conscience.

In fact she was willing to bet that was it.

"I know this is an affair. A little blip in time—just meant to be fun."

He stared at her for a minute. Then his lips were back on hers, devouring her as if he was starving. He walked her backwards until her back bumped into the courtyard wall, cool brick, earth-scented vine curling over it.

Ren's hands moved over her almost frantically as he wadded up her skirt, bunching the material in one hand as his other hand slid underneath, finding her panties.

She would have thought this kind of frantic, forceful attack would have scared her. Instead, she found his desperation incredibly exciting.

His hand left her to unfasten his jeans. She felt his hard length against her bare thigh as he pressed her harder against the wall, kissing her, licking her, nipping her lips. Maggie gasped as his hand pushed aside her panties and he began to stroke her. His touch was firm, excited, and felt so, so good.

Desire tunneled through her, filling her, leaving no portion of her unaroused or unaware. Her whole body was his, reacting only for him.

Vaguely, as his mouth teased and tasted hers, she became aware of his materializing a condom. He shifted against her, his weight pinning her to the wall, his desire for her as palpable as his arms around her.

With one push of his hips, he was buried deep inside her. Her body squirmed and writhed against him, instinctively trying to find the best position to accept him as fully as possible.

"Maggie," he murmured against her mouth. "Maggie, darling."

She kissed his face, raining kisses on his cheeks, his jaw, his lips.

He lifted his head, and in the dim light, she could still see that haunted look of his. Suddenly his frantic movement calmed.

His eyes held hers as he rocked slowly in and out of her. One arm moved to hold her waist, balancing her, angling her. The other hand came up to caress her cheek and her hair.

His tender attention was just as thrilling as his desperate lovemaking. More so, because he never broke eye contact as he rocked her to her release. Even after she cried out, he kept moving slowly, bringing her to another orgasm.

Only this time when her head fell back and a pleasured moan escaped her, Ren's own release joined hers. He gripped her tight, and she burrowed her head against his neck. The fresh scent of his hair, the green, earthy scent of the courtyard; it all somehow joined in the wave of satisfaction that swept through her.

She remained curled against him, and he remained holding her.

She must have dozed, because the next thing she knew Ren was placing her carefully into his bed.

She smiled sleepily up at him, her eyelids feeling as if they had weights attached to them.

"Thank you," she managed to mumble, still riding the wave of delighted bliss, even in her exhausted state.

She closed her eyes, and as she drifted back into darkness, she thought she heard Ren whisper, "What am I going to do?" She wondered what he meant for a fraction of a second, then a lovely darkness, warm and comforting, enveloped her.

Ren watched Maggie drift easily back to sleep and knew rest would not come so readily to him. He'd not be able to relax until the sun forced him to sleep.

Again he found himself pacing, something he'd done quite a bit since meeting Maggie.

It was as if he had no control where she was concerned. Vittorio's comments about her had made clear he really had to tread lightly with her. Hell, if he had been honest with himself, he wouldn't have needed his brother to suggest he was feeling more for Maggie than he should.

Of course, he could feel whatever he wanted. His affection for her wasn't the risk. He could be head over heels in love with her, as long as she didn't love him back.

He walked to the bathroom and stood in front of the medicine cabinet, his reflection in the mirror vaguely see-through, as if he was fading away.

Except he didn't fade away—he just remained like this, almost human, almost a ghost. Not quite either.

He studied the eyelashes, the white ones, that were hard to make out in his opaque state.

He touched the spiky lengths. It hadn't always been that way. There was a time when the left eye had been the same as the one on the right.

He'd only been half kidding when he'd asked Maggie on that first night if she thought it was an evil eye. It wasn't evil in and of itself. But it was a strange outcome of this curse.

He'd mentioned voodoo as a source for his unusual eye as well, but there was no voodoo involved.

Only a petty, selfish, and spiteful woman.

And now, Maggie had wandered into his life, and he couldn't stand what he was. He didn't want to be this see-through, empty person. He wanted to be worthy of her.

He wanted her love.

No! He gripped the edge of the sink, leaning in to glare at himself. No. He couldn't think like that. He couldn't want her love. Even thinking it made him as selfish as the one who'd made him this ghost of a man.

He would never hurt Maggie. Never.

He pushed away from the sink and headed back into the bedroom. Maggie still slept soundly, nestled in his bed like she belonged there.

He watched her for a moment. She did look perfect, burrowed deep under his covers, curled on her side, her hand under her cheek, her lashes dark, her pink bow lips parted. She looked like a cherub. Young, innocent. So how could she possibly be perfect for a creature like him? She couldn't.

Even if love was a possibility for them, what could he offer her? He'd never be normal, and she needed normal.

He paced the room again. What was he going to do?

Pausing, he ran his fingers through his hair, still tangled from their earlier tryst in the courtyard. His eyes stopped on the piano. And as on the night before, he found himself wandering over to it. He hesitated, wondering why the antique instrument that he'd very rarely noticed over the years suddenly called to him.

He sat down and opened the lid. The keys shone mellow in the lamplight. Maybe he was using something familiar to calm himself.

He held his hands over the keys, then began to play.

He lost himself in the delicate weave of notes and keys. When he finished, he just sat there, wondering what was getting into him.

"That was lovely," a sleepy voice said from behind him.

He spun on the bench to see Maggie sitting up in a nest of rumpled bedding. She pressed a sheet to her ample breasts.

His chest immediately tightened at the sight—as did other parts of his body.

"That was the piece you were playing that first night."

He cursed silently to himself. Why had he done that? Why had he played the one song that would possibly pique her curiosity again?

"Yes. It's just something I wrote years ago," he said, hoping that if he admitted to writing the song, she'd realize it couldn't be the same piece she was researching.

Except—maybe it could be. Although he couldn't for the life—or the undeath—of him figure out how she'd have a copy.

"It seems so much like that piece I looked at before leaving."

Ren shrugged. "Couldn't be."

She studied him for a moment, then nodded. She yawned, then smiled at him, adorably drowsy.

"Want to come to bed?" she asked.

Even in his agitated state, that was not an invitation he could turn down.

He walked to the bed and undressed. Maggie wiggled closer, once he was under the covers with her.

"I like when you play," she murmured. "You are so good."

The compliment pleased him. He'd once derived his whole identity from his music. But instead of letting her know that, he said, "So I've heard," and it was clear that he wasn't talking about his piano playing.

But she didn't smile. Instead she reached out and brushed back his hair, tucking the long strands behind his ear.

"So how many women do you think you've been with?"

He hadn't thought there was any topic he wanted to discuss less than his past compositions. But apparently, she'd found one.

"Quite a few." Honestly, even that was an understatement.

She nodded, her gaze focused somewhere over his left shoulder.

"Do you think you could ever be faithful?"

This was the moment to say something that would put all of his worries to rest. Given what Maggie's fiancé had done to her, at the altar no less, if he just said he couldn't be faithful, she'd never fall in love with him. She couldn't love a man who couldn't offer faith and loyalty and love . . . things she deserved.

"I'm not sure." That was hardly the definitive answer he should have given her. It left room for hope, if she should want it. And he knew better than anyone that hope was just another form of self-torture. Hope kept you longing for something you couldn't have.

But his answer didn't seem to satisfy her. Her lips turned down slightly as she considered it. Then she rolled onto her back, crossing her arms over her chest.

"Do you think you will want to get married again one day?" he asked, maybe feeling a need for a little self-torture himself.

She didn't hesitate. "Yeah, I think I will."

Fidelity, loyalty, love—none of those things would ever be an issue for Maggie.

Ren tried to imagine the man she would end up with. Someone handsome enough, intelligent, reserved. Not a long-haired lead singer of a cover band. That was for sure. And certainly not a cursed vampire.

And that should be a good thing, but he found himself wanting to kill the Mr. Right who'd appeared in his head.

He glanced at Maggie. She still stared at the canopy above them, lost in her own thoughts.

"Do you want to know something?" she suddenly asked.

He rolled over to face her. "What?"

"I could see myself living in New Orleans."

He didn't speak for a moment. He didn't breathe. This was not good.

But instead of saying anything to stop this train wreck they were headed for, he just reached out and touched a lock of her hair.

"I can see that."

Chapter 20

Maggie woke feeling no better than she had falling asleep. This morning she was thankful for the dark shroud of the curtains surrounding the bed. She rolled over, resisting the urge to pull the covers up over her head. The darkness wasn't enough to block out her embarrassment. She wanted to curl up and hide.

Why had she thrown out the comment about living in New Orleans? Especially after Ren had basically admitted that he couldn't see himself in a monogamous relationship?

Was she utterly stupid? Wasn't everything that happened with Peter enough of a humiliation? Did she need to repeat her stupidity with Ren?

Ren had said more than once this was a fling. Over as soon as she got on that plane back to D.C. Why was she even abstractly considering something more long-term?

Ren hadn't even made it sound like he was offering friendship when all was said and done. Maggie just needed to let her silly fantasies go.

She didn't even look over at Ren as she crawled out of bed. Her first thought was to call Erika or Jo; they'd know the best way to brush all this aside and get things back to where they'd been before she'd opened her big mouth. But her friends were gone, probably on the plane back home.

She fought back a groan as she again recalled announcing

that she could see herself living in New Orleans. Could she have been any more obvious?

She tiptoed around gathering her clothes, then she headed into the bathroom. From the look of the light outside, she had again managed to sleep until afternoon. Even in her horrible state of embarrassment. God, she was a fool.

She tugged on her skirt and sandals. She wanted to get out of here for a while. Just to clear her head, and get herself sorted out and calmed down, so she could actually enjoy her night with Ren. He had the night off, and he'd told her he was going to take her to another nice restaurant.

She walked carefully to the piles of magazines stacked in nearly teetering towers on the end tables by the sofa in his bedroom. She scanned them, searching for something she could write him a note on, in case he should wake up before she got back.

All she saw were music magazines—interestingly enough, about every type of music but rock.

She flipped through one about opera, then headed down the stairs. She continued her search, finally finding a small notebook buried under more music magazines.

She found a pen and flipped open the notebook, her fingers pausing as she saw musical notes.

She studied the handwritten notes. From the tempo and style she could see it was a classical piece. He'd said that piece he played again last night was one of his own compositions. He was not only interested in classical music, he was very good too.

She studied his notation for a moment longer, then flipped to a blank sheet further back in the pad. Tearing it off, she wrote a brief note telling him that she'd gone for a walk and would meet him back here for dinner.

She placed the note on the kitchen table, along with the pen and the pad of paper.

Then she found her purse and stepped outside. It was drizzling, although the air was still warm.

The gates that led to the sidewalk couldn't be bolted back into place behind her without a key. She hated to leave them unlocked, but she didn't want to wake Ren, and she really needed this time alone.

Her emotions were in total upheaval, and being in his presence even when he was asleep was jumbling her thoughts. She wanted to walk and clear her head. Even the light rain dampening her skin somehow helped.

She opted to shut the gates firmly behind her and hope that no one tested them and discovered them unlocked.

The street was relatively quiet. Maybe it was the weather, or maybe it was because it was a Monday afternoon and even things in the Quarter quieted down on a workday. Whatever the reason, she was grateful for the general lull.

She wandered, pausing under store awnings and balconies to peer in the plate-glass windows at all the strange and fascinating assortments of items. Antiques, jewelry, paintings.

"Good afternoon, precious," a smiley older man greeted her. Maggie smiled back, realizing that if some stranger said that to her on the streets of D.C. she would have assumed him crazy and/or homeless. Here, the man's greeting seemed natural. A part of the weird and wonderful atmosphere.

Instead of rushing away, which would have been her natural reaction back at home, she stopped to peer into the store where he stood in the doorway. A bookstore. One of her favorite places.

"We've lots of superb books. About the history of New Orleans. About the architecture." He leaned closer. "And about all the hauntings and other spooky things that happen here in the Big Easy."

Maggie found the man's mysterious and conspiratorial whisper entertaining.

"I think I will look around," she told him, offering another wide smile.

He nodded, giving her an approving look. "You'll find something of interest. I guarantee."

She stepped into the book-lined store. Actually, "lined" implied order. This store was utter chaos, books piled in every inch. The wooden floor was warped, and creaked under her feet as she navigated the narrow aisles. The scent of aged paper filled the air, mixed with newsprint. She liked the place immediately.

She wandered aimlessly, stopping occasionally, tilting her head to read the titles embossed on the spines. Everything ranging from bestselling fiction to voodoo as a form of self-help.

She smiled.

Then she spotted the section dedicated to local authors and New Orleans itself.

She picked up one of the hardcover books with an interesting picture of New Orleans from the 1800s. The street was crowded with women in bustled skirts and men in top hats.

She smiled at the image, trying to imagine how different the city was then. She suspected the mechanical legs on Bourbon Street were not there. But then, other adult entertainments had been available, just not so blatantly displayed.

She flipped open the book, the pages parting at a section about the French Opera House. The building had once been right where the hotel she was staying in stood now. The Opera House had burned to the ground in 1919.

The hairs on her neck rose. A cold chill ran over her rain-moistened skin. She glanced around, looking for a window or an air vent to explain the sudden coldness. All she spied was more books.

She continued to read, discovering that several people had been killed in the blaze. One of whom was one of the performers, Annalise Broux, a young woman of Creole descent. The opera being performed at the time was *La Conzoni di Vita*. Maggie vaguely recognized the title. In fact, she had heard other pieces by that composer. What was his name?

Her eyes scanned the paragraph, landing on his name.

Renaldo D'Antoni.

Another shudder not stemming from a draft shook her whole body.

Renaldo D'Antoni. Ren Anthony.

She snapped the book shut, fumbling to stack it back with the others. No. It couldn't be.

She backed away from the shelf, still staring at the spine of the book. Hadn't she just said that coincidence and signs ran rampant in this city?

But this was too crazy to be part of the peculiar vibe of the city. This would mean that Ren was . . . she tried to calculate roughly the age he'd have to be.

That opera was roughly ninety years old by the time it was performed at the French Opera House. So that would make Ren well over 150 years old.

She blinked at the shelf, the books now only a colorful sea in front of her as her rattled mind tried to decipher what she was thinking.

Nonsense, her mind finally told her. Utter nonsense.

He couldn't still be alive. And only in his late twenties. A weak laugh escaped her—she must be mad to even consider this idea.

"Did you find anything interesting?"

A small squeak escaped Maggie as she turned to see the man from outside.

She pressed her hand to her chest, laughing nervously. "I'm sorry. You startled me."

"I'm sorry, my sweet." He did look genuinely regretful. "Anything you like?"

She nodded, managing to sound relatively normal. "Yes. You have a lot of fascinating books."

He nodded. "Well, let me know if you have any questions."

She told him she would, and then she forced herself to wander some more, absently browsing the aisles.

Finally, she purchased a book of postcards, feeling like she should buy something. Then she stepped back onto the street. The sky had darkened to a slate gray and the rain was coming down in earnest now.

She hurried down the sidewalk, avoiding the largest of the ominous filth-filled puddles, making her way back to her hotel to get clean clothes. The hotel that now stood where the Opera House had once been.

When she entered the lobby, she went right to the service desk. Jo and Erika had said they would bring her suitcase down to the front desk when they checked out, so she could then check back in to a single.

At the front desk, the woman told her that Jo and Erika had already had her room changed, and her luggage was waiting for her there.

Maggie smiled. She could kiss her friends. All she wanted was to get into her room, into a hot shower and talk herself out of the absolutely crazy theory she'd developed—all because of a similarity in name.

She accepted her new key card, gave her thanks to the desk clerk, then headed to the elevators.

Her mind still buzzed with the fact that she'd actually considered that she might—and this truly was the craziest might ever—be having sex with a man who was nearly two centuries old.

She stepped off the elevator, trying to recall what room number the lady had told her.

"Two . . . two-twenty?" she said to herself, trying to recall, when she turned the corner and saw a figure sitting on the floor in the hallway.

She hesitated, and considered turning around and heading back down to the lobby as the figure rose.

"Maggie."

Feeling ridiculous at her jumpiness, she realized it was Ren. Of course, if Ren was two centuries old maybe she should be jumpy. She almost laughed at her silly thoughts earlier today.

"What are you doing here?" she asked as she approached

him. He didn't look dead or old, she decided. He looked gorgeous, his hair damp, his shirt clinging to his broad chest.

He gave her a sheepish smile. "When I woke up and you were gone, I was afraid you decided to end things early."

Part of her wondered if that might not be a good idea. Safer for her heart. She had to admit she was shaken. Last night had been so intense. So right. And she did feel very invested in him, which was not a good idea. An even crazier idea than him being some sort of undead creature.

But as she looked at him, she knew she wasn't going to end it. She'd take whatever time she had, whatever way she could have it.

"No. I just woke up and decided to go for a walk. I left you a note."

He frowned. "You did? Where?"

"On that kitchen table."

"Oh," he said. "I missed it."

"So you came here to camp out until I finally returned."

His expression was again very sheepish as he nodded. "Sort of stalker-ish, huh?"

Maggie laughed. "Sort of. But in your case, more romantic than stalker."

"I'll take that."

He kissed her.

"Come in while I take a shower. Then we'll go to that restaurant you mentioned?"

"Sure. Do you have a fancy dress?"

"Yes," she said as she slid the keycard into the door and pushed it open. "Is it that fancy?"

She gave him a questioning look, then noticed he was wearing one of his funky sort of rocker-style shirts and faded jeans. Which looked fantastic but not fancy, exactly.

He shook his head, giving her that Cheshire cat smile. "Not necessarily. I just want to see you all dressed up."

She rolled her eyes, but then went to her suitcase to pull out a black dress that Jo had given her because it didn't fit right. The dress was better suited to Maggie's lush curves—a rare find in fashion. She rummaged around for undergarments and the heels she wore with the dress.

Behind her, she noticed Ren waiting around, seemingly agitated, as he had been the last time they were here.

"Did you know this was the site of the French Opera House? It burned down in 1919."

She sensed rather than saw him stop.

"Yeah, I did know that. The French Opera House was a beautiful building."

Maggie turned to look at him.

"Or so I have heard," he added.

She nodded, another chill running down her spine. But as she looked at him, she just couldn't reconcile all that warm skin and live muscle with her strange theory based on a name in a book. It was nuts.

She picked up her clothes. "I'll be quick. Feel free to check out the mini bar if you want."

Ren watched her disappear into the bathroom. Relief at being with her again almost calmed his tense muscles, but not quite. He forced himself to sit on the queen-size bed in the center of the room.

He'd woken up earlier than usual, because of the storm blotting out the sun. He'd actually panicked when he'd realized Maggie was gone.

His first thought was that his reticence with her comment about moving to New Orleans had driven her away, that she'd decided to end things.

He'd thrown on his clothes and headed straight here. And then he'd waited, sitting in the hallway, leaning on her door like a desperate teenager or a deranged stalker—neither one a role he'd ever thought to find himself in.

When she arrived, and didn't order him to leave, his muscles had weakened with relief, making him nearly sag against the wall.

Ren heard the shower start, the rush of water a calming sound. He listened to her movements in the other room.

He looked around the room, wondering what prompted her to mention the structure that had once stood in this building's place. Probably one of the staff mentioned it to her; since it was a tourist town, everyone considered themselves a guide.

He heard the scrape of the shower curtain. He imagined Maggie standing in the shower spray, water cascading over all those lush, soft curves. His discomfort and worries faded with the vividness of the image. As had been the case since meeting Maggie, good sense took a backseat to his desire. He rose from the bed and knocked lightly on the door.

"Yes?"

He pushed the door open. "I was thinking." Was he really going to suggest this? How would this help either of them? It wouldn't. Still he couldn't not ask. "Why don't you spend the rest of your vacation with me?"

Maggie peeked out at him from behind the shower curtain, her face rosy and wet. "I was planning to."

He smiled. "No. I mean not even keep this hotel room. Just bring your stuff to my place."

Maggie's smile deepened. "Okay."

His body reacted instantly. "Did you happen to need help in there?"

Her wide grin transformed into a sexy smile. "I was just thinking I might."

Ren smiled. "Good. Because I'm just your man."

He closed the door, leaving behind everything but warm water, slick soap, Maggie, and total ecstasy.

"Did I mention how much I love that dress?"

Maggie laughed. "Just once or twice."

Now that she was in his company, after the toe-curling sex in the shower, and now this incredible dinner, she wondered what had her so keyed up earlier today. She felt good with him.

"Want to go get a drink?" he asked as they stepped out of the restaurant. The rain had stopped and actually managed to take a little of the humidity with it.

"Sure." Her veins already buzzed with the warm merriment of two glasses of chardonnay, but she felt so good and happy, she wanted the night to go on forever.

And she had to admit that she loved being seen with Ren. Several times she'd noticed women doing double takes as he walked by. He didn't seem to notice, probably because he was used to it, but Maggie had never been on the arm of a man who garnered so much female attention.

Peter had been handsome. Average height, blond. But he wasn't the same kind of dynamic, truly beautiful handsome that Ren was.

She knew they must make an odd couple. Probably part of the double takes, too. But she didn't care. She was pleased with this time. She planned to enjoy it fully. And if she left to go back to D.C. with a hefty crush to get over—she'd deal with that then.

As she expected, Ren led her back to the small bar they'd gone to on their second night. When they entered, she also wasn't surprised to see Vittorio seated on one of the stools at the bar. He chatted with Sheri, although they acknowledged them with a nod when they entered.

"Leave it to you to show your lady the best that New Orleans has to offer," Vittorio teased.

"Hey," Sheri said, feigning offense as she snapped at Vittorio with a bar towel.

"Yeah, hey," Ren agreed, waiting for Maggie to take a stool. She did, and found herself sandwiched between the very attractive Anthony brothers. Then she paused. Vittorio was Ren's half brother. Maybe they had different last names.

"Ren said that you are half brothers."

Vittorio nodded, not making eye contact with her. Instead he focused on running his index finger along the rim of his highball glass.

"Yeah," he said, and again she was surprised at how deep his voice was. It just didn't match his face.

"So is your last name Anthony too?"

He smiled at that. A strange, almost enigmatic curve of his lips. "Nope. It isn't. It's actually Ridgewood."

She nodded.

"Same mother, different dads."

Maggie nodded. "Ren doesn't seem to be overly fond of your mother."

She regretted the comment as soon as it was out. Maybe she shouldn't have said that, but Vittorio's reply squelched any worries that she'd said too much.

"Our mother is a very difficult woman to love." He took a sip of his drink. "Or even like, for that matter."

Maggie was intrigued. Could she really be as awful as they said? She supposed she must be, since neither brother had reason to lie.

"Where does she live?"

"She moves a lot." He took another sip of his drink. "I'm not really sure where she is at the moment."

"That's funny, that's what Ren said about you. Should we expect her to show up before the night is over?"

Vittorio grimaced. "God forbid."

"What are you two talking about?" Ren asked as Sheri, who he'd been chatting with, left to wait on the only other patron, in the back of the bar.

"Our mommy dearest."

Ren grunted. "Joan Crawford would have been a god-send."

Vittorio nodded.

"What did she do that's so bad?" Maggie knew she was asking far too sensitive a question, but she couldn't help her-self.

The brothers exchanged looks.

"It's all pretty hard to explain," Ren finally said.

Vittorio nodded, taking another drink.

"Did you two grow up together?" It was clear to Maggie that they loved each other, and it made her feel better to think that even with a terrible mother, they at least had each other.

Ren shook his head. "We met when we were—in our twenties. I was in my late twenties actually."

Maggie frowned, then glanced at Vittorio. She caught him giving Ren a sharp look, which disappeared when he realized Maggie was watching him. Instead he smiled almost smugly. The expression would have been amusing if it wasn't so puzzling.

But she let that go, returning to what Ren had said. "Late twenties? How old are you now?"

Ren gave her a look that was just as amusing in its stunned quality.

"Umm, I'm thirty. I guess I must have just lost track of time. We met in our early twenties. Right?"

Vittorio nodded. "Yeah. I wasn't even twenty yet."

Well, that Maggie could believe. He only looked about twenty-three or so even now. But he did have an angelic quality to his features that made it hard to guess his age. And something in his dark eyes could, at times, make him seem almost old. An old soul, maybe.

She glanced at Ren. He had that look too. She'd thought of it as haunted, but maybe that wasn't quite the right description. Maybe it was the look of an old soul.

She considered that for a moment, then realized the brothers had moved on to talking about the band.

"So have you gotten a keyboardist yet?" Vittorio asked.

"No. We are just having whoever can fill in, or just set the keyboard up to play on its own. Last week we had Merrick."

Vittorio made a face. "God, you're better off not having a keyboard player at all."

"You could come back," Ren said, giving his brother an inviting look.

"No." Vittorio's answer was definite, as if this idea had been posed before.

Ren didn't push the issue. Instead he took a sip of his drink.

"You play keyboards?" Maggie asked, knowing the answer was obvious, but feeling the need to dispel the tension between the two of them.

Vittorio nodded. "I do—but not like Ren. Isn't that right, Renaldo?"

Ren's head shot up, and he glared at his brother. He didn't answer. Instead he ordered another drink.

Maggie stared at his profile. Renaldo? A cold chill curled down her spine. Renaldo.

She studied him, only stopping when Vittorio said, "Ren says you also play piano."

Maggie glanced back at Ren for a moment, then turned to Vittorio, nodding. "Yes. Not well."

Ren's attention, which seemed focused some place faraway, returned to Maggie.

"She's great. She plays better than most people I've ever met. But she tries too hard. She doesn't allow herself to enjoy the music."

Maggie blinked, surprised by Ren's words. She hadn't realized he thought so much about her playing. He'd said it was terrific, but not much else. She didn't react, though. She couldn't. She'd had too many years of Peter's telling her that she wasn't good to let go of.

"That's an easy thing to do," she heard Vittorio say.

Ren touched her, placing his hand over hers, his fingers and palms encompassing hers.

"She needs to believe she's good." His eyes were intent as they held hers. She could believe his sincerity, his absolute belief in her.

She suddenly felt overwhelmed by her feelings for this

man. She stared into the amber and green eyes. Eyes of an old soul, and she knew in that instant that if she allowed herself to dream, to imagine, she could fall in love with this man.

She broke their gaze, shaken by the very idea. Shaken by the idea that she could be falling in love with Renaldo Anthony. Renaldo D'Antoni.

"Umm," she tried to gather herself. "I-I have to go use the restroom."

She slid down off the barstool, her legs rubbery and weak under her. She held the edge of the bar for a moment to steady herself.

Ren still looked at her with that intensity of his. She could feel Vittorio's eyes on her too, but she couldn't look away from Ren long enough to read his expression.

She gathered herself and squeezed out from between them, heading blindly in the direction of the bathrooms, she hoped.

She needed a moment alone to get this stupid idea of love out of her mind. She would let that random thought go. She had to. She couldn't take any more heartbreak. And Ren had made it pretty clear that's all he had to offer.

And there was the fact of the name. That was still a stretch—to say the least. But that had her shaken too.

Ren watched Maggie walk away. Her movements seemed calm, but her agitation filled the air like a sudden cloud of thick smoke.

Once she disappeared into the restroom, he turned back to Vittorio, glaring at his brother.

"Why the hell did you use my real name?"

Chapter 21

Vittorio hardly looked remorseful as a rare wide smile curved his lips. "You do know that you are in love with her, right?"

The question threw Ren. No, he wasn't.

"You are," Vittorio said, as if Ren had spoken his denial aloud. Then he nonchalantly took a drink from his highball glass—as if he hadn't just made an announcement that was so ludicrous, so insane, that Ren couldn't have spoken if he wanted to.

"I have to admit," Vittorio said, after he finished swallowing his drink, "I never thought you'd get the sense to pick someone like Maggie."

Ren, whose mind was still swirling with the idea that Vittorio believed he was in love, frowned at him.

"What are you talking about?"

Vittorio's lips twisted. "I'm talking about the fact that you've finally gotten a clue. Maggie seems perfect for you."

What on earth was his brother talking about? Vittorio had never struck him as a particularly romantic—or delusional—person.

Ren shifted away from his brother. "I think you are reading way too much into this, bro."

"You've done it with her."

Ren gave him a disbelieving look. "Well, yeah. But I've

done it with a hell of a lot of women." He leaned forward to peer into his brother's eyes. "Vittorio, are you feeling all right?"

"I'm not talking about sex, you idiot." Vittorio shook his head, giving Ren a look that stated he was truly doubting his intelligence.

But then Ren was starting to doubt it, too. He had no idea what his brother was talking about.

Vittorio sighed, setting aside his glass. "You shared energy with her. You gave yours to her."

Ren nodded. "Yes. But that doesn't mean I'm in love with her. Hell, I was just thinking I wanted to make her come like she never had before."

Vittorio nodded, seeming to agree that was a good plan. "But you've never wanted to do that before, have you?"

Ren had already considered that fact. But now, with his brother making it into some monumental moment, he considered his past. Surely, somewhere in two centuries he'd shared his energy with another woman. Although off the top of his head he couldn't recall who.

"Ren, I can feel your energy in her. It's as much a part of her life force as her own energy now. You've branded her. You've marked her as yours."

Ren's brows drew together so tightly he could practically feel them meeting in the middle of his forehead.

"Sharing energy doesn't brand the person."

"It does if you love that person."

Suddenly irritation that Ren didn't even understand coursed through his body. "Why the hell are you telling me this?"

"Because I can't believe you are so stupid that you don't actually know it yourself." Vittorio was totally unshaken, his quiet confidence irritating Ren even more.

"You have no idea what you are talking about."

Vittorio's attention, however, wasn't on Ren. He looked past his right shoulder, smiling politely.

"I'm sorry," Maggie said from behind Ren. "Should I give you guys a minute?"

Ren turned on his barstool to see her standing a few feet away. From her expression, he didn't get the feeling she'd actually heard what they were discussing, just the agitation in their voices. Okay, his voice.

He stared at her for a moment. Tousled hair, intelligent eyes surveying the situation, her lush body and tentative smile clinging to bow-shaped lips.

He pulled in a deep breath, stealing a little of the energy in the room with the inhalation. And then he felt it. Her energy mingled with his. His vibe on her, in her.

Fear tightened his chest. He *had* marked her. He had made her his.

He did love her.

Maggie walked silently beside Ren, still confused by what she'd returned to in the bar. Ren hadn't given her much chance to decipher the strange tension hanging in the air between the two brothers. He'd said their good-byes to Vittorio and Sheri, and herded her out the door.

She'd attempted small talk, feeling the need to fill the air between them. But she only received one-syllable answers.

Even in the courtyard, he didn't acknowledge her any more than to move back for her to enter. And again, as on the previous night, she had the strange feeling that whatever he and Vittorio had been discussing involved her.

Tonight, he actually seemed even more remote.

She stepped into his house, then turned to look at him, grateful for the light. Now, maybe she could read his expression.

But she couldn't. Not in the least.

"I'll be right back," he said, even his voice distant, cool.

"Okay." She frowned. What had happened in the brief time she'd been in the restroom?

She watched as he headed up the stairs. When he was no longer in view, she wandered around his living room, trying to decide what she should do.

She glanced back to the stairs, listening. She heard him walking around above her, his footsteps making the floorboards creak.

She immediately got the image of him up there pacing, as he did when he was agitated.

For a moment, uncertainty held her still. Worry kept her feet from moving. Was he upset with her? Did he want to tell her something, but didn't know how? Did he regret asking her to stay here with him?

Then she grimaced at her insecure thoughts. If any of those concerns were true, well, he needed to tell her. She deserved to know what was going on—what had changed so abruptly.

She headed for the stairs, not allowing her self-doubt to slow her pace. Something was bothering him, and he was going to tell her.

When she reached the top step, she saw she'd been exactly right. Ren was indeed pacing. Maggie was surprised the varnish wasn't worn away along what appeared to be his favorite path.

He paused when he saw her. He ran a hand through his hair, the gesture another sign of his agitation.

"What's going on, Ren?" She managed to sound calm, despite the tightness in her chest.

What if he told her they were done? That he didn't want her? That strange, almost pained look on his face—she was sure it was something bad, something he truly dreaded telling her.

She knew she only had three days with him, but she wasn't ready to end it any sooner than she had to. She wasn't ready to let go of this kind of passion. This kind of . . . she didn't let her thoughts go there.

"Ren, what happened back at the bar?"

He didn't answer her. He only looked at her with an expression that broke her heart—as if he wanted to tell something her so very much, but just couldn't.

For a moment, she could swear she saw love in his eyes,

but she quickly squelched that idea. After all, he'd made it very, very clear love was the last thing he had to offer.

Still she couldn't stop herself from walking over to him. That expression called to her. He wanted to say something and couldn't.

She understood that. She had things she wanted to say to him too. That he'd made her feel more beautiful than anyone ever had. That he'd given her back so much that she'd lost. That she loved him.

But those things could never be said. She knew that. She knew that would force him to end what time they had left.

So instead, she rose on her tiptoes and pressed a kiss to his lips. Her hands framed his face, stroking the raspy skin of his jawline.

She loved him with her fingers and her mouth. She poured every ounce of her love for him into that single kiss, willing him to feel her emotions, even if he couldn't hear them.

He remained still for a moment, then growled deep in his throat. His arms came up to capture her, and then he was devouring her.

Their touches always built to this sort of wildness, this sort of passion, and she reveled in it. She did love him, God help her. She didn't want to feel this way. She wanted to keep herself removed from anything other than their passion, but she couldn't.

She pressed kisses to his cheek, trailing along his jawline. Down his neck to the curls on his chest. Her fingers moved to his shirt, plucking open the buttons, exposing more and more of his muscled chest. She pushed the shirt off his shoulders, running her palms over the hard muscles as she did. Then she slowly ran them back down his chest, reveling in the strength of him.

Ren made a noise low in his throat, then reached for the hemline of Maggie's shirt. Her hands left him to catch his fingers.

"No," she said, smiling naughtily. "I want to touch you."

His brows pulled together. "I want to please you."

There was so much concern in his voice, so much masculine need to be sure she was taken care of, that her heart leapt in her chest. This was one of the reasons she couldn't keep her heart separate from their passion. He made her feel treasured, adored—and she had wanted that her whole life.

"And I want to please you." Her fingers released him and nudged his hands out of the way. To her surprise, he let his hands drop loosely to his sides.

She slipped the fingers of one of her hands into the waistband of his jeans, while the other worked the button open. The rasp of metal against metal mingled with his exhaled breath as she tugged down the zipper.

She pushed his jeans down over his narrow hips, taking his boxers with them.

She stepped back to admire him. Long muscular legs dusted with dark hair, a rock-hard stomach and chest. Her eyes wandered back down him, to his erection, thick and heavy, prodding his belly in tiny hops of anticipation.

She smiled slowly. Good Lord, he was gorgeous. And he was hers . . . for now. But maybe for forever, if she could just convince him.

For a moment, her smile slipped and her confidence wavered, but she pushed her doubts aside.

Something was keeping Ren from falling in love, but she didn't think it was her, and she would work to help him get over whatever it was that was keeping his heart distant and aloof.

She stepped forward and touched the steely muscles of his stomach, letting her fingers slide slowly lower. She wasn't giving up any of this without a fight.

Ren watched in dazed silence as Maggie's little hands roamed over his body. Desire gripped him so tightly, he felt like he had to hold every single muscle within him in check, or he'd throw her down on the floor and drive himself into her over and over, until they were one. No separation, no beginning, no ending.

Maggie trailed her hands down over his hips, and kneeled in front of him.

He swallowed, watching her, never experiencing anything as arousing, as intense as this woman, on her knees before him. He should be the one kneeling before her. Bowed before the altar of Maggie.

She looked up at him, her hands framing his erection, touching him, but not quite touching where he most wanted her to.

She smiled, a slow sexy spread of her lips. His body tightened even more at the sight.

"You've become quite a tease," he managed, his voice hoarse and low.

Her smile widened as if that idea pleased her. It pleased him too—as long as her teasing was for him alone. A violent wave of possessiveness joined his arousal, heightening it, making him nearly mad for her.

"Is it really teasing," she asked, her fingers gently caressing, "if I intend to give you whatever you want?"

He made another noise in his chest. Damn.

Then Maggie leaned forward and ran the tip of her tongue up the sensitive underside of his cock.

He could no longer keep his hands down at his sides; they reached for her shoulders, buried themselves in her hair.

She took his rock-hard length into her hands, angling him so she could take him into her hot, excruciatingly delicious mouth.

His fingers knotted in her hair, and his head fell back as he lost track of anything beyond what her mouth was doing to his body.

She licked him, sucked him, her tongue swirling and tasting.

The muscles in his thighs bulged as his release surged closer and closer. In the back of his mind, he told himself that he didn't want to orgasm this way, without her, but his body didn't listen. His hips bucked forward and she took him deeper between her lips. Her hand curled around the rest of the length that her mouth couldn't take; both continued to stroke, consuming him.

He shouted out her name as he spurted into her throat, wave after wave of ecstasy washing over her. She didn't pull back, she rode the waves with him, guiding him back to earth.

Finally, he opened his eyes to see her still kneeling before him, a small satisfied smile on her glistening lips.

His body immediately reacted again. He reached down, catching her under the arms, pulling her to her feet. Then he swung her up into his arms, intent on laying her on the bed and undressing her slowly. He attempted to take a step, only to realize his pants were still wrapped around his ankles.

Maggie's beautiful laughter filled the room as he fumbled with his shoes, trying to toe them off so he could kick aside his pants.

Ren laughed too, and realized there was something incredibly sexy and appealing about laughing at a moment like this. Appealing and addictive.

His laugh faded.

Maggie noticed immediately, her own laugh fading too. "What's wrong?"

He didn't answer immediately, because he didn't know what to do—he couldn't let her go, but he couldn't keep her.

One of Maggie's hands came up to gently touch his cheek. "Are you okay?"

No. No, he wasn't. But he nodded.

She leaned up and pressed a sweet kiss to his lips.

"Are you no longer in imminent danger of tripping?"

Despite the turmoil inside him, he smiled. "Yes. I think I've got things under control."

"Good. Let's go to the bed. I've got other things I want to do with you tonight."

Again, despite himself, he smiled. "I have created a monster."

She laughed, but then shook her head. "No. You've made me happy."

Her words should have made him uncomfortable, but instead, he just felt proud, and really, really good.

Maggie awoke, cocooned in the usual darkness of Ren's bed, although it was no longer a source of confusion. Now, it was a comfort. A nice place to be.

She curled up against his side. As was his way, he didn't move; he was sleeping like the dead.

She sighed contentedly, with well-earned exhaustion. Even now, the memories of last night were enough to curl her toes. They'd made love, slow and steady and mind-blowing. The entire time, he'd watched her, as if memorizing every nuance of her reactions to him.

She stroked his hair and couldn't suppress the words bubbling up in her chest, desperate to be spoken.

"I love you," she whispered, still touching his silky locks. Ren slept on, oblivious to her feelings, which was probably for the best.

She sighed again and stretched. She should be tired, but she felt great, her whole body alive.

Carefully, she crawled out of the curtained bed. She wandered downstairs, hoping that she'd soon feel like crawling back into bed with Ren, But every cell in her body was vibrating with energy. It wasn't an unpleasant feeling, but she was finding it hard to stay put.

She considered going back up and waking Ren for a little more lovin'. She rooted around in her purse, finding her cell phone to check the time. Yep, "afternoon delight" certainly fit.

She crossed over to the windows. Watery sunlight filled the courtyard. Wispy clouds drifted across the sky. It didn't look like rain again, but it didn't look as if the sun would totally prevail, either.

She glanced back up to the stairs, again debating going back to bed. She decided against it. Ren was an incredibly deep sleeper, possibly a sign that he didn't get enough rest, and he did have to work tonight.

Besides, she had something she wanted to check out. She knew it was crazy, utterly crazy, but since Vittorio had called him Renaldo, that far-fetched thought about Renaldo D'Antoni had refused to go away. She had to prove to herself that it was nothing more than a coincidence.

She hurried back upstairs, moving on tiptoes, even though she knew there was really no purpose. Ren would never wake. That realization lingered, adding to this outlandish idea she had.

She dismissed it, but didn't dismiss her plan. At the very least, a little research would get rid of this crazy idea. And it was crazy. As if Ren could be—she couldn't even say it in her mind. Ren wasn't some sort of immortal being.

She shook her head at her own craziness. But she did hurriedly get dressed.

Chapter 22

Finding the library was relatively easy. Stepping inside had been a little more difficult. She couldn't believe she was doing this. Yet, she knew she had to, for her own piece of mind.

She stared at the large front doors of the library. Research wouldn't hurt; it was what she did for a living, after all. Just not usually on the men she was sleeping with. Of course, she'd never suspected that she was sleeping with a person who should have been dead over two centuries ago.

"This is nuts," she muttered to herself, even as she moved up the steps toward the door.

She walked inside, strolling up and down the stacks, probably appearing to any of the other browsers like someone casually looking for a good read. But she knew what she wanted.

Renaldo D'Antoni. A lesser-known composer. She perused the shelves, half-expecting a book about classical music to leap off the shelf in front of her. After all, coincidences had happened since she set foot in this city. A book toppling off the shelf in front of her wouldn't be that strange, would it?

But no books offered themselves up to her. So she stopped her wandering and headed to the bank of computers at the front of the library near the checkout desk.

Carefully, she typed in Renaldo D'Antoni, only pausing once at her own insanity. But once she was finished, she hit Enter with decisive force. She wouldn't discover anything, and she would be able to laugh about the ridiculousness of the notion.

And if she did discover something? Well, of course, she wouldn't.

She printed out the list of books with references to Renaldo D'Antoni, then headed back to the stacks to find the books.

Once she had four books piled in her arms, she headed to the back of the library to a table. She set down the books, then settled herself onto one of the tweed-covered chairs.

Taking a deep breath, as if she was getting ready to dive into a deep pool of water, she opened the first book and searched for the section about the composer, who was long gone. And certainly not back in the French Quarter sleeping in a decadently comfy, red velvet bed.

She paused. She really should be back there with him, not on some wild goose chase.

But she forced herself to focus on the words in front of her. She softly read the words aloud.

"Renaldo D'Antoni was born in 1785. Believed to be the illegitimate son of John Frederick Stansfield, the fifth Duke of Ashfordshire, and Italian opera singer Orabella D'Antoni. D'Antoni disappeared in 1815, right at the cusp of achieving real success."

Maggie considered that. So there was no actual date of death? The hairs on her arms rose. She attributed the reaction to the humming air-conditioning overhead.

She read on, but the book told little more about him other than discussing his better-known pieces, including the opera playing at the Opera House the night it burned down.

She pushed that book aside and reached for the next.

This book also noted who his father was suspected to be,

and made mention of his disappearance. Maggie was some-what familiar with a few of his pieces, but she'd never known he had disappeared. Interesting.

She flipped through another book, this one showing copies of his compositions, actually done in his own hand.

Maggie stared at the nuances of the handwriting. The flares at the end of the notes, the varying pressures of the quill.

This was one of the methods she used to identify com-posers. That and the style of the music itself. Composers often had favorite note combinations, favorite keys, even fa-vored instruments to highlight in their compositions.

But without the pieces back in her office, she couldn't do an in-depth analysis. She could compare the pieces in the book to each other, and she could see recurrences in style. Renaldo D'Antoni had a real flair, signatures in his music he maybe didn't know about himself.

One of them being a partiality to the minor keys—the key of the piece Maggie had heard Ren playing.

Then she recalled the beginnings of a song written on the pad back in Ren's apartment. Written in a minor key.

She shook her head at her own thoughts. That was hardly incriminating evidence. Pushing that book aside, she moved on to another. This one again mentioned his disappearance and his illegitimacy. His presumed father sponsored much of his music. Renaldo, when not entertaining the aristocracy, stayed at one of the Duke's estates in Essex.

Maggie's fingers froze. Where had the compositions she'd been sent been found? In the attic on an estate in . . . Essex sounded right, although she couldn't quite remember.

Another chill stole over her. Darn air-conditioning.

She suppressed a shudder and read on, mumbling the words aloud.

"His mother eventually married the fourth son of an earl, and gave birth to another son. Although D'Antoni's half brother was a musician of some renown himself, Vit"—Maggie stumbled over the name, ice pouring into her veins—"Vittorio Ridgewood never achieved the fame of his older brother."

She shivered. Okay, that was a coincidence that was pretty hard to explain. Very, very hard to explain. In fact, everything up to this point could be explained away. Strange, but not proof of anything. But Vittorio Ridgewood—that she couldn't ignore.

She stared at the words on the page, just to prove to herself that she didn't make up what she'd just read. The words stared back at her in bold black. But what was she looking at? Was she really and honestly thinking Ren was Renaldo D'Antoni, and somehow still alive? And not only alive but . . .

She looked at his birth year, then the year he disappeared. He would have been thirty years old. The age Ren said he was.

Okay, this was nuts. Absolutely nuts. She shoved the book away from herself, then stared blankly, trying to decide what to do with this information.

Ren Anthony was Renaldo D'Antoni. And he was . . . immortal. A ghost? A vampire? A monster of some sort?

She immediately dismissed the monster theory. He wasn't that. She'd certainly never felt fear in his presence. Good Lord, she'd been more comfortable with him than any man in her past. And he was dead? Or undead? Or . . .

She made a noise in the back of her throat.

These all had to be weird coincidences, right? After all, there really wasn't any other feasible explanation. Vampires didn't exist.

She continued to sit there, stunned. Then she reached for the final book. Surely something in this one would prove that all she'd read thus far was just strange happenstance.

She checked the index at the end of the book, then turned to the page where the segment on Renaldo D'Antoni began. She didn't have the section even fully open when she froze. In front of her was the only known picture of the composer

Renaldo D'Antoni, a rough charcoal sketch. It was completely undeniable proof. She was looking at Ren. Her Ren.

Maggie had just spent several evenings making love with Renaldo D'Antoni.

Ren awoke and knew immediately that Maggie wasn't in the house. He wasn't sure if he should be worried or relieved. He definitely couldn't say he was happy.

She'd told him she loved him. He'd heard her whispered words even through the blackness of his slumber. And somehow he knew they weren't a dream. She had said them.

Not that he'd needed to hear the words to know it. He'd seen it on her face last night as they'd made love. The emotions was there as clear as day—or as clear as he remembered day. And had he continued making love to her? Had he ended their lovemaking with a kiss in which he again filled her with his energy?

He'd done both. Even knowing she loved him and was in imminent danger, he hadn't stopped. What the hell was he thinking? And what the hell was he going to do?

Maggie had no idea how long she wandered around the French Quarter, trying to digest what she'd just discovered. How did one deal with finding out that the man you were insanely attracted to, *and* in love with, should have been dead many decades ago?

She didn't know. She had no idea whatsoever.

But she knew one thing. If Ren had meant her any harm, he'd had more than his share of opportunities to do so. From the first night on, no one had known where she was. Erika and Jo had never been to his place. Maggie had never told them where it was.

She knew she was probably being completely naïve—that woman in the horror movie who went to the basement to see what the strange noise was—but she didn't believe Ren meant her any harm.

Nor did Vittorio. Who she'd deduced was the same supernatural creature that Ren was—because he should be long dead too.

She also deduced Ren, and thus Vittorio too, must be a vampire. The name of his band, the Impalers. His penchant for sleeping like the dead, all day. His lack of appetite, for food, anyway. They all pointed to his being a vampire. Even Emile at the restaurant mentioning Ren's dislike of garlic. All vampire lore.

Still, Maggie was pretty certain Ren had never bitten her . . . she didn't think. She sighed. Who knew anymore?

Maggie stopped at a street corner, peering around her to get her bearings. It was getting dark, and she needed to decide what she was going to do. She still had no idea.

Should she just stay away from Ren? Or should she confront him with her knowledge? Would he think she was crazy? But *he* was the one who was undead.

She laughed at her own reasoning. The sound was a little crazed. Not good. This was so not good.

Then a thought hit her. What if she approached him with her knowledge and he killed her? Maybe it was one of those situations: "Now you know the truth, so you must die!"

Okay, she really must be naïve and crazy, because she had a hard time believing that one. Why, she really couldn't say.

She peered up into the waning light to read the street sign. Chartres.

She squinted down Chartres, realizing she was close to the fortune-teller's shop. Without thought, she moved in that direction.

Bells jangled as she pushed open the door to the shop and stepped inside. The calming scent of sandalwood immediately filled her nose, and she pulled it in deeply. She need calming. Boy, did she need calming.

An older, almost frumpy, woman greeted her from behind a counter where there was a register and several racks of crystal pendants and other mystical jewels. "How are you this evening?"

Maggie managed a smile, although it felt brittle and forced. "Is Hattie in tonight?"

The woman gave her a regretful smile. "She is, but she's just finished up her last reading."

Maggie nodded, turning to leave, just as Hattie and another woman stepped out from the back of the store.

Hattie was still speaking to the woman, but she lifted a hand toward Maggie, indicating that she saw her.

Maggie wasn't sure if that meant she was supposed to wait, but she wasn't sure what else to do, so she remained, studying a shelf of crystal balls, seeing her distorted reflection in a few of them.

Did Ren have a reflection? She'd been in bathrooms with him, but she couldn't remember. Another slightly crazed laugh bubbled up in her throat, but she suppressed it.

Hattie finished up with the woman, telling her that her instincts on this matter were totally right. Maggie wondered if that was a sign for her too. The woman thanked Hattie, then left the shop with another jingle of bells.

"Hello, Maggie," Hattie said, surprising her.

Maggie turned to smile at the older woman.

Hattie smiled in return, but Maggie could see her smile was filled with concern. "Come back with me."

"Oh," Maggie said, surprised. "I thought you were done for the evening. I don't want to hold you up."

Hattie shook her head. "You aren't. I think we need to talk."

Another chill snaked through her, a sensation which was becoming very familiar to Maggie today. She followed the older woman into the back.

"Sit," Hattie said, gesturing to the chair in her small closet of a room. Maggie did, perching on the edge of the seat, holding herself rigid.

"A lot is going on, huh?" Hattie said, as she took the seat across the round table from her.

You could say that, Maggie thought wryly, but she only nodded.

"I think I should use the leaves again, just to help clarify what I'm seeing."

Maggie nodded again, regarding her with a little uncertainty. She wondered what Hattie was seeing. Was it as weird as what she was seeing?

As she'd done the other day, Hattie prepared the tea leaves. Maggie turned the cup over, then watched as Hattie peered into it.

"So you did meet the new man."

Maggie nodded, even though Hattie was stating rather than asking.

Hattie looked up from the cup, narrowing her eyes. "I don't need the tea leaves to see that. I can sense him on you."

Maggie frowned at that. "You can?"

"He's inside you."

Maggie supposed that should sound slightly naughty, given the things they had done together, but she knew Hattie didn't mean it that way. And given her suspicions, she did wonder if there was more to them being together; him being inside her. She did feel different since meeting him, but was that really anything supernatural?

Maggie couldn't contain her own questions, her own need to understand what was going on.

"Can you see him?"

Hattie nodded, looking back into the cup. "Yes."

"Is—is he . . ." Maggie couldn't even say that words. It was just too insane.

"Maggie, you have nothing to fear from your differences."

Maggie's breath caught. "What are our differences?"

Hattie smiled at that, her expression indulgent. "You know. And you are right to believe he would never use his . . . oddities to hurt you. If anything, he wants to share them with you. He has already."

Maggie paused at that. He had? Then she suddenly knew it was true. Every time he'd made love to her, she felt a bonding, a connection, that seemed beyond anything she could have imagined.

"But I do see here," Hattie said, again gazing into the cup, "that you have a hard time ahead. Something that will shake you greatly. And you need to learn to trust totally."

She shook her head. "And I don't know if you can do that. The leaves are not clear on that count."

Maggie frowned. She knew trust wasn't easy for her, but what could happen that would shake her that much? After all, she was still considering remaining with Ren, and she wasn't even sure what he was.

"Just remember," Hattie said, holding Maggie's gaze, "not everything is as it seems."

Boy, was that true. Not comforting. Not helpful. But obviously true.

"This is all I can really see," Hattie said, her voice low and serious. "You have to trust yourself, and you also have to let him sort out what's holding him back. Give of yourself, and then let the cards fall into place."

Maggie left Hattie feeling oddly calm, but also still a little unsure. What did she do with all of this information? She walked a little longer, realizing from the darkness that Ren had probably gone to the bar to work.

She headed in that direction, taking her time, mulling over what she would do.

When she reached Bourbon, she picked up her pace, suddenly needing to see him. As she got closer to the bar, she recognized his voice, and that made her feel better. It made her realize that no matter what, she did trust him. Hattie said she needed to do that.

She had to tell him what she knew.

She walked into the bar fully expecting him to be aware of her the moment she stepped into the room. But instead, he continued to sing, not even looking in her direction. There was no sign he knew she was there.

How *not* vampire-y of him.

Maggie studied him from where she stood in the doorway. He certainly didn't look like a vampire, or whatever he was. And he'd never bitten her, at least not in the way she'd thought a vampire would. She didn't think nibbles here and there counted.

She strode over to the stage. She waved at him. He waved back, his expression neither surprised nor relieved to see her. His mouth was set in a grim line.

Did he know she knew? Her heart thumped in her chest, but she calmly walked to the back of the room to find a seat and wait to talk to him.

The set seemed to take forever, but finally Ren did announce they were taking a break. But like the first night, Ren didn't approach her. Instead he fiddled with the equipment.

Did he know something? He was certainly avoiding her. His demeanor was beyond chilly.

But she wasn't going to be frightened by his behavior. She walked up to the stage.

"Ren, can I talk to you for a minute?"

Ren glanced at her, almost looking surprised she was still there. She half-expected him to tell her no.

But he nodded, stepping down off the stage.

Maggie headed toward the side door that led to the sidewalk. Ren followed, but she noticed he kept his distance. Even when they faced each other on the street, he didn't get within arm's length of her. Something had happened to both of them since last night.

"What's up?"

Maggie stared at him for a moment. His tone was so cool and disinterested that her confidence wavered.

But she didn't buckle. Instead she met his aloof gaze.

"I know who you are," she stated. "Renaldo D'Antoni."

Chapter 23

Ren fought to hide his reaction. Shock that she had figured that out. Surprise that she wasn't recoiling from him in horror. Dismay that after finding out who he really was, she didn't appear to be willing to let him go, to flee of her own accord.

Didn't this woman have a lick of sense or self-preservation? And he'd actually believed ignoring her was going to send Maggie packing? If finding out he was a composer who should have been dead 150 years ago didn't do it, the cold shoulder sure as hell wasn't about to work.

"You do realize what you've just said is crazy," he managed to say, too stunned to think of anything else.

"Yes, I do." She sounded so calm, so accepting, that it totally unnerved him. "But somehow, some way, you are him."

"I don't know what you are talking about," he said, trying to add as much disdain as he could.

"Yes, you do. And I think that's why you are afraid to have a relationship beyond a fling. It is a rather large secret," Maggie admitted.

Ren stared at her. She really did have an uncanny way of shocking him. She couldn't wrap her mind around the fact that he found her sexy, that he wanted to have sex with her, but she accepted that he was undead for nearly two centuries.

He frowned at her. She gazed back, regarding him with a calm and contemplative expression.

"So are you a vampire?"

"Maggie—"

"I'm deducing that from the band's name." Then realization widened her eyes slightly. She left him to peek in the doorway at the stage. Only Dave, the bassist, was up there, the rest down mingling with the crowd.

"They're all vampires too, aren't they?"

Ren didn't answer right away. Maggie was the first mortal to know the truth about him in over 150 years, and frankly, he didn't know how to react.

When she turned back to him, to his absolute shock, she reached for his face and tugged up his lip to inspect his canines.

"They look normal." She didn't seem relieved or disappointed, just matter-of-fact.

Ren jerked back and glared at her. Not a goddamned lick of sense.

"So are you going to just stand there and pretend you don't know what I'm talking about?"

Where had the timid, uncertain Maggie gone?

He shook his head.

"No. I'm not going to."

"And is that why we can't have something more between us?"

Ren widened his eyes. "Isn't that enough?"

"Not really," she said. "After all, you could have hurt me at any time, and you never did."

"No," he agreed, and that was why she had to go now—if it wasn't already too late. He glanced around, half-expecting a car to career out of control and hit her. Hell, a meteor to fall from the sky. His vampirism wasn't going to kill her, but her love for him would.

That was his curse. He considered telling her that outright, but from the look on her face, her trust and determination, she wouldn't listen. She might believe him. Hell, she should believe him.

She believed he was a vampire. But somehow he didn't think even impending death would deter her. And frankly, he was afraid he was too late. She'd said she loved him . . . and he loved her too.

So what the hell did he do?

He looked over at the hotel. Maggie's hotel. The site of Annalise's death.

He ran a hand through his hair. How the hell did he let this all happen? He'd known he was playing with fire from the moment he saw Maggie.

He had to save her. He had to make sure his curse didn't hurt her. Kill her. And her death was imminent unless he got her to leave. Got her to fall out of love with him.

He studied her face, seeing her feelings for him clearly in the set of her mouth, in the depths of her eyes. She wasn't going to walk—and even if she did, she wouldn't stop loving him.

Wasn't that something he'd been drawn to about her? The obvious loyalty he could feel in her energy. Maggie didn't fall in love easily, and she didn't fall out of love easily either.

What the hell was he going to do?

Maggie stepped up to him. Her small fingers touched his face, grazing his cheek, his hair, back to the curve of lips.

"Is it so terrible to imagine us having something more than a fling?"

He closed his eyes. No. God, no. Then he froze under her caress.

What the hell was he doing?

Maggie rose up on her tiptoes and pressed her lips lingeringly to his.

"I'm not afraid of whatever you are," she murmured against his mouth.

He pulled back. "You should be."

She stared at him, her eyes roaming over his face. "I just can't believe that."

"That's what scares me," he told her honestly. "Maggie—"

She came forward and kissed him again. Damn, he loved ever single thing about how she felt, how she tasted. The small noises she made when he deepened the kiss. But he couldn't continue this. She couldn't love him. He had to think of something to stop this.

But he couldn't think with her so close. With her knowing what he really was. Who he really was.

And that, in and of itself, was wonderful. He had never shared that with another mortal. Not Nancy. Not Annalise. He hadn't wanted to—yet, Maggie knowing about him felt absolutely right.

He took another step back from her. He was doing it again, allowing himself to believe that he could have this woman. That her acceptance of his vampirism was all he needed to allow him happiness, love.

But being a lampir was never the problem. Not really. It was his curse, and that he couldn't control.

He had to find a way to make her fall out of love with him. It was the only way to save her. The only way to ensure that the woman he loved remained safe.

"Maggie, this is a lot for me." He didn't have to lie about that. "I know that sounds really stupid, considering that you just discovered the man you've been sleeping with for the past week is actually 223 years old."

"Is that how old you are?" Again, she didn't sound upset. Just curious. Amazed.

"Yes."

"Who made you a vampire?"

Ren stared at her for a moment. Her calm curiosity really was unnerving. Which did seem a little strange, given that he should be the one freaking *her* out.

"My mother," he admitted. "And she made me a lampir, actually."

Maggie seemed stunned by that. "Really?"

"Yes," he said. "Maggie—"

"Is that why you hate her?"

His mouth snapped shut at her question. This really wasn't going well.

"In part," he answered, then attempted to move on. To buy some time until he could think of what to do. It really was impossible to think with Maggie here. "Maggie?"

"Was your father really the Duke of Ashfordshire?"

Ren nodded, growing a tad frustrated. He had no idea Maggie could be so tenacious.

"And he never accepted you as his son?"

"No."

Maggie shook her head, clearly disgusted. "That's terrible."

For a moment, her irritation with his illegitimate father blotted out his own frustration, filling the air around them with warmth. Acceptance.

Damn, she made him feel good. Really good.

He straightened. Get a friggin' grip. He needed to stay focused. He needed to protect her.

"Maggie?"

This time, she actually seemed to listen to him.

"Yes?"

"I know this sounds really strange, given what you know about me, but I need a little while to figure out how to deal with this."

Maggie didn't seem to find it strange at all. She nodded. "Okay. Do you want me to wait for you back at your place?"

He wanted to say no. Knowing she was there waiting for him was just too much of a temptation. He liked her being there far too much. Of course, whose fault was it that she was staying there with him? She really had nowhere else to go.

Not to mention, she was literally in danger. He shouldn't allow her out of his sight. He couldn't. What if the curse happened, and he wasn't even there to attempt to save her? Like with Annalise. He had been with Nancy, but he'd been no help. He couldn't send Maggie away.

There was no choice but for her to stay here. He had to keep an eye on her while he found a solution. A way to make her fall out of love.

There had to be a way to do that—although the thought of hurting her killed him. But heartache she'd get over. And then she'd be safe from him, safe from this goddamned curse.

"Come back inside," he said.

"Are you sure?"

No. He wasn't sure about anything. But he nodded.

When they went back inside, the Impalers were playing. Dave, the bassist, had taken the mic.

Ren could easily just take the night off again. It wasn't as if the band really cared. The owner cared more, but he wouldn't be that concerned. To be honest, it was a pretty quiet night.

But Ren couldn't deal with Maggie yet. And his only chance to get any thinking done was to go back on stage.

He walked her over to a vacant high-top table and waited with her while she got settled. She smiled at him when she was done. He must have sported a concerned look, because she touched his face again in a way that made him want to nuzzle against her open palm. Not a familiar feeling for a man who prided himself on being removed from emotions.

"Don't worry," she said.

Easy for her to say, but he nodded, turning to head back to the stage. He had to worry enough for both of them. And he had to think of some way to save her.

Maggie watched Ren as he waited at the edge of the stage for the song to end. Then he took the mic again. Tonight he didn't look at her as he performed, and she got the feeling he simply couldn't.

Was he ashamed of what he was? Why should he be? After

all, his mother turned him into a vampire. Or, what was the word he used? A lampir.

She kept waiting for fear and even disgust to hit her. She was seeing a vampire—or a lampir, for heaven's sake. But neither emotion appeared. She couldn't see him as a monster or an aberration. He was just Ren. The man who made her feel sexy and smart and talented and protected. The man who was everything she'd ever wanted in a man.

Did that make her weird? She smiled to herself. She didn't feel weird. She felt in love—and while that was pretty different, she didn't see it as strange.

Ren lifted the mic, belting out a portion of the lyrics, his voice raw with emotion.

She knew he was shaken, and she could understand why. After all, she'd managed to figure out his secret. She had the feeling not many people had.

But his secret was safe with her. He had to know that.

She just wanted the chance to love Ren. She didn't care who he had once been. She just wanted the man he was now. The one who'd never hurt her. She knew that, deep inside.

"Dude, you've got to stop letting your woman come here," Drake said with a sigh and a shake of his head. "She way frigs up your concentration."

Ren couldn't deny that. If he only knew how to get rid of her. He suppressed a groan. Just imagining her gone was hell. But he had to, he had to come up with a plan to drive her away. A plan to make her hate him.

He suggested a song—"My Own Worst Enemy" by Lit—then he tried to juggle the lyrics and his own thoughts.

What could he do that would make her hate him?

Just then, the redhead from a few nights earlier entered the bar. She immediately tried to catch his attention, pausing at the edge of the stage, her fingers curling around the railing.

He absently acknowledged her, and she grinned back. A

broad, inviting smile. One that stated exactly what she'd like to do with him.

He ignored the grin, until realization hit him. What was the one thing that Maggie would never forgive? What would kill every emotion she had for him, dead?

He glanced at Maggie. She smiled at him, her own smile as inviting as the redhead's—just in a more lovely and generous way. A way so deserving of love.

For a moment, he shoved his plot aside. He couldn't hurt her like that. Then he glanced out the window at the symbol of his past mistakes. The hotel. His mistakes that were unforgivable. Annalise had died because of loving him. He couldn't let that happen to Maggie. He loved her far too much.

His eyes locked with Maggie's once more. Pain so crippling that it stole his breath shot through him. But then he refocused on the redhead. He had to do this.

He had to find a mistake that Maggie couldn't possibly forgive. A "mistake" that would kill any love Maggie felt for him.

He smiled down at the redhead, putting as much open interest into the look as he could.

Maggie turned on the faucet in the women's restroom. The rust-stained porcelain and gunk-caked knobs hardly gave a person the sense of truly cleaning one's hands. But given what the bathroom stalls looked like, she had to attempt some sort of cleanliness.

Of course, she'd actually come into the filthy bathroom to do exactly what the facility was meant for—unlike the couple who'd come in after her and now held residence in one of the other stalls.

She turned to glance in the direction of the gray pen- and marker-scrawled door. At the moment, all she heard was the occasional shift of bodies, small breaths and moans, and soft giggles.

Maggie raised an eyebrow. She was insanely hot for Ren, but this bathroom was the last place she'd want to do that with him.

A low moan, definitely feminine, echoed through the filthy room. Maggie glanced that way again, seeing a black patent-leather, four-inch sandal in the space under the stall door.

Maggie shook her head, but had to smile. Okay, maybe, if Ren was very, very persuasive, she'd risk the filth to be with him here. But he'd really have to beg.

She laughed at that, then returned her attention to washing her hands.

She caught her reflection in the dirty mirror. Touching her hair, she realized that she hadn't even had a shower this morning. She'd been in such a hurry to go research Renaldo D'Antoni that she hadn't gotten to her usual ablutions. And then with what she'd learned—well it wasn't too surprising she hadn't thought of showering.

She fiddled with her wavy locks a little longer, then gave up. Given what she had discovered, she supposed she didn't look too bad.

Again the couple in the stall made noise. This time a low, very masculine moan joined the female one.

"Oh, yeah, baby," the woman whispered.

Maggie blinked at the door, then decided she'd shared the room with the amorous couple long enough. Once she started to hear their actual dialogue, she was getting far too involved.

Quietly, she opened the door—not that people who decided to shag in a public restroom were concerned with privacy. Still, Maggie felt the need to afford them a little.

The dance floor was only filled with ten or fifteen revelers, grinding and gyrating to the DJ's music. Maybe another six or seven people lined the bar, but otherwise the place was empty. And the band was on break.

Good, maybe Ren was feeling better and they could talk a little.

Maggie wandered toward the stage, seeing the drummer and the bass player still up there. The rest of the band members had disappeared, Ren included.

She stepped outside onto the sidewalk. Often the band went out to grab a breath of air, and she suspected that was where Ren waited. The two other guitarists were out there, leaning on the wall, chatting. But still no Ren.

She cast a look around the street, thinking maybe he decided to take a little stroll. She knew he was shaken by the fact that she'd pieced together who he really was. Which hadn't actually been that difficult. It was a wonder someone else hadn't figured it out before this.

A warm wave washed over her, adding to the flush that the humid air had already created on her skin. She knew she was the only human who knew the truth about him. She'd seen it in his eyes. She couldn't say why or how, but she'd sensed it in him, as if the truth was radiating off his body and she could "read" it.

The fact that this was their secret was thrilling to her. Thrilling and significant. She wasn't as sure about Ren's feelings for her, however. She did believe he cared for her, and that his true nature was what was holding him back from allowing things to deepen between them. But he hadn't told her what he felt. He hadn't used the "1 word" as she had—not that he'd heard her. But she did feel that he could love her. It might just take a while. After all, he hadn't allowed love for so long.

"You looking for Ren?" the guitarist with the goatee and shaved head asked.

She nodded. "Yes. I thought maybe he came out here."

The guitarist shook his head. "Not that I've seen. Last time I saw him he was talking with the red—"

The other guitarist, the one she'd never heard speak, elbowed the chatty one. The gesture, of course, put Maggie on alert.

Red? She considered that. The redhead. Oh, Maggie had noticed the woman from the other night had returned to the bar. Maggie had seen her leaning on the stage. She was hard to miss in her four-inch-high heels and skintight animal-print dress. This time a tiger print. She apparently favored exotic cats in her wardrobe.

Maggie had also noted that Ren was paying a little attention to her. But she had thought it was because she was indeed hard to miss. She also knew Ren was avoiding her; he was having a hard time with her knowing the truth, and Maggie understood that.

But Ren had been talking to the redhead? And had gone somewhere with her, obviously.

Suddenly she recalled the glimpses of feet under the stall door of the bathroom. High heels—ones she recognized. Worn with a tiger-print dress.

Without thinking over what she would do, what she would say if her suspicions were true, she rushed back to the women's restroom.

When she shoved open the door, she was greeted by the sounds of moans, the wet smacks of deep kisses. Revulsion washed over her. At least she hoped they were wet kisses.

And God, please God, don't let it be Ren in there with the redhead.

She hesitated at the stall door, then reached out a trembling hand and pushed. The gray, graffiti-covered door opened easily.

Her first limited glimpse revealed the woman pinned against the wall, her dress hiked up around her waist, her head flung back, auburn hair cascading around her, her red lips parted. The picture of wanton lust.

Then Maggie's gaze turned to the man, his head at her neck, kissing her. His hand between her thighs, his own shirt pushed down around his arms to reveal broad, muscled shoulders and back.

Even as Maggie stared at the man, at the long chestnut hair reaching the middle of his back, she told herself it wasn't him. It wasn't Ren.

Then he moved, kneeling down in front of the woman until his face was level with her . . .

He flipped his hair, and she saw Ren's tattoo. Cards, aces and eights. Right between his shoulder blades.

The dead man's hand.

Maggie stared at the flesh and ink, feeling like she was the one who'd died. Was dying.

Nausea hit her, and she shoved a hand to her mouth, trying to hold back the wretched feeling. But she couldn't hold back the wretched sound that escaped her lips.

Ren turned. His hazel eyes met hers. She heard the other woman make a shocked cry, but Maggie couldn't tear her eyes away from Ren to see her reaction.

"Maggie," Ren said.

Maggie still couldn't move. Her body wanted to run, just escape, but her feet didn't seem connected to her body. They remained still.

"Why?"

For a moment, she didn't realize the question came from her.

Ren shifted, and she vaguely noted his jeans were undone. The redhead had touched him. And he'd very obviously touched her.

Maggie swayed, feeling lightheaded.

"Maggie, this is who I am."

She stared at him. That was his explanation? That was it?

She stepped back from the stall, her movements clumsy, jerky, as if her feet still weren't truly a part of her body.

She half-expected Ren to follow her, but he remained, kneeling in God knows what, his head still level with the woman's. Another disgusted sound gurgled in the back of Maggie's throat.

The woman hadn't even covered herself. And Ren had remained in position. Maggie realized that when she fled that bathroom, these two were going to continue exactly what they'd been doing—as if she never existed.

Maggie battled the tears and the rush of nausea that threatened to strangle her. She turned from the sight, hoping that would help her gather her wits. But she knew that image would be forever burnt into her mind.

She somehow managed to find the door handle and pushed the bathroom door open, then she was free. She stepped through the doorway, and then she ran, not even sure where she was going. Not even seeing. Just trying to escape.

Chapter 24

Ren remained kneeling, watching as the bathroom door swung closed, seemingly in slow motion. And once it shut, he knew it was done. Maggie was gone. He'd never see her again.

His plan had worked. Any love she'd felt for him was dead. He remained motionless—unable to breathe, unable to react.

"She was rude," the woman stated from beside him, her nasal voice the vocal equivalent of nails on a chalkboard.

Ren felt her fingers tangle in his hair. Maggie had loved his hair. Played with it after they made love. Stroked it to comfort him.

Ren jerked away from the woman's touch, pure, undiluted disgust flowing into his veins as if a valve had been opened.

He rose, not even looking at the woman. "Get out."

The woman gasped, and didn't move. "What the hell's wrong with you? Don't tell me that little bit of nothing is going to ruin the good thing we had going here?"

Ren closed his eyes, more revulsion washing over him. This was what she considered a good thing? Had he really been with women like this for decades?

"Come on, baby," she murmured, again touching his hair.

This time he shoved open the door so hard it hit the wall with a deafening slam. "Go."

He heard her rustling behind him, adjusting her clothes.

"This is the ladies' room," she pointed out, as a hint he should be the one to leave. But Ren wasn't in the mood to be polite—or nitpick.

"Leave, goddamn it!"

The woman finished arranging herself and then teetered across the dirt-crusted tile floor. She didn't say a word as she stepped back out into the nightclub. In fact, no one would even guess what had just happened in there.

Funny that the ending of a man's existence could appear so uneventful.

Maggie wandered around the streets until she summoned the coherence to find a hotel. Fortunately, the first one she entered had a room—and fortunately, she had her purse. She didn't have the rest of her stuff. Her suitcase was still at Ren's. And she had no intention of going back to get it. The hell with her clothes. She had her wallet. She had everything she needed to get home, and she could live without everything else.

She managed to hold herself together long enough to check in and make it to her room.

But once the door clicked shut, she collapsed on the bed and the tears began to fall. Big, fat, frustrated tears, rolling down her cheeks.

How could she be so stupid? Not for being with Ren. Not even for trusting him. But for ignoring the things he told her from day one. That he'd never love her.

She made a noise, then rolled onto her side, bunching the pillow up under her head.

She really was a schmuck. She'd thought she had him all figured out. That he was holding himself back because of what he was.

She made another noise, pulling the pillow over her head. On top of everything else, she'd fallen for a vampire. And she'd thought Peter was a bad choice.

God, she was a mess.

She remained that way, the pillow over her head, half hoping the weight of it would eventually smother her. It didn't work, of course.

She tossed the pillow aside and stared up at the ceiling. Gradually, her disgust with herself, with her neediness and trust, morphed into irritation with Ren.

She hadn't imagined his feelings for her. He had been caring and attentive. His feelings were real.

She knew he'd felt as strongly about her as she did about him. So why would he take a chance? What made him want to destroy what they'd had?

She pushed upright, reaching for the pillow she'd flung aside, hugging it to her chest.

The image of him in that horrible bathroom stall, his hands on the most private parts of that woman. The image made the nausea rise up in her chest again. But she also recalled the look in his eyes. She focused on that, rather than the overall awful image.

He'd had that haunted look. That heartbroken look.

"Why?" she asked the empty room. Why had he done that? Why had he ruined what they'd had? Why?

"We're having a fucking great time tonight," Ren shouted out to the crowd. A crowd that consisted of about twenty people—most of whom didn't appear to be partying quite as hard as Ren was.

He weaved slightly, using the microphone stand to steady himself.

"Stacy," he shouted to the bartender, his voice over the mic deafeningly loud. "More Jäger! Shots for everyone! On me!"

That got the crowd cheering, which was good. Who the hell liked to drink alone?

Drake came over to him, placing a hand over the mic to speak to him privately. "Ren. I think maybe you should take off for the night. You ain't right, my friend."

Ren smiled, swaying as he did so. "You are right, my friend. I'm a fucking vampire. And I'm fucking cursed. I'm so not right. Not at all."

Drake frowned at him, then cast a look out at the audience, checking to see if any of them had heard Ren's announcement.

Like Ren gave a shit if they did. Maybe one of them would come up with the bright idea of staking him through the heart. He could go for that right about now. A stake had to hurt a hell of a lot less than the pain that was already there.

And the damned booze wasn't helping at all. He needed more.

He peeled Drake's hand off the mic. "Stacy!"

Then he noticed Vittorio in the doorway. What was it with his brother? He had this way of appearing so randomly. And frankly, tonight he wasn't in the mood for his brother's searching looks and know-it-all commentary on Ren's life.

Ren ignored him, turning to Drake. "Let's sing 'No Sugar Tonight' by the Guess Who."

Drake raised an eyebrow, perplexed. "We don't do that one."

Ren groaned, disappointed. "We really should."

Drake stared at him for a moment, then Wyatt, the always-quiet rhythm guitarist, joined them.

"Ren. I really think you should take the rest of the night off."

Ren blinked at the one band member who never voiced an opinion.

"Why?"

"You are drunk."

"So?" Hell, they were rockers on Bourbon Street; they'd all performed drunk before.

"You are a mess," Wyatt stated.

Ren blinked again. "I like you better when you don't talk."

Wyatt glanced at Drake and then backed away.

Drake leaned in toward the mic. "Hey dudes, we are going to take a break."

Ren frowned at the guitarist, then out at the crowd. Man, his band was a freakin' buzzkill tonight.

He watched as the band left the stage. Then he decided to follow. He'd get a drink faster if he went directly to the bar anyway. He stumbled across the stage, nearly tripping on some of the cords duct-taped to the floor. He also had to catch himself on the few steps leading down. When had all of this gotten so damned difficult?

"Ren?"

Ren stumbled to a halt, not suppressing his groan. He'd forgotten about his brother. Turning slowly, in part because that was the best way to keep the room from spinning and in part because he really didn't want to talk to Vittorio, Ren faced him.

"Where's Maggie?"

Ren groaned again and rolled his eyes. See, he knew he didn't want to talk to him.

"She's gone?"

"Gone where? I thought she was here for another two days."

"Was she?" Ren twisted back toward the bar. He needed a drink. Now.

But before he could take a step, Vittorio caught his arm.

"What's going on? What happened?" Vittorio demanded.

"Why do you do this?" Ren asked.

Vittorio frowned, clearly confused. "Do what?"

"Show up now. You disappear for weeks at a time, and then when I really don't want to see you, you show up. And meddle. You are a meddler."

Ren expected Vittorio to be hurt by his words, but instead he smiled. "And you are a drunk."

Ren stared at him, swaying a bit. "Fair enough. Then leave me to it."

"No." Vittorio tugged his arm, hauling him easily away from the bar. Several times Ren thought to struggle, but it was really hard enough just to concentrate on keeping his footing. He remembered Maggie when she'd slipped on the Mardi Gras beads. She'd been so mad. So mad and so cute.

He'd been able to fix that mad. He'd never fix what he'd done tonight.

"Where are we going?" he finally thought to ask, but by then Vittorio was pulling him into his favorite bar and toward the room in the back.

"Sit." Vittorio gestured to a barstool. Gladly, Ren did. God, he was drunk.

"So what's going on?"

Ren frowned at his brother. "Didn't you already ask that?"

"Yes. And you didn't answer."

Ren considered that. "Are you sure?"

Vittorio shook his head. "Man, you are a stupid drunk."

Ren tried to muster up some indignation, but he had to agree. Hell, he was just plain stupid. So totally and utterly stupid.

"Where is Maggie?"

"Gone," Ren stated, waving a hand. "Gone forever."

This information actually seemed to irritate Vittorio. "What do you mean? What asinine thing did you do now?"

Ren frowned at his brother. "This wasn't asinine. I saved her life—thank you very much."

Vittorio stared at him for a moment, took a deep breath and then perched on the seat next to him.

"Explain."

Ren shook his head. No. But for some reason his mouth didn't listen to his brain. "I saved her life." He took a deep breath. "I broke her heart, but I saved her life."

Vittorio again made a face—bewilderment and irritation at the same time.

"Explain. More."

"Maggie told me she loved me."

Vittorio's drawn eyebrows and grimace made it clear, even to Ren's addled mind, that he wasn't following.

"Sheri, I need a drink." Ren waved to the bartender.

Vittorio waited for him to continue.

Finally, Ren sighed and said what he hadn't said to anyone but Maggie—and she hadn't believed him. Little fool. "Dude, I'm cursed."

Again, Vittorio didn't react even remotely the way Ren thought he would. He laughed, his deep chuckle filling the back of the bar.

"What the hell are you talking about now?"

Ren stared at his brother. And he'd always considered Vittorio the sensitive one. The ass.

"I'm cursed. Mother cursed me. The bitch."

Vittorio studied him for a moment, then raised an eyebrow. "She made us both vampires, but I really don't think, in this case, that has to be a curse. I think Maggie would understand if—"

"She knows about that." Ren still couldn't believe she knew that. And that she hadn't even been remotely frightened by the idea. She could be so spunky, his Maggie.

His Maggie. He had no right to think of her that way. He nearly snatched the drink out of Sheri's hand as she went to place it on the bar in front of him. He took a long swallow, hoping the alcohol burning his throat would drive from his mind the memory of her face as she'd discovered him with the other woman.

It didn't.

But he'd done the right thing. He had. It felt like hell—it felt so completely wrong. But it wasn't.

"So did she freak out when you told her? Is that why she's gone?"

Ren shook his head. "No. She figured it out herself." He placed his drink on the bar. "She's so damned smart. Too smart for me." He shook his head just thinking about the intelligence he could see in her eyes. Smart, sweet, sexy. Perfect.

"So she was okay with it."

Ren nodded. "Yeah."

Vittorio stared at him, then sighed. "So what the hell are you talking about a curse for?"

"Because I'm cursed."

Ren got the feeling Vittorio wanted to scream—or maybe hit him. Vittorio's fingers clenched where they rested on the bar. Yeah, definitely hit.

Ren took another sip of his drink, which Vittorio then extricated from his hand and set further away.

"Explain this so it makes some sort of sense."

Ren looked longingly at the drink, but then pulled in a deep breath. "About ten years after Mother made us lampirs, she came to me to write her an opera. It was right after *La Conzoni di Vita* started to receive some attention. She wanted me to write an opera for her. Starring her. I refused. She was furious. A few days later, she returned and began chanting some sort of gibberish. You know, this was when she was in her dark-arts phase."

Vittorio nodded, then sighed. Their mother had been involved in everything from Satan worship to the kabbala.

"I just thought she was being ridiculous and melodramatic. Until I woke up the next morning with this." He pointed to his white eyelashes.

"I did wonder how that happened, actually," Vittorio said.

"Mom's curse." He pointed to it again, a way of reiterating his point.

Vittorio looked impressed. Frankly, aside from the vampirism, their mother hadn't been much good at her other supernatural pursuits.

"So what is the curse?"

Ren took another deep breath. "If anyone falls in love with me, they will die."

Vittorio immediately looked dubious. "Are you sure that's the curse? That doesn't sound like a Mom curse."

Ren nodded. He was sure. Far too sure.

"Remember Nancy? She was in love with me, and she died."

"She had the pox. Which she had long before she hooked up with you."

Ren tilted his head, trying to recall. "Did she?"

"Yeah," Vittorio said, as if Ren was the dumbest person on the face of the earth. Which he'd already decided he was.

"Wow. I didn't remember that. I guess it was a good thing I was already dead before I started shagging her."

Vittorio nodded.

"Okay, well maybe my curse didn't bring on the demise of Nancy. But what about Annalise? She died in that freak fire at the Opera House."

Vittorio actually seemed to pale at the mention of the long-dead opera singer.

"You didn't have anything to do with her death."

"You can't be sure." Ren pointed to his eye again. "Huh? Huh?"

Vittorio stared at him for a moment, then shook his head, a dry laugh escaping him. "I really cannot believe that you have believed this for years. Based decisions in your life on this cockamamie idea."

"It's true," Ren stated, reaching for his drink, but Vittorio lifted his arm to block him.

Ren grimaced at the drink—so close, yet so far away.

"Ren, Annalise didn't love you. She came on to any man who got in a hundred-foot radius of her."

Ren stopped grimacing at the drink and frowned at his brother instead. "No, she didn't."

Vittorio laughed again, another humorous bark. "She did. She hit on me on a regular basis. She hit on dozens of men while you were together. She was just like our mother, for God's sake. Greedy, shallow, narcissistic."

Ren considered that, then shuddered.

"Was I really attracted to someone like our mother?"

Vittorio gave him a remorseful look, then nodded.

Ren made a gagging noise. "Good God."

"Ren, I really don't think that is the curse Mother put on you."

Ren considered that, then actually felt ill. Had he really hurt Maggie that deeply, that intensely, for no good reason? He swiped a trembling hand through his hair.

Vittorio reached out and touched his arm. "Are you okay?"

Ren shook his head. "No. No, not at all." He tried to calm the swell of pain rising in his chest. "I hurt Maggie. I hurt her very badly."

"What did you do?"

Ren relayed the whole story to his brother, including the part about how she'd been left at the altar by her fiancé.

"I knew this would be unforgivable to her. It would absolutely kill any love she might feel for me."

Vittorio looked appalled. "Well, if that had been your curse, that certainly would have done the trick."

Ren nodded. "She's gone, Vittorio. I can't fix that."

Vittorio was silent for a moment. "You have to try. Drinking sure as hell isn't doing you any good."

They sat there silent for a while.

"You know, I think you are cursed, too," Vittorio finally said. "But I know it isn't the curse you thought."

"Oh yeah. What do you think the curse is?"

Vittorio took a drink from Ren's glass. "I remember Mother, when she was on one of her benders—something she passed on to you, by the way."

Ren grimaced.

"She said that you would never be a success. She'd seen to that. What if her curse had something to do with your music?"

Ren considered the idea. Now that he thought about it, he hadn't composed anything new in decades. Was that his curse?

"What if you are cursed to never write your own music again?"

"Cursed to only play other people's music," Ren said, mulling over the idea. It made sense.

And in retrospect, seemed far more like something his mother would wish on him, since she'd always envied his talent.

"Brother, you are cursed to play "Jessie's Girl" for all eternity."

Ren stared at him, suddenly realizing Vittorio was right. He'd destroyed his only chance at true love for nothing.

Chapter 25

Maggie hung up the phone. Just her luck—she hadn't been able to change her airline ticket for less than $312 dollars. And 57 cents. Which was money she was willing to part with—but not when the first flight she could get on wasn't until the next morning anyway.

She might as well stay the extra day, save the money, and just avoid Bourbon. It wasn't as if Ren was going to come looking for her. And she now knew she was utterly safe in the daylight. No chance of meeting him then. So she just had to survive tonight and the next. No big deal.

Except New Orleans had really lost its charm for her.

She lounged on the bed and considered staying in for the next two days. Then her stomach growled—a reminder that she did need to eat, even if she didn't feel hungry.

She rolled over and grabbed the room-service menu off the nightstand. Absently, she flipped through the meager menu, finding nothing the least bit appealing.

She tossed the menu on the mattress and stared at the ceiling—a portion of the room she'd nearly committed to memory.

Suddenly the walls seemed to be closing in on her. She pulled in a deep breath and looked at the windows. The sun was setting. She should just stay here.

Then she thought of Peter, of how she'd reacted after his announcement to all of their friends and family that he was dumping her for someone else. She'd gone to her apartment and hid, buried herself in her work. She'd cut herself off from the world, from life.

She sat up and flung her legs over the side of her bed. She wasn't going to do that now. She'd loved New Orleans from the moment she'd stepped into the city. She was going to take her time here and enjoy it. She wasn't going to hide anymore. Or ever again.

She walked to the bathroom and checked her hair. Sure, she was wearing the same clothes as the day before. Sure, she had on no makeup. But she wouldn't let that stop her, either. She was tired of feeling bad.

She pulled in another deep breath, gathering her determination. She was heartbroken—far more so from Ren's betrayal than anything Peter could have done to her. But more than that, she was disappointed in Ren. Because they could have been happy, if he'd allowed it.

She still believed that, and she knew that alone showed how much she'd changed. She wouldn't take the blame for what Ren had done. He should have trusted her the way she trusted him. He should have seen what they could have had.

Oh, part of her wanted to curl up in a ball and hide. And she knew the ache in her chest wasn't going to go away anytime soon. How could she feel this much pain after a five-day relationship? This ache also made her realize that Peter had wounded her ego more than he'd broken her heart. Ren had definitely broken her heart. Shattered it.

But she also learned from the very man who devastated her that she was worthy of true love and loyalty, and nothing less than both.

She used her fingers to brush out the tangles in her wavy hair, then went to grab her purse. She left the hotel, glancing up and down the street, deciding which way she wanted to go. Getting her bearings—which was a little difficult, since she wasn't quite sure where she was—she decided that Bourbon was probably to her right. She went left.

She wandered down the street, peering into windows, absently admiring artwork, jewelry, and the other wares in the shops. A painting of a view of Bourbon done in broad, thick brushstrokes and vivid colors caught her attention. She stopped and stared at it. Pain welled in her belly, rising up to her chest.

She closed her eyes, breathing in slowly, suppressing the tears that threatened to slip from beneath her closed lids. Shake it off. Be tough.

She opened her eyes and turned to keep walking, not even sure where she was going. She took several steps only to realize she was looking at Ren's brother.

Vittorio leaned on a signpost at the corner. Maggie stumbled to a stop, staring at him. He nodded, and Maggie still couldn't react.

He took a step toward her, and somehow his motion seemed to spur her into movement too. She pivoted and headed away from him, walking quickly, trying to decide where to go, wondering why he was there.

Vittorio easily caught up to her, falling into step beside her.

"Maggie—"

"What are you doing here?" They both kept walking, probably looking for all the world like professional speed walkers in the heat of competition.

"Please come with me to see Ren."

"No." She wasn't going to hide, but she was not going to put herself back out there to be hurt again. She was trying to be strong, not masochistic.

"I know what he did."

Maggie stumbled to a stop, glaring at Vittorio. "Then you know full well why I never want to see him again. Ever."

"Yes, I do understand that. Completely."

Maggie's eyes roamed over Vittorio's beautiful face. His

dark eyes were filled with pain and disgust. Pain for her, disgust for his brother. But mixed with that was love.

And suddenly she was remembering Ren kneeling on that filthy bathroom floor. Again she wasn't seeing the scene in its entirety, she was seeing Ren's eyes. He'd had the very same look as he'd watched her.

Her own gaze dropped to the ground. She wanted to see Ren, but she had to admit she was scared. Terrified. Ren had the power to devastate her—even more.

"Maggie," Vittorio said, "he did what he did for a good reason."

Maggie's head snapped up. "There could be no good reason for what I saw."

Vittorio sighed, then ran a hand through his hair, long and thick and several shades lighter than Ren's. But the gesture was so reminiscent of Ren that Maggie's heart seemed to constrict.

"I know it looks that way, but . . ." Again Vittorio swiped his fingers through his hair, a helpless expression on his face. "Hell, my brother can be a huge idiot, and in this case, he was a colossal idiot, but he really did hurt you to help you."

She gave him a disbelieving look.

"He did. He's dying over what he did. He'd dying to see you."

"He's already dead," Maggie said, trying not to be moved by Vittorio's words.

"No, he isn't. He just happens to have all of eternity to feel this pain over you. To regret losing you."

Maggie stared at him, wanting to believe him. Before she even really understood what she was going to do, how she was going to react, she nodded. "Okay."

"Okay?"

"Okay, I will go see him."

Vittorio, even though he didn't move, seemed to sag with relief. "Thank you."

She just hoped she wasn't setting herself up for more pain. She'd learned she could take a lot, but she knew she couldn't take much more.

If Drake thought having Maggie in the bar was messing up Ren's concentration, *not* having her there tonight was really wreaking havoc on his focus. God, he hoped Vittorio had found her and convinced her to come here tonight. Ren had mangled pretty much every song he sang tonight. And frankly he didn't care. All he cared about was Maggie coming back, and somehow making her believe that he loved her. And that he'd never hurt her again.

He'd told his bandmates about what he would be doing if she came in. That was probably the most of himself that he'd ever shared with the guys . . . that he was going to grovel for the woman he loved.

And honestly, given that they lived a life of meaningless one-night stands and endless partying, they actually seemed hopeful for him. He noted they all seemed to be watching the doors of the bar. And they all were ignoring his horrible performance tonight. Who knew you could totally botch the lyrics of "You Give Love A Bad Name"?

Apparently what he'd done to himself was far worse than his mother's curse. And he'd verified that Vittorio was probably right. He hadn't been able to write a thing last night. He'd tried to write a sonata for Maggie, but nothing would come. The notes sounded discordant, unnatural.

He hoped his second choice at an apology would work. If he got the chance.

He turned to talk to Dave, asking him if he'd be willing to step in for the next couple of songs. He really owed the other musician. Dave had been covering for him for half the week.

As they discussed which song to do next, and Dave prepared to take off his guitar to hand it over to Ren, Ren felt a tap on his shoulder. Almost simultaneously, his skin, his whole body, prickled with awareness.

ANY WAY YOU WANT IT   265

"She's here," Wyatt said, his voice low and full of anxiety.

Ren would have smiled if he wasn't so anxious himself. Who would have guessed Wyatt, the gunfighter, once a wanted man, could be so anxious about repairing a romance.

Ren turned to see Maggie walking toward one of the back tables with Vittorio. She didn't look at the stage until she was seated, and even through the milling people and the distance, Ren could clearly see the doubt and distrust in her eyes. And the pain.

His chest tightened, because he knew he had put those emotions there. He handed the bass back to Dave and headed up to the front of the stage.

His fingers actually trembled as he curled his hand around the microphone. He'd performed for princes, for dukes, for other esteemed composers. None of them had shaken him. Maggie had him terrified. But then, Maggie held his life, his heart, in her hands. And he'd actually used her past, her biggest heartbreak, against her. Maggie could forgive a lot. Hell, she could forgive his being a two-century-old lampir. But he just didn't know if she'd ever forgive him for cheating.

"Hi there," he said, his voice hoarse, catching like a nervous schoolboy's. He cleared his throat, then took a deep breath, trying to calm himself. He had to make this good. He had to make her believe him.

"I'm going to play a song for you tonight that isn't the usual fare. Please bear with me." He spoke to the audience, but his eyes never left Maggie. He stared at her a moment longer, taking in her pale skin, the smudges of exhaustion under her eyes.

More pain filled him, but he broke eye contact and moved to the keyboards. He poised his fingers over the keys, then began to play, pouring every bit of emotion into the song, putting all his love into every note.

Maggie tried to remain distant, and she'd managed it until Ren began to play. The song that he'd played that first night.

The song that had led her to him. And her heart began to ache just watching him.

He was beautiful to watch, and so incredibly talented. The song was as haunting and intricate as she remembered. A song of heartbreak and forlornness. She could feel it with every note, she could see it on his face as he played.

He looked up from the keys, seeking her out. Their eyes locked. She could see the pain, the regret, the . . . she didn't dare give the other emotion a name.

What if he hurt her again? She just didn't know if her already fragile heart could take another trauma like that.

He brought the song to an end, and the crowd applauded and whistled, having no idea that they had just seen a composer genius perform a masterpiece. They just cheered because it added to their own fun.

"Thank you," he said, and Maggie noticed how husky his voice was, as if he was holding back those emotions in his eyes, and it was nearly strangling him.

"I wrote that piece a long, long time ago. I actually wrote it for my father, a man I loved, who never even acknowledged me as his son in return."

The crowd grew silent, some perplexed, some drawn in by the story. Some, like Maggie, waiting for him to continue with bated breath.

"Tonight I want to give this song to someone else. This person gave me her love—openly, fully. And I stupidly, very stupidly, gave it up."

Ren pulled the mic off the stand and walked to the edge of the stage. Maggie watched, her heart ceasing to beat in her chest.

"Maggie"—his eyes held hers—"if you give me another chance, I swear, I will never, never hurt you again. I want to give you an eternity of the love you deserve."

Maggie didn't react. She couldn't. All she could do was stare at him. God, she wanted to believe. She did.

"Maggie, I am crazy in love with you. And I know this

sounds like the lamest excuse, but I only did what I did in a misguided attempt to protect you."

"He's telling the truth," Vittorio said from beside her. "And I can also attest to the fact that it was seriously, seriously misguided."

Ren had stepped down off the stage and now stood a few feet away. "He can. And he can also attest that I'm so damned in love with you, I don't know what to do."

"I can," Vittorio agreed.

A broken laugh escaped Maggie, and for the first time, she realized tears rolled down her cheeks.

"Please, Maggie, I can't write anything new, but every sonota, every concerto, every symphony, they are for you. Only you."

Ren stood directly in front of her, his eyes pleading. And Maggie knew he was telling her the truth. She could feel it in the very depths of her soul. But all she managed to give him was a nod.

His eyebrow rose. "Is that a yes, you'll give me a second chance?"

She nodded again, and then she found herself pinned tight to Ren's hard chest. He lifted her, spinning her around. His mouth kissing her forehead, her nose, her cheeks, and finally her lips.

When they broke apart they were both laughing, although both of them had suspiciously moist eyes.

"Don't ever hurt me again," Maggie warned.

Ren kissed her again, then murmured against her lips. "Never. Never."

Epilogue

"So what did Erika and Jo think about your decision to move here?" Ren asked as he placed the last of Maggie's boxes in the living room of his carriage house.

"Erika wasn't surprised at all," Maggie said, dropping her own box next to his. "And Jo wasn't surprised; more concerned. She's a mother hen, you know."

Ren moved over to pull Maggie against him. He kissed her neck, finding the sensitive spot just below her earlobe that he knew drove her crazy.

She tilted her head, allowing him better access.

"Did you tell them anything about what I really am?"

Maggie shook her head, then pulled back to look at him. "No. And if I did tell them, it wouldn't be to tell them what you are, but rather who you are."

"Are you just attracted to me because I was once a nearly famous composer?" Even though he asked the question jokingly, Maggie sensed the small bit of real concern there.

Poor Ren still believed he'd never been loved for anything other than his talent. Which apparently had been true of his mother. Maggie had been shocked when she learned that Ren really did have a curse on him and why his mother had done it. Orabella D'Antoni Ridgewood truly was a horrible, selfish woman. It was a wonder she'd given birth to such a sweet and generous son as Ren. And Vittorio too.

But Maggie had a surprise for Ren. One that she hoped would help him see his own self-worth, just as he'd done for her.

"Where are you going?" Ren's hold tightened as she tried to wiggle free. She laughed, enjoying his attention very, very much.

"I need to show you something."

"Hmm, does it involve taking off your clothes?"

Maggie laughed again. "Not this particular thing, no." She wriggled free, and moved to one of the boxes that had just been shipped here.

"We've been apart for a week. I have no intention of doing anything that doesn't involve touching you."

Maggie sidestepped him, as she tugged at the packing tape.

"Behave yourself," she half-heartedly scolded him. Frankly, she wanted nothing more than to touch him too. But this was too important not to show him. "A week cannot be that long to a vampire, after all."

"Ha!" But he did let her finish opening the box.

She pulled out a rather large, ungainly chest. Carefully she placed it on the floor.

"This is all of your original sheet music."

Ren stared at the chest, his skin actually growing pale.

"I called the person who shipped it to me, and they verified that it was found at the estate that your father owned. The one in Essex."

Ren crouched down, and touched the lid of the old box. The lid was carved with a pastoral scene. His long, tapered fingers traced the carvings. "This was my toy box." His voice was so quiet, she almost didn't hear him.

"It was a part of his estate. And it turns out that if I'd looked at the contents of the box closer, I would have realized that I wasn't sent this to figure out the composer. I was sent it just to validate the sheet music's authenticity."

Ren looked up from the box. "What do you mean?"

Maggie reached down and opened the box. On the top she'd placed the letter, yellowed and barely legible. Carefully, she picked it up and handed it to Ren.

She watched his face as he read what it said. Then he reread it. Finally he gaped at her.

"My father saved these."

She nodded. She knew what the letter said, word for word.

It was his father's apology for never claiming him as his son publicly. It explained why he did it. Because of his position as duke, because of his other children and his legal wife. But that he'd loved him so very, very much.

"Your father did love you. And he saved every single thing you wrote. Even things you balled up and tossed in the bin."

Ren stared down at the piles and piles of music, stored in his very own toy box.

When he looked back up at Maggie, his eyes were suspiciously glittery.

"He did love you, Ren."

Ren stared at the note for a moment longer. Then he hugged Maggie tight against him.

"And somehow he also brought you to me," he murmured in her hair.

She smiled. "Maybe you are right."

She squealed at he swept her up into his arms and headed for the stairs to the loft.

After he placed her on the bed, she gazed at him, all humor lost. "Will you make me like you?"

"If you want me to," he said. "I want forever with you."

"I want that too. Can we do it tonight?"

Ren didn't hesitate. Obviously the idea of love didn't scare him in the least now.

"We can do it now." He wiggled his eyebrows.

She playfully cuffed him. "Not *that* it. Although I do want that too."

He smiled. "Good." But then his expression grew serious. "Are you sure you want to be like me?"

"I just want you. Forever."

Ren pulled her tight again him. "I *am* yours. Any way you want me."

If you liked this story,
you've got to try
THE BLACK SHEEP AND
THE HIDDEN BEAUTY
by Donna Kauffman,
available now from Brava.
Turn the page for a sneak peek . . .

Elena backed down the ladder from her loft apartment over the outer stables, yawning deeply and wishing like hell she'd remembered to set the timer on the coffeepot the night before. The sun was barely peeking over the horizon and last night the temperature had dipped down a bit further than it had recently making for a chilly late spring morning. She shivered despite the long underwear top she'd donned under her overalls this morning. Teach her to be a smartass and offer up a dawn class. But then, she hadn't really expected him to take her up on it. He struck her as more of a night owl, than an early bird. Serve her right if he stood her up. With her luck, Rafe was probably still tucked in his nice warm bed. Which was where she should be. Well, not in Rafe's bed, but . . .

No way could she stop the visuals that accompanied that little mental slip. It wasn't a shot of warm coffee, but it did have the added benefit of getting her blood pumping a little faster. Of course, if she were in the same bed as Rafe, she wouldn't need any coffee, just . . . stamina.

"Morning."

His voice surprised her, making her lose her footing on the last rung. An instant later two strong hands palmed her waist and steadied her as both feet reached the ground. She could have told him that putting his hands on her was not the way to steady her at the moment, but she was too busy trying to rally her thoughts away from imagining him manhandling her like this while they were both naked among tousled sheets.

Then he was turning her around, and she was getting her first look at a scruffy, early morning Rafe. And whatever words she might have found evaporated like the morning mist under a rising sun.

Goodness knows her temperature was rising.

He wore an old forest green sweatshirt and an even older pair of jeans, if the frayed edged and faded thighs and knees were any indication. It was standard weekend morning clothing for most men, but, until that moment, she'd have been hard pressed to visualize it on him. Of course, on most men, that combination would have given them a disheveled look at best. In fact, she was feeling incredibly disheveled herself at the moment. Rafe, on the other hand, without even trying, looked like he'd just stepped off the pages of the latest Ralph Lauren ad. She resented the ease with which he made scruffy so damn sexy, except she was too busy fighting off the waves of lust the look inspired.

"So," she said, her tone overly bright. "You ready for lesson number two?"

"As I'll ever be."

She led the way down the aisle toward Petunia's stall. "It's been a while since your first lesson, so keep in mind that you'll probably need to reestablish your report with Petunia."

"Check." He said nothing else, just followed behind her.

She stopped at the tack room door and went inside. "I haven't set anything out, so we need to get her saddle, pads, bridle, everything."

He followed her into the smaller room. "Just point to what we need."

She could feel him behind her, her awareness of him as finely tuned as her senses were to the animals she worked with. Except with him, there was all that sexual energy jacking things up. She cleared her throat, maybe squared her shoulders a little, then made the mistake of looking back at him before reaching for the first of the gear.

Something about the morning beard shadowing his jaw, the way his hair wasn't quite so naturally perfect, made his eyes darker, and enhanced how impossibly thick his eyelashes were. And she really, really needed to stop looking at his mouth. But the ruggedness the stubble lent to his face just emphasized all the more those soft, sculpted lips of his.

Her thighs were quivery, her nipples were on-point, and the panties she'd just put on not fifteen minutes ago, were already damp. The morning air might have been head-clearing, but her body hadn't gotten the message at all.

"You take the saddle there," she said, trying not to sound as breathless as she knew she did. Dammit. "On the third rail," she added, pointing, when he kept that dark gaze of his on her.

"What else?" He didn't even glance at the rack.

"Grab one of the pads. Same kind that we used last time. I'll get the halter and bridle."

"Okay."

She waited a heartbeat too long for him to move first. He didn't.

So they were officially staring at each other now. The silence in the small space expanded in a way that lent texture to the very air between them. The room was tiny, the temperature warm, with little ventilation. The sun hadn't risen enough to slice through the panels on the roof, leaving the room deep in shadows, with thin beams of gray dawn providing the only light. There was a lightbulb overheard, but she'd have to reach past him to get to the switch.

He stepped forward. "Elena—"

"Rafe—"

They spoke at the same time, and both broke off.

He paused. "Yes?"

She really wanted to know what he'd been about to say,

before she potentially made a very big fool out of herself, but went ahead before she lost her nerve. "I can't—I mean, not to be presumptuous here, but I can't—don't—mix business with pleasure."

"Are we?"

She didn't back down. She might not be the most experienced person in the world when it came to relationships, but she knew the way he was looking at her wasn't of the innocent teacher–student variety. "It feels like more than a simple riding lesson to me." *There. She'd said it.*

He took another step closer, and her breath suddenly felt trapped inside her chest. So much for being brazen.

"It is a simple riding lesson," he said. "Not a corporate merger. So what if there is more? I don't really see a conflict of interest here."

"You're a close friend of my boss."

He stepped closer still. It was a small room to begin with. He was definitely invading her personal space. Again.

"And you're not planning on staying here long term anyway, right?"

"What is that supposed to mean?"

"Meaning that as potential conflicts go, that one is temporary at best. As is anything that may happen between us. No commitments, right?" His voice was all just-rolled-out-of-bed rough.

"What are you saying, then?" she asked, tipping her chin up slightly as he shifted closer. She felt the bridle rack at her back. "What is it you want?"

"I just want to learn to ride." His lips curved then, and her thigh—or more accurately, the muscles between them—suddenly felt a whole lot wobbly.

His eyes were so dark, so deep, she swore she could fall right into them and never climb back out. And that smile made it dizzyingly clear that horses weren't the only thing he was interested in riding.

It was too early in the day for this. She couldn't handle this kind of full-out assault on her senses. Or on her mind. Or . . . hell, what part of her didn't he affect? He muddled her up far to easily. Muddled was definitely not what she needed to be right now.

But when he lifted his hand, barely brushing the underside of her chin with his fingertips, and tipped her head back a bit further . . . she let him.

"I think about you," he said, his voice nothing more than a rough whisper.

Her skin tingled as if the words themselves had brushed against her.

"Too often. You distract me."

"And that's a bad thing."

"It's . . . an unexpected thing."

She wasn't sure what to think about that. And his neutral tone made it impossible to decipher how he felt about it. "So, this is . . . what? An attempt to exorcise me from your thoughts?"

His smile broadened as his mouth lowered slowly toward hers. "Either that, or make all this distraction a lot more worthwhile."

She had a split second to decide whether to let him kiss her, and spent a moment lying to herself that she was actually strong enough to do the right thing and turn her head away. Who was she kidding? Her body was fairly humming in anticipation and it was all she could do to refrain from grabbing his head and hurrying him the hell up.

Like he said. It was just a kiss. Not a contract.

His lips brushed across hers. Warm, a little soft, but the right amount of firm. He slid his fingers along the back of her neck, beneath the heavy braid that swung there, sending a delicious little shiver all the way down her spine at the contact.

He dropped another whisper of a kiss across her lips, then another, inviting her to participate, clearly not going any further unless she did. She respected that, a lot, even though part of her wished he'd taken the decision out of her hands. It would make all the self-castigation later much easier to avoid. Given his aversion to commitment, somehow she figured he knew that. They were either in it together, or not at all.

He lifted his head just enough to look into her eyes, a silent question in his own. *Will you, or won't you?*

She held his gaze for what felt like all eternity, then slowly lowered her eyelids as she closed the distance between them and kissed him back.

Don't miss Jill Shalvis's
STRONG AND SEXY,
out this month from Brava . . .

"Why do you look so familiar?" His mouth was close to her ear, close enough to cause a whole series of hopeful shivers to rack her body. He was rock-solid against her, all corded muscle and testosterone.

Lots of testosterone.

"I don't know," she whispered, still hoping for a big hole to take her.

"Are you sure you're all right?"

"Completely." *Except, you know, not.*

"Because I can't help but think I'm missing something here."

Yes, yes, he was missing something. He'd missed her whole pathetic attempt at a kiss seduction, for instance. And the fact that she was totally, one hundred percent out of her league here with him. But his eyes were deep, so very deep, and leveled right on hers, evenly, patiently, giving her the sense that he was always even, always patient. Never rattled or ruffled.

She wanted to be never rattle or ruffled.

"Am I?" His thumb glided over her skin, sending all her erogenous zones into tap-dance mode. "Missing something?"

"Yes. N–no. I mean . . ."

He smiled. And not just a curving of his lips, but with his whole face. His eyes lit, those laugh lines fanned out, and damn, that sexy dimple. "Yeah," he murmured. "Definitely missing something."

"I'm a little crazy tonight," she admitted.

"A little crazy once in a while isn't a bad thing."

Oh boy. She'd bet the bank he knew how to coax a woman into doing a whole host of crazy stuff. Just the thought made her feel a little warm, and a nervous laugh escaped.

"You're beautiful, you know that?"

She had to let out another laugh, but he didn't as he traced a finger over her lower lip. "You are."

Beautiful? Or crazy?

"You going to tell me what brought you to this closet?"

"I was garnering my courage."

"For?"

Well wasn't that just the question of the night, as there were so many, many things she'd needed courage for, not the least of which was standing here in front of him and telling him what she *really* wanted. A kiss . . .

"Talk to me."

She licked her lips. "There's a man and a woman in that first office down the hall. Together. And they're . . . not talking."

"Ah." A fond smile crossed his mouth. "You must have found Noah and Bailey. They've just come home from their honeymoon. So yeah, I seriously doubt they're . . . talking."

"Yeah. See . . ." She gnawed on her lower lip. "I was hoping for that."

"Talking."

"No. The *not* talking."

Silence.

And then more silence.

Oh, God.

Slowly she tipped her head up and looked at him, but he wasn't laughing at her.

A good start, she figured.

In fact, his eyes were no longer smiling at all, but full of a heart-stopping heat. "Can you repeat that request?" he asked.

Well, yes, she could, but it would make his possible rejection that much harder to take. "I was wondering what your stance was on being seduced by a woman who isn't really so good at this sort of thing, but wants to be better . . ."

He blinked. "Just to be clear." His voice was soft, gravelly, and did things to every erogenous zone in her body. "Is this you coming on to me?"

"Oh, God." She covered her face. "If you don't know, then I'm even worse at this than I thought. Yes. Yes, that's what I'm pathetically attempting to do. Come on to you, a complete stranger in a closet, but now I'm hearing it as you must be hearing it, and I sound like the lunatic that everyone thinks I am, and—"

His hands settled on her bare arms, gliding up, down, and then back up again, over her shoulders to her face, where he gently pulled her hands away so he could see her.

"I saw the mistletoe," she rushed to explain. "It's everywhere. And people were kissing. And I couldn't get kissing off my mind . . . God. Forget it, okay? Just forget me." She took a step back, but because this was her, she tripped over something on the floor behind her. She'd have fallen on her ass if he hadn't held her upright. "Thanks," she managed. "But I need to go now. I really need to go—"

He put a finger to her lips.

Right. Stop talking. Good idea.

His eyes, still hot, and also a little amused—because that's what she wanted to see in a man's eyes after she'd tried to seduce him, amusement—locked onto hers. She couldn't look away. There was just something about the way he was taking her in, as if he could see so much more than she'd intended him to. "Seriously. I've—"

He turned away.

Okaaaay . . . "Got to go."

But he was rustling through one of the shelves. Then he

bent to look lower and she tried not to look at his butt. She failed, of course. "Um, yeah. So I'll see you around." Or not. Hopefully not—

"Got it." Straightening, he revealed what he held—a sprig of mistletoe.

"Oh," she breathed. Her heart skipped a beat, then raced, beating so loud and hard she couldn't hear anything but the blood pumping through her veins.

His mouth quirked slightly, but his eyes held hers, and in them wasn't amusement so much as . . .

Pure staggering heat.

"Did you change your mind?" he asked.

Was he kidding? She wanted to jump him. *Now.* "No."

With a smile that turned her bones to mush, he raised his arm so that the mistletoe was above their heads.

Oh, God.

"Your move," he whispered.

She looked at his mouth, her own tingling in anticipation. "Maybe you could . . ."

"Oh, no. I'm not taking advantage of a woman in a closet, drenched in champagne." He smiled. "But if she wanted to take advantage of me, now see, that's a different story entirely."

He was teasing her, his eyes lit with mischievousness and a wicked, wicked intent.

"I'm a klutz," she whispered. "I might hurt you by accident."

"I'll take my chances."

She laughed. She couldn't help it. She laughed, and he closed his eyes and puckered up, making her laugh some more, making it okay for her to lean in . . .

And kiss him.

Tensions are running high
in Charlotte Mede's
EXPLOSIVE,
available now from Brava . . .

"What exactly is the nature of your agreement with de Maupassant? Is it money? The promise of notoriety?"

Devon turned her head sharply to look up at him, absorbing the stark lines of his face, the wide mouth above the strong jawline. She pivoted gracefully in his arms, holding herself stiffly as though more conscious than ever of a confused upsurge of unwelcome sensations, of fear and desire. Blackburn felt her invoke her steeliest reserve.

"My relationship with Le Comte has nothing to do with us."

"He has everything to do with us," Blackburn muttered. "He's thrown us together quite deliberately. And he's prepared to give you access to the Eroica, despite your denials," he said just as the orchestra struck up a lively minuet.

"It's not that easy." Her mouth was set in a firm line. "I don't want or need your offer of money, or anybody else's for that matter."

"Don't take me for a fool, Mademoiselle. And I won't take you for the innocent that you pretend to be," he said in a softly uttered threat. "You know how to play Le Comte for a puppet, and you know exactly how to convince him to relinquish the score to you."

The confusion and embarrassment clouding her eyes was a

fine bit of acting, he thought, looking at her drift away from him a few steps, in perfect time with the music's rhythm.

"Tell me, is Le Comte sparing with the purse strings?" he continued ruthlessly as his strong arms propelled her back toward him. "One should think those emeralds around your lovely neck would keep you satisfied. Or are you trying for diamonds?"

"Stop it," she whispered under her breath, then in the next instant lifted her gaze to him boldly as though changing her mind. "Rubies, actually," she said with a brittle voice. "I'm trying for rubies, if you must know."

He didn't like the answer or her bravado. "Then perhaps we should turn up the heat."

She gave him a mockingly sweet smile, for his benefit or for their audience, he wasn't sure. "And how do you propose we force Le Comte's hand?" she asked.

"With the utmost discretion, of course," he said, fooling neither her nor himself. "As strategies go, you of all people must know how potent the combination of seduction, jealousy, and deception can be, Mademoiselle," he explained, his voice rough velvet as he led her from the center of the ballroom to the protective shadows of a grouping of leafy plants.

She was a tall woman but he still towered over her, backing her into a corner. In the wavering candlelight, he thought he glimpsed uncertainty and fear in her eyes as she refused to lower her gaze, staring steadily, courageously into his face. Vulnerability was difficult to feign and for a moment, Blackburn questioned his own powers of observation. He watched the tip of her tongue slide from her lips, the gesture deliberate, he didn't know. All he knew was how his body reacted with a blast of heat.

As though to make it easier for her, his shadowed face moved fractionally closer as he slid his fingers deep into the mass of her hair to tilt her face upward. It was just one way to fight the battle, he persuaded himself, before taking her face in both palms. Her mouth trembled beneath his, moist, pliant, and intensely female.

The tension eased out of her by slow degrees as his lips brushed lightly against hers. Instead of drawing away, Devon drew unconsciously closer, her lashes lowered, closing her eyes. He teasingly nipped her lower lip, his tongue licking inside. She surrendered her mouth, opening to the voracity of his deepening kiss while the strains of violins and the protective covering of fronds receded in the distance.

More insistent and demanding, the pressure of Blackburn's lips increased in a velvety heated stroking as his tongue suggestively explored, caressing her sweetness, tasting her mouth with a lazy greed. Slow and inexorably consuming, his mouth devoured hers until she gasped for breath. He heard her groan as she pressed her breasts against him, oblivious to the sharp edges of the pilaster biting into her back, sighing against the succulence of their hot, ravenous play.

"We should have done this from the very first," Blackburn whispered roughly, and plunged again for her pliant tongue as his hands stroked their way down her back and to the sides of her breasts.

Against his mouth, she whispered, "This makes no sense . . ." But she wound her arms around his neck, shuddering at the feel of his palms molding her breasts. She sank into his kisses, long, leisurely, wet incursions that left her so weak he had to hold her up in his arms.

As if he had all the time in the world, and as if a good number of Le Comte's guests had not spied their impromptu rendezvous, Blackburn traced a voluptuous trail along her parted lips, her smooth cheek, the curl of an ear, the highly sensitive, he discovered, curve of her neck. He moved his mouth to the softness of her shoulder and felt Devon shiver at the touch of his mouth, his teeth, the soothing stroke of his tongue.

No longer distant nor in complete control of the encounter,

Blackburn felt himself become harder, tauter, his body contemptuously mocking his attempt at detachment. Her skin was like rich cream beneath his lips, her body sinuously lush as it melted into his. She drew a shuddering breath and, against his will, his hard fingers slid from her breasts to the back of her head, where they tangled in her thick hair. His mouth, a hot brand, closed over hers once again.

His eyes closed in self-defense and he immediately saw her naked beneath him, warm and soft and ready. He groaned against the tidal wave threatening to overtake them both. Her open and ardent sensuality startled him like nothing had in a very long time, and he had drunk from the very depths of decadence, manipulating, controlling the most sophisticated of carnal games.

He forced his eyes open, pulling back and releasing her by slow degrees with small kisses, erotically tugging at her lips, willing himself to ignore the clamoring of his heated blood, willing his erection to subside. She was just another of de Maupassant's women. His pulse slowed, he tensed and ice water began to replace the blood in his veins.

The objective was to have her secure the Eroica, at whatever cost.